Protection

JAMES

Copyright © 1988 by Bill James

This edition published in 1992 by Foul Play Press, an imprint of
The Countryman Press, Inc., Woodstock, Vermont 05091

Library of Congress Cataloging-in-Publication Data

James, Bill.
    Protection / Bill James.
        p.   cm.
    "A Foul Play Press book."
    ISBN 0-88150-231-6
    I. Title
PR6060.A44P76   1992
823'.914—dc20   92-4978
                                                          CIP

10 9 8 7 6 5 4 3 2 1

Printed on recycled paper in the United States of America

1

Jack Lamb rang him at home, wanting to arrange a meeting, and sounding as comfortable and breezy as ever, his voice rich on endless dark victories. And, also as ever, Harpur listened and said not very much, because his part was only to agree with whatever Lamb proposed. Harpur's older daughter, Hazel, had answered the phone first and, probably without covering the mouth-piece, bawled upstairs: 'Dad, it's for you. Sounds like one of your finks? He asked for Colin.'

He picked up the receiver and Lamb said, 'My mother's over from the States again.'

'Grand, Jack.'

'You met her once.'

'I remember. Lovely lady.'

'Well, she likes to keep an eye on me. She worries. As a matter of fact, did I ever tell you, mother always wanted me to go into the police, myself?' Lamb guffawed. 'She thought you were lovely, too.'

Harpur stayed silent.

'She's very keen on hearing Billy Graham. At the football ground, you know? Preaching – it fascinates her. Always has. Anyone. She never misses that afternoon service on radio. Nothing like it in the States. "As may be most expedient for them", all that. I thought I'd take her to Graham tonight.'

'Why not?'

'Oh, a lot of people about, but not many you or I'd know at a show like that, Col.'

'It'll do.'

'I'll have Helen with me, too, I should think.'

'Helen?'

'Ah, what happened to Fay, you'll ask. That had to end, didn't it? Her husband became resentful and distressed, eventually. But an amicable break. Fine wholesome person, Fay. Well, we're mature people. You'll like Helen. She used to work in catering. Full training. The girls won't be in the way. They'll want to listen to the service. We can talk in private somewhere. They always have a room where the converts are taken. See you outside there, about half an hour after the sermon starts.'

'You did say outside?'

He laughed again. 'I think so, at this stage. Mind you, I quite like the notion of unloading all my troubles on some genuinely sympathetic counsellor. Now and then I see myself like that one who fell among thieves. Never feel wearied by sin, Col? How's the wife and children? All well there?'

'Fine, Jack.'

'Excellent. What I like to hear. Didn't I always say it would come good again?'

'I think you did.'

'Oh, still not too great, is it?'

'It's fine, Jack.'

'OK. None of my business. As a matter of fact, I miss Fay. True, Helen's very beautiful and younger, yet gentle, and younger's so important, of course, but Fay knew about art and pool and hanging baskets, and her sister's quite well placed in the Royal Automobile Club office. These things add up. Never mind, a husband has rights. I can't deny it. He wanted her back, and Fay was quite touched. I didn't stand in her way. I mean, this is a long-time marriage we're talking about. Have to show respect. I gave her a very pretty Brabazon-Brabazon water-colour of Venice as a farewell, to help soothe hub.'

'So I'll see you at the ground.'

'Am I rambling, Col?'

Meeting Lamb was always a risk, wherever it took place, but all the same Harpur expected to enjoy the Billy Graham rally, like Jack's mother. It was the kind of simple, salvation preaching he had known as a child: although his parents never went near a church or chapel, of course, they had made him attend Sunday school at the local Gospel Hall, and in fact some of the most frequently quoted Bible verses from those days still lurked in his memory, and could still trouble his sleep: 'the dead in Christ shall

6

arise first', 'without shedding of blood is no remission.' On blood the Gospel Hall had gone very strong. 'Wash me in the blood of the Lamb and I shall be whiter than snow,' they sang. That used to upset him when he tried to visualize it and make sense of it. He must have been a sensitive kid and, maybe, a stupid kid. Some of the sensitivity had been filleted since, but only some, he hoped. Some of the stupidity must have hung on, too, or he probably would not be going to meet an informant at a crowded rally. There was the blood of *Jack* Lamb, plus his own, to worry about these days.

Jack was already in place when Harpur arrived, waiting huge and kindly-looking near the home side's dressing room, taken over by the spiritual advisers tonight. He wore a very superior grey leather bomber jacket and a navy beret. It was one of Jack's few drawbacks as an informant that he did stand out in crowds. His non-stop, deeply perilous optimism and confidence could be alarming, too, and so could his businesses, which Harpur never wanted to hear much about: once, Megan had asked him whether the only two physical qualities essential for high rank were an ability not to vomit drink – especially not in public – and ownership of a blind eye. Even after fifteen years with Harpur, Megan did not understand how police worked. Or, perhaps she understood but hated parts of it, especially those shadowy parts required to deal with the biggest villains and the biggest jobs. She came from a family of benign Highgate doctors, who believed in the perfectibility of Man, despite all the senility and ulcers they saw, and Megan still gamely harboured many of their principles. When she and Harpur married he was at the bottom, investigating stolen scooters and pub brawls and there had been no tricky aspects of the job for her to swallow. As he moved up, though, things had grown tenser; now, against all the problems and dangers that Jack Lamb certainly brought, Harpur had to weigh the brilliant, eighty per cent accurate information he supplied, and regularly supplied. No other nark approached his class, and for such service Harpur would put up with pretty well anything. Most policemen would. Or most policemen who got ahead would. A copper lived and died by his whispers.

Over the public address a clear-voiced boy soprano sang a sad, slow hymn which Harpur remembered well, 'Just as I am without one plea.' The people he stalked these days always had a plea, along with a crew of QCs and side-kicks to package it in the prettiest wrapping for the jury.

'They've been talking about you from the platform, Col,' Lamb said.

'Yes?'

'The man taken in adultery.'

'I thought it was a woman.'

'Yes. But there must have been a man. You're not looking as good as I've seen you.'

'Got some trouble, Jack?'

'Me? Of course not. Trouble! Would I bother you with that? Have I ever?'

A pleasant-looking girl in a yellow anorak and jeans came out from the counselling room and approached them. 'You've decided to give yourselves to the Lord? And are you here for advice? Please, do come in and we'll speak to Him together.'

'Perhaps in a moment, love?' Lamb said.

'Don't fight it. This may be the last time you'll ever hear the call.'

'Yes, I know,' Lamb replied.

'Open your heart.' She turned to Harpur. 'Well, both of you, I mean. It's all that matters.'

'Yes, it is,' Harpur said.

'Two grand, big chaps like you: it would be so nice if you were working for the Lord.'

'I agree,' Harpur said.

The singing had finished and there was a sudden rush of people looking for counsellors. The girl in the yellow anorak went to help deal with them.

'She's a very winning kid,' Lamb said. 'Think, she might have been home listening to the giggling fucking gabble of disc jockeys, but, no, she's here to reclaim souls for God. Myself, I'm warmed by that. What I wanted to see you about is Tenderness, Col.'

'Mellick?'

'Bernard Tenderness Mellick, yes. Ever been to his place?'

'No, not personally. But we keep an eye. Big new house on the Elms Enclave?'

'So you've not met his son?'

8

'Didn't know he had one. It will be on the dossier.'

'Boy of eleven. Not quite sixteen ounces to the pound. He's called Graham, but not after Billy, I shouldn't think. Delightful child, like so many of them are. Mellick worships him. How he got to be called Tenderness?'

'No, that's from when he cut up someone years ago and gave him a face like Clapham Junction. Bit of a savage, Tenderness. We think he did Ivor Wright lately with a blowlamp. Tenderness – it's like calling a tall bloke Tiny. Megan would tell you it's irony. Big thing, irony. So, what's happened, Jack?'

'The boy's missing.'

'How long?'

'Eight days.'

'We haven't been told. I'd have heard. Mellick's a name.'

'Why I'm telling you, Col.'

'Not a case of the boy wandering off? I mean, if he's not right in the head.'

'He was snatched.'

'From where? Isn't the house like a fort? And the whole Enclave's got private security.'

'All the same he was snatched, Col. Mellick's upset a lot of unstoppable people, hasn't he? Not just Ivor's team and relations. Top-class claws all over. Are a couple of fat lads with peaked caps and walky-talkies going to keep them out?'

'Eight days? He's still alive?'

'Col, I know he's gone, I know he was taken, and that's all. I don't know who or where. If I knew who I might know why, but I don't. And I don't know if he's been killed, either.'

'Is Tenderness trying to do a deal?'

'He's got his people out looking. The gang who took the boy might be in touch with him. I don't know that, either. Do you and yours keep a tap on his phone?'

'Not that I know. A permanent thing like that's tricky without authorization, and we wouldn't be granted it, of course. But I'll check in case we're running something privately.'

'I hear Tenderness is offering a hundred grand for information. No questions.'

'That going to be enough?'

'Not so far.'

9

'Has he got that much, anyway?'

'It's what he's offering,' Lamb replied. 'He's done all right, hasn't he?'

'A hundred grand is a lot to have in the bank when you spend like Tenderness.'

'So it might be bullshit, but he's got to talk loud and big if he's going to reach the right ears.'

'He's playing about with the life of his child. If he had come to us – '

'Would he, Col? You really think he'd involve the police? Do they ever, operators like Tenderness? In any case, they might have told him the boy's finished if he brings your lot in.'

'So, how do I know all this, Jack?'

'Here's mother now and Helen.' Lamb waved.

'Jack, how do I know this? Can I act on it and say you're source?'

'You don't know it. Not yet. Do nothing until I give the word'. He went forward and put an arm around his mother's shoulders. Helen took his other hand. She was pale, slightly punk and less than twenty. 'Wasn't he fine?' Lamb exclaimed.

'Well, simplistic,' his mother replied.

'The saved and the lost, ma. Hasn't it got to be simple? No fancy footwork can dodge round that.'

'So, who's this?' Mrs Lamb asked.

'Saved or lost, you mean? Who can tell? Don't you remember Colin Harpur? He remembers *you*.'

'Cop?'

'One of the best, ma.'

'How come he's here? For the preaching? I don't believe. This just a rendezvous outing, Jack? You need somewhere to spill again? You using us, using God? You do your deals here, like the money-changers in the temple?' She had on an old, once-good silk suit, with a large, navy cravat. The outfit made her look grave and unforgiving.

Harpur said: 'Wherever there's a crowd you'll find a cop, Mrs Lamb. Who knows what we might discover there?'

'So you discovered Jack. Such luck.'

'This is Helen, Colin,' Lamb said.

'Jack says you were in catering.'

'Catering?' she replied. 'Me?'

10

'Wasn't it something like that?' Lamb asked.

'This was quite an experience here tonight,' Helen replied. 'About Lazarus and rolling away the stone at the tomb. Things must have been pretty good in those days. Did people know how lucky they were? Oh, St Mark and the others wrote it all down, so they must have known it was interesting, but what about all the other people? I mean, the sick made better and all that. Great.'

'Yes, things have gone a bit down hill since then,' Lamb said. 'Life may have got trickier.'

The girl in the yellow anorak approached them again. 'Do all of you require counselling?'

Harpur said: 'We're in people's way here. We're leaving now.'

'It may be the last time you'll ever hear the call.'

'Thoughts like that make me sad and very fearful,' Mrs Lamb replied.

'Me, too,' Harpur said.

2

Nobody came if he screamed in the night so he never did now. Every morning a man called Rick arrived to let him out and take him to the toilet in the house. He had breakfast with the men. They gave him bread with Marmite or jam. He could have more than one piece. Graham's father had taught him counting and he knew that sometimes he had four pieces.

There were three men. He did not know how many days and nights he had been at the farm and sleeping in a building near the farm house. His counting went only to four, and it was more. There was a sleeping bag in the room on the floor and he thought it was new because it smelled like new clothes.

At first the building where he slept had made him very frightened. It did not have a window or any curtains. He had seen a building like this on television and knew it was called a cowshed but the men said this was his room now. It had been disinfected. To him it had a smell like when his mother cleaned the toilet.

When Rick came to let him out in the mornings Graham would look at the big lock on the outside of the door. On the first night in

11

the shed he had panicked. He did not know if they would ever let him out again and he cried and yelled. That night, he left the sleeping bag and tried to get to the door. But he bumped into a wheelbarrow in the dark and fell, cutting his face, and when he gave up and went back to the sleeping bag he made it wet with blood. He did not tell the men about that, fearing it might make them cross if the blood spoiled the new sleeping bag. When they were angry they shouted and sometimes they hit him. Each morning he put some of his clothes on the bag to hide the bloodstain.

He had been hurt another time. That had happened when the men came to take him from his mother and father's house. He did not want to go and he fought, but they put him in a green van. His mother had taught him colours. Green was not hard to remember, because it was like grass and the big table on television when the men were playing snooker. There were a lot of balls on that table. He did not remember all the colours but he knew blue, red and green.

The men had come for him when he was playing on the grass at the back of the house. He shouted for his mother and father but they did not hear. One of the men had picked him up and carried him along the lane, then pushed him into the back of that van. It was then that he had hurt his head. He was kicking and trying to stand up, struggling to get away. He knew now that the man who carried him was called Dave. The other one's name was Milton. Dave was always laughing and to the boy he seemed elderly, with grey hair like Graham's grandmother. He did not understand how someone so old could be pushing a boy into the back of a van. Dave had a grey moustache and small grey beard.

When Dave carried him down the lane to the van he had seen Sam the dog lying on the ground, and he had an arrow sticking in his throat by his collar, and his tail was lying out, very still and very straight in the mud, like a brown branch. He knew about arrows. He had seen them in *Robin Hood* on television. Usually, if anyone approached the house, Sam would bark a lot but he did not bark that day.

Sometimes Dave called him Podge. That had upset him for a while. It baffled him that someone who knew his name should want to call him something else. Now, he felt better about it. He thought it might show Dave liked him, and he wanted that. He felt safer then. In the fight at the van he had bitten Dave hard near the nose, and he knew people remembered bites. The teacher at his school did, and afterwards he could be very nasty. Sometimes when he bit somebody and he was friends later he used to kiss the spot, but he had never kissed the teacher or Dave. Now, he was glad if Dave did not feel angry with him all the time because of the biting.

Dave used to touch the place of the bite sometimes with his finger and laugh. One day when he did that he said: 'Podge, you're a terror. You're just like your dad.' He said something else as well. He said 'your fucking dad', but Graham's mother used to tell him that word was not needed.

When they spoke about his father it made him want to cry. He could tell they did not like him, but could not understand why. It troubled him to think that his father and mother would not know where he was and would be worried. They would go out in the car and look for him because they did not like it if he left the garden. One day, a long time ago, he did go into the street and they came and found him. He was playing with some children. He liked that, but his mother and father said he must go back to the house with them. But a farm was not in the street, and he was afraid his mother and father would not know their way in fields.

When somebody came to this house the men made him hide. They sat upstairs and watched from the window. There were no houses and they could see a long way. If a car was coming they told him to hide and keep quiet. They said he must stay in the bathroom and if he came out or if he made a noise they would lock him in the cowshed all day as well.

They gave him some toys to play with but the toys were in the house, not in the shed. He liked the toys very much, and especially the Lego building kit and little horse soldiers with bright helmets, so when they told him to hide and be quiet he did because he dreaded being locked in the shed all the time.

For dinner they had chips and sausages and sometimes meat and beans. They had their dinner upstairs. He thought this was very quaint: upstairs was for going to bed and for having a bath. In one of the upstairs rooms, there were photographs on the wall. He was delighted to see one of himself, in his red T-shirt and the trainers bought him by his mother. A few photographs showed the garden in his mother's and father's house, with all the flowers and the climbing frame. He liked climbing. There was a big picture of Sam the dog before he was shot and some others of his mother and father and his father's car.

Milton came in one day when he was looking at those pictures and he said: 'Don't cry, you'll be back there soon, Graham, if everything goes all right.' Sometimes Milton touched him on his trousers, when he was talking to him. He disliked that but did not know what to do about it. Milton said Sam was dead now but there were shops for buying new dogs, so that would be all right.

When Milton was talking to him that day, Rick came in and said the pictures could come off the wall now. He said they should be burned because they were not needed any longer. But they did not do it.

Rick talked more quietly than Milton and Dave and had a lot of pretty rings on his hands. His soft voice made him sound kind, and Rick never hit him, but Graham was not really sure whether he was kind. Only Dave and Milton hit him. Sometimes Dave said sorry. Milton never said sorry.

Sometimes Milton was quiet and sometimes he was very loud. When he sang he had a cigarette in his mouth but he could still sing and it did not fall out. That amazed and thrilled Graham. Sometimes Dave and Milton played darts, throwing things at a thing on the wall, and the things stuck in it. Milton had some hair in his nose. The boy's mother had told him people could not help it when they had hair in their nose or pimples on their face. She said he must not talk about it to them, they did not like it, so he never mentioned the hair to Milton.

3

Harpur disliked farewell parties but thought he'd better go to Hubert Scott's. Twelve years ago, when Harpur was a newly promoted detective sergeant, they had been close colleagues, with Scott much the senior. He had stayed at that rank, apparently happy to transfer his ambitions to Free Masonry, where he was now a flashy eminence of some sort, often getting his name and title heavy typed in the *Daily Telegraph* announcements. He used to say that if Masonry was good enough for Rudyard Kipling it was good enough for him. The boys who did the office posters for his leaving thrash mocked up a picture showing him in gorgeous Masonic regalia and half throttling a masked man holding a sawn off shotgun: Hubert could still turn dangerously rough with villains once in a while. He was hard and he did not mind people knowing. Three or four times lately, though, Harpur had worked with Scott again and found him restrained enough, capable enough, loyal enough, and very brave. For his retirement he had landed a porter's job at the polytechnic, but always refused to talk about it. It was the kind of embarrassment and sadness which made Harpur very uncomfortable at send-offs and so inclined to dodge out. But Hubert was Hubert, and he went.

At Scott's wish, this one was 'a wives do'. People brought their spouses, and that pleased Harpur: outsiders stopped things getting too grim and mawkish. The décor team had festooned the bar with more pictures, one enlarged from a newspaper shot featuring Scott's torn and swollen face after he was cornered and beaten up by a hired crew on a vengeance outing not long ago. Another, lifted out of television film, showed him at a window with a knife at his throat during the two-day Royal Street siege, when he voluntarily took the place of a girl hostage. From a mock-up gibbet hung a nicely made dummy of Councillor Maurice Tobin, left-wing chairman of the police committee who had frequently raised questions about Hubert Scott's methods. The committee were not invited tonight. At the moment, Mark Lane, the Chief Constable, and his wife were standing near the gibbet, talking to Scott, Lane with his back to the effigy and pretending not to notice it. He had to live with Tobin, and he had to live with his men and women, too.

Benign-looking and beautifully dressed, as ever, Lane's Assistant Chief, Desmond Iles, was alone at the end of the bar and beckoned Harpur. 'How depressing to see Sally Lane losing a most courageous battle with that ever spreading elephant's arse of hers, Col. I'm not saying it doesn't suit her. No, Sally's all of a piece. Megan with you?'

'Circulating, sir.'

'Grand. Sarah had one of those previous engagements. Yes. Where she goes, God knows, possibly. She tells me she has her own life to live. They read these things now, don't they?'

'We'll all miss Hubert,' Harpur replied.

'Ah, I see: seek the safe ground. All right – yes, good old Hubert. I'm very fond of Hubert, and not just because of the Lodge. Mind you, the Chief's been blathering lately that he should have got out sooner.'

'What the hell does that mean?'

Iles leaned forward a little so that a sheaf of grey hair fell across his brow. He pushed it back, then froze with his hand still there. 'Put a bullet in each of my knees if you ever see me perform that gorgeous Heseltine gesture again, Col, will you?' he snarled.

'Why should Hubert have gone sooner, sir?'

'I'm supposed to sit on this for the time being – you know the Chief and that mean little taste for secrecy.'

'Sit on what, sir?'

'Apparently we have a big visitor coming down to look at . . . well, look at certain allegations.'

'Oh, Christ, Hubert got heavy once in a while. It's water under the bridge.'

'Maybe, but that's not the point, as I understand it.'

'What else?'

The Assistant Chief made a small, brief unclenching movement with one hand. 'It's a grief, Col.'

'On the take?' Harpur said. 'Hubert? Oh, that's got to be wrong, sir.'

'That's the tale. Lane seems very eager to believe it, in that unwholesome way of his. He comes into the Force and begins looking for corruption before he's got his feet under his desk.'

'Taking who from?'

'Nobody minor.'

'Who?'

'The only word I have on it is Lane's.'

'OK. So who?'

'He says our friend Tenderness.'

'Taking from Mellick?'

'Alleged.'

'And who's the Chief's source?'

'Over a period of at least two years.'

'Who says?'

'Lane wouldn't tell me. After all, I'm only his Number Two.' He nodded at the hanged effigy of Tobin. 'I wouldn't be surprised if this questing, point-scoring rag-and-bone man were behind it. Anyway, they're sending some Assistant Chief from outside to investigate. That's not going to satisfy Tobin and his like – police judge and jurying police and all that formula – but it's the best they'll get. Naturally, the Chief's not too bothered. He's half in favour of anything that does damage to the Craft. We keep a bit of an eye on Tenderness?'

'Yes.'

'Something special going on there?'

'Not that I heard.'

'He just coins it and coins it, no hassle. A protection team protected? Maybe someone from this quarter really is giving him comfort and succour.'

'Hubert's going out to a nothing job, for God's sake, sir. If he was being paid by Tenderness – '

'Hubert's a very bright and very experienced old lad, Col. Is he going to send signals? Next year the Bahamas, maybe, not next week. He probably knows people are watching.'

'You believe all this? I thought he was a mate of yours.'

'A Brother.'

'So?'

Iles did not answer. Instead, he said: 'Lane's afraid the shit will start flying all ways if this visitor does some earnest digging. We could do without that. Are you still having happy times with Ruth Cotton, or Avery that was? Of course you are. Who's going to ditch a pair of thighs like those, for God's sake? And are you still running your perilous reciprocities with assorted undisclosed grasses, all that grey area activity. Of course you are. How else do you get convictions? But, you see what I mean, Colin? Why, there's Ruth and her husband now. Isn't she looking healthy? You're very good for her.'

Iles grinned across the room and waved. Ruth responded. Harpur waved, too, and Ruth gave one of those very tiny, dead-and-alive smiles she could always produce for him at public occasions. Then she turned away and began talking sweetly to her husband and their group. It was wise, it was discreet, it was the only behaviour possible, but it still hurt him. Ruth and

17

Harpur had been running these disguises for a long while now, but the sight of her temporarily out of reach and seemingly happy with Robert Cotton always depressed him.

'They can haul Hubert back whenever they like for questioning,' Iles said. 'How's that going to look to his new employers? And do you think he, or anyone else, can count on support from Lane if matters get sweaty?'

It did not sound as if Iles expected a reply, and in any case, Harpur was still watching Ruth.

'Well?' Iles demanded.

Harpur had forgotten that Iles did not ask questions which might be left unanswered. 'Sir, I believe the Chief would do everything legitimate to look after the proper interests of any officer who became the subject of inquiry.'

For a second, Harpur thought the ACC would hit him. Iles's body tensed inside the grand suit and he half raised his left arm, the fingers of his hand tight in a fist. Then he relaxed them and pretended he had been reaching for his drink on the bar. 'Are you taking a correspondence course in spokesmanship, Harpur? What were those creepy terms – "legitimate", "proper"? This is a police force, not *Sense and* fucking *Sensibility*.'

'I think I'll find my wife, sir.'

'Boasting again.'

Harpur made his way through the crowd towards Megan, who had joined the Chief and Sally Lane with Hubert Scott. Megan looked to be in very good form. She and Harpur had drunk a couple of bulky gins at home before they left, and now she was laughing and waving her arms about and amiably poking Scott in the chest with her finger to emphasize some point. Harpur liked it when she drank. He could not persuade her to do it very often, though. Some of her worthy worry about the world could disappear for a while when she had taken a few on board, and some of that biting uneasiness she felt among police in the mass. When they first met fifteen years ago she had been drinking a bit, and perhaps that had helped bring them together. Occasionally these days he could not think of very much else that might have done it.

She beckoned Harpur: 'Colin, love, we're discussing ethics. It's all right. Don't panic – not police, political ethics.'

All the same, he groaned and slowed down, and was glad to be intercepted by Francis Garland. In that special, overwhelming

18

way of his, Garland at once began talking urgently, as if Harpur's only wish in life was to hear his words: 'I took a swift look around the Mellick place, sir. Outside only, as you suggested. No boy of eleven about, and the dossier says there should be, so your informant might have things right. They use a dark glass Merc and I couldn't tell who was going in and out. Megan not with you tonight, sir?'

'What? For Christ's sake, yes, Megan is with me tonight, just behind you. Iles first, now you, why the concern?'

'People have your welfare at heart, sir.'

'What about you? No bird tonight, Francis?'

'Picking records.' He nodded towards the juke box and Harpur saw a dark-haired girl he did not recognize.

'You'll be relieved to hear Sarah Iles isn't here.'

Garland shrugged. 'Long time ago, sir.' A Randy Crawford record came on, *Now We May Begin*.

'She has taste, too,' Harpur said.

'I talked to kids in the street near Mellick's house, just very gentle stuff, nothing head-on. They didn't know anything about the boy: almost never saw him, so they'd have no idea if he was missing. "A head case", they call him, poor little bugger. Apparently, he only ever played with them once in the street, and Tenderness and his missus arrived in a big sweat, afraid he was lost. The kids reckon an Alsatian has disappeared from the house – it used to bark, but hasn't for more than a week. They had some idea it could have been got at by men a couple of them saw with a green van. Probably three. The descriptions are feeble, but they might fit a trio of Ivor Wright's boys – Ancient Dave, Rick the Intelligent and Milton Bain. There's a lot of trouble between Ivor and Tenderness, isn't there?'

'Yes, you could say that. If someone goes for your balls with a blowlamp you might want to give a reply. But, Christ, three men, a strange van – I thought the Enclave was built with its own security. Wasn't that the idea? All sorts of vulnerable money lives up there: Tenderness, Mr Porno, high-tech wizards, the fruit machine king, a snooker champ – '

'The security's a farce, sir. More ways in than a blow-up doll. If – '

His girl returned from the juke box and pulled him away to dance. Harpur saw that she was very beautiful, with fine dark

19

eyes and lovely, pale skin. She scarcely glanced at Harpur, though, and that nettled him. Christ, was he starting to look old? Garland was such a catch, for God's sake? Did she fancy being jawed to death?

Megan went out on to the floor with Scott and Harpur followed with Scott's wife. It was better than talking ethics, any ethics. Jessie Scott beamed about the crowded room, a tall, square shouldered woman of fifty, wearing ornate spectacles and biggish pieces of wine-coloured costume jewellery. In a pause between records, Harpur said: 'It's a great turn-out. Well, what you'd expect, Jess. Everyone likes Hubert.'

'The Chief's been really ever so nice. I mean, all the things about Hubert he was saying just now, and Mrs Lane. They're caring, no side. What does it matter they're RC? Mr Iles goes on about "the Micks", but it's not pleasant, not nice. Take as you find. Mr Lane thinks the world of Hubert, that's obvious. It makes some of the rough bits like in these photos seem sort of worthwhile.'

'And you're glad to be going?'

She nodded. The music was about to restart. 'Of course, we've got regrets, especially Hubert. But – he'd kill me for saying this, you know – but he's getting a bit old to take these hammerings, isn't he? Soon he won't be giving as good as he gets.' Ella Fitzgerald began to sing *Every Time You Say Goodbye*.

'So sweet of them,' Jessie Scott said. 'Hubert's been putting it off, putting it off. It's a way of life, isn't it, Mr Harpur, not just a job? And there are one or two things he would have liked to finish.' She was moving slightly to the music. 'He really wanted to nail that bleeding Tenderness for the incendiary raid on Ivor Wright's face, neck and balls.'

So, if Hubert was in Tenderness's pocket, she did not know about it, or she was a top-class actress. He had always thought of her as totally straight. But, then, he had always thought of Hubert as totally straight.

'All right, we all know Ivor's offal,' she said, 'and this was just part of some endless, dirty gang war, but he was entitled to a love life, too. You've got to draw a line. It was a big mission with Hubert.' She added something which Harpur did not hear properly above the record, possibly 'Win some, lose some.'

20

He let it go, but could not really believe things always evened out. They didn't. You lost more, a lot more. She and Hubert might soon discover that for themselves. It was when you thought you'd just about managed to come out on top that you could suddenly lose everything.

The music ended and they made their way off the floor. Jessie said: 'Megan looks so lovely tonight. Well, always.'

'Yes.'

'I think of you two and the girls as the perfect family.'

'That's very kind, Jess.'

'I mean it: the two or three times I've been to your house – I could feel the love and happiness there. It really hit me.'

'Yes, the kids are a great help.'

'Not just the kids. You two. Somehow you've kept it alive after how many years of marriage—fifteen, sixteen? The kids are so lucky. And I know you'll go on like that.'

'Yes.' Did anybody know anything about anybody, really know it?

Lane was getting ready to lead Hubert and her up to the platform for the speeches and a presentation. Iles, master of ceremonies for the night, was already there, alight with special goodwill, team feeling in glorious spate.

Megan took Harpur's arm in a loving, slightly tipsy way, leaning into him, and stretched up as if to speak fondly, close to his ear: 'There's something very bloody wrong, Col.'

'Is there?'

'Isn't there? You know it. Don't kid about.'

'Tell me exactly what you think it is, Meg,' he said.

'No idea, but looking at Lane, I can feel it. What does he know?'

'Shall we make a move, then?' the Chief said and he and his wife and the Scotts began to push gently through the crowd.

'Hubert knows it, too,' Megan said.

'Knows what, for God's sake?'

'Anyone can see it in his face.'

'He seems fine to me.'

'Well, yes, he looks a bit better than in some of those pictures on the wall. But poor old bugger, who's he crossed, Colin?'

Iles tapped the microphone and began. 'Ladies and gentlemen, we're in the presence of a legend tonight. I'm still a comparative newcomer to this fine Force, but in the time I've been here I've come to recognize in Hubert Scott all the most worthwhile principles of policing, and especially detective policing.'

'Shoot first,' someone yelled, and there was a big, long laugh from the audience.

'Well, one duty of an officer is to stay alive, with all his members unimpaired,' Iles said. 'As far as I can tell, he's done that, despite I don't know how many near things, and it's grand that he should look so durable and happy here tonight.'

Harpur studied Scott, trying to spot the signs of distress Megan claimed to see: Hubert was sharp enough and informed enough to have picked up any threatening rumours that might be about. He did seem a little tense and pale, but only what might be expected in someone leaving a job he loved after thirty-odd years and going out to become a nowhere nothing. He had a round, sallow face, almost genial when he was with people he regarded as his friends, and set rigid when he was not. Tonight, there were moments when he looked cheerful enough, but Harpur thought he was having to work at it. Megan obviously felt the same.

Iles was talking about the changes Scott had seen and adapted to. 'This patch is damn wealthy territory now, thanks to the lush flowering of high-tech factories with their coin-op owners. And, despite black days on the Stock Exchange, we host all sorts of the mega-loaded, looking for an out from London's crime and property prices and Aids to bijou, provincial fortress estates, like our Elms Enclave. Of course, where you get the prosperous you will also get the clubs and the casinos and the drug dens and the super-rat villains. Vegas-on-sea. Well, I'm not telling you anything new: you've seen it, and learned to deal with it. Policing for us has become more dangerous and a lot rougher. Nobody has coped with these new conditions better than Hubert Scott.'

'They don't come rougher,' a voice called.

'We all have to fight harder,' Iles said, 'or the filth will drown us. We're snorkling in shit – if Mrs Lane will forgive the imperfect alliteration. There are villains fighting us, and fighting each other, and somehow out of this nettle, danger, we have to pluck the flower, safety, for the general, decent populace. There are a few of them left, and they're worth worrying about, even if they do elect crud kings like Tobin. There's nothing personal against Maurice Tobin, I know the Chief would not like to think that. It's

22

just that he and so many others whom we have to take some note of are intellectual derelicts, cheapjack moralisers. However, we do take note of him and those like him and, were he here, I would be happy to assure him – reassure him – that we always strive to work within the rules. Yes.' He gazed over respectfully towards the hanged effigy of the police committee councillor and, speaking with heavy reverence, said: 'We enforce the law and are wholly bound by that law.'

Lane nodded.

'To Hubert Scott this precept has always been especially meaningful and dear,' Iles declared. Lane nodded once more and briefly applauded. A group of men near the bar began to sing, 'For he's a jolly good Grand Master.'

Iles held up a hand and quelled that. 'Society looks at its problems and asks, "Whom shall we send, who will go for us?" And Hubert Scott replies, "Here am I, send me." Of course, when the job is done, and the problems resolved for the moment, so that people feel safe again, society is liable to turn round and kick the man who did it. Gratitude? The word's not in their fu . . . is not in their dictionaries. So, do we retaliate? Are we bitter? No, we smile patiently, accept these things as part of our role, wait for the next task. This is what makes men like Hubert Scott great.'

Lane would speak next. Behind him on a table were a golf bag and clubs, a video machine and a large bouquet in cellophane wrapping. Iles came down from the platform and stood with Harpur and Megan.

'Very resonant, Desmond,' she said.

'Now and then my heart takes over.'

'Same for all of us.'

Lane beamed out at the crowd in that affable, winning style of his and said: 'Of course, this is a sad occasion tonight, but I feel – '

Suddenly, Scott who was standing close to him put a hand on the Chief's shoulder and shoved him hard away from the microphone. Lane stumbled and almost fell, then recovered.

'Let's stop all this, Mr Lane,' Scott yelled. 'Stop it right now. It's a bloody farce.' Harpur saw that Hubert was weeping. The gnarled, unshockable face shone with tears. His wife had hold of his coat and tried to tug him back but he didn't shift. For a moment Lane seemed bemused.

Scott gripped the stalk of the microphone and bellowed into it:

'I'm being set up. They smarm me here and make out I'm perfection, and all the time they're slitting my throat.'

People had suddenly become totally silent. Nobody barracked now, nobody joked. Some turned away, unable to watch him.

'What are you saying?' his wife screamed. 'What's this about, Hubert, for God's sake? So crude, so unnecessary.'

'The old story with this lot,' Scott told the crowd. 'I'm the sacrifice. You've all heard? It could be any of you next.'

The Chief had recovered and gently tried to reclaim the microphone, muttering calming words. Scott fought him off. 'There's rottenness here, all through and far up,' he shouted. 'I'm not carrying the can for them. I'm not being bought off with a fucking set of clubs and a video. "Thanks very much, Hubert, so long now, and stand by for a knock on the door and a hand on your collar."'

He turned away and pulled a club from the bag. When the Chief moved towards him, arms stretched out in a consoling gesture, Scott swung the club at him, a sweeping, one-handed blow which caught Lane high on the cheek with the metal head. The Chief staggered but again did not fall. Scott put both hands around the club handle. 'Keep away,' he bellowed. 'All of you.' His wife was weeping, too, now and she stepped towards him. 'No, Jess. Stay there.' He swung the club again, this time bringing the head crashing down on the video machine and the flowers, then repeated this and repeated it. Iles swiftly climbed to the platform.

'Hubert, this is only entirely understandable stress,' he said.

'You, you bastard. You're deeper in it than any of them. You've got some coming, too. You're supposed to be a hard man, aren't you? I'm the hard man, but they all say you're harder still. We'll see how hard you are now, when you're not sitting behind a desk and rotaring others to take the risks.' He spun to face the ACC but before Scott could switch the club from his attack on the gifts, Iles ducked in fast, grabbed him hard by the lapels of his blazer and pulled him close, then cracked down with his head on the bridge of Scott's nose. The club fell to the floor. Scott folded forward for a moment, blood pouring from both nostrils. He put his hands to his face and groaned. Iles held him by the hair, perhaps to keep him still, perhaps to save him from falling further.

'What the hell are you doing, Hubert?' he said. 'You're really in decline, old lad. A bit of blood and pain and you leave yourself as wide open as the Book of Remembrance. I could have taken you apart. How in God's name have you lived so long? Well, it's time to retire, with or without a video, I'd say.'

He pushed a chair under Scott, then turned to look at Lane, who was still on his feet and also bleeding. His wife had folded a handkerchief and the Chief held it against the wound. Carefully, Iles removed this pad and looked at the cut. 'Nothing too bad, sir. Hubert's got a hopeless, rheumatoid swing, especially one-handed. I imagine we won't be bringing charges? It wouldn't look too good in the papers.'

Harpur saw Ruth go to the juke box and select records. Very briefly she grinned at him and shrugged, as if such a fracas was run-of-the-mill at these parties. For tonight, that moment of special communication would have to do. He was grateful for it. This was the kind of life they had settled for.

At first, nobody danced, but then Garland and his girl started and others followed. Things picked up again. The platform was cleared and Harpur and Iles sat with Scott and his wife near the bar. Hubert had more or less stopped bleeding now, but his blazer and shirt and shoes were stained. 'Why won't he tell me anything of what it's all about, Mr Harpur?' Jessie Scott asked. She was close to weeping again.

Iles said: 'We're going to take care of him. Don't worry.'

'Oh, come on, Mr Iles,' Jessie said. 'Is Mr Lane going to take care of him after this?'

'The Chief doesn't bear grudges, Jessie,' Iles replied. 'It's one of the great things about him. Forget his funny way with clothes and the unctuousness. He really is a good man, a father figure since birth.'

'Who is it that's coming?' Scott asked.

'The visiting eminence?' Iles said. 'We don't know yet. We can handle him. We're a team here. We look after one another. Is he going to take us all on, for God's sake?'

'Maybe you'll know him – I mean, friends,' Scott said. He was speaking a plea.

'It's possible. Not many of my friends are cops. Police are all so damn grave,' Iles replied.

Soon afterwards the Scotts gathered up the golf equipment, their scarred video and broken-backed flowers and prepared to leave.

'I'd go home myself if I thought she'd be there,' Iles said to Harpur. 'Once in a while I envy Lane for picking a wife nobody else is ever going to want.' He and Harpur stood at the bar with port and lemons, Iles's favourite: what he called 'the old tarts' drink'. Megan danced with an inspector from Drugs, Ruth danced with her husband, again. Iles glanced at Harpur. 'Christ, you moralizing sod, you're debating whether I should have hit Hubert so hard.'

'I don't think his nose is broken.'

'I'm supposed to hold back until he's pulped my skull?'

'No, sir, we must keep you in top form, in case any more keynote speeches are needed.'

4

Mellick had a red-brick, Queen Anne style corner house on the Elms Enclave, the picture window of the big rear lounge looking down towards where the elms themselves used to be before they grew sick and were felled. He had never liked the place: too flash, too large, too dear, too much of a target. It was the sort of thing Jane wanted, though, so he had bought it with a murderously high interest loan from a fast-buck banker at the plans stage. Who would give him a proper mortgage, for Christ's sake? Was he going to disclose his income and say how he got it?

The Jacuzzi and wrought iron work and sunken bath and security system and the rest were standard, but Jane had asked them for an extra room downstairs next to the kitchen where Graham could play and never be far away. To her disappointment, the boy scarcely ever used it and always wanted to be outside. He would have preferred to go in the street and find friends, but they managed to keep him in the garden most of the time. She feared that other children would be heartless and rough with him and that he would not know how to cope with traffic. Of course, he met boys and girls at his school, but it was a special school and he did not stand out.

Now Graham had been taken, Jane Mellick suddenly began to share her husband's hatred of the house and he had promised to put it on the market as soon as their son was found. Since he went she had been unable to do any cooking or cleaning and Mellick prepared rough meals or brought home take-aways, and occasionally did a bit of tidying and dusting. The work helped keep him sane. They were in the rear lounge now, blue floral curtains drawn across the picture window, although it was day, because she could not bear looking at the garden where Graham had been snatched. They were sedating her but Mellick was scared she might slide into a real breakdown if this went on much longer. Already there were moments when she couldn't get her words out, and when her body looked as if she'd lost all strength and coordination. He needed her to be right. At home he depended on Jane very heavily, and especially now there was trouble. He came from a family where the wife and mother had unusual power and used it to help deal with all major domestic crises. Always he had looked for that sort of support from Jane, more than ever since Graham was born, and now she could not give it he felt lost. 'There might be a call, any time, love,' he said.

'Oh, God, another dud?'

'I got good people looking and listening everywhere, Jane. They'll ring as soon – This sort of thing, all sorts of people wants to help. They don't like it when kids are drawn in, it's not on, so the next call could be the one, Jane. Eventually, it's going to be the one. Bound to be. We been getting close. I know it.'

'It could be the one,' she mimicked. 'Eventually. How long's eventually, Bernie? Nearly nine days now and – '

He made himself remain patient with her. 'I know, love. It's – '

'Is it going to be nine weeks, nine months. Would it be best if I started a new baby?'

'Jane, love, no, not so long, I swear.'

'Another phone call, another answer to it all, just around the corner,' she whispered, almost as though talking only to herself. 'How many telephone calls? We know less now than when we started. Isn't that right? People ringing up and saying, "Sorry,

Tenderness, it's a dead end." Yes, they're good boys, but they can't do what they can't do.'

He was sitting on a settee opposite her and would have liked to go and comfort her, put his arm around her shoulders, give her some warmth and perhaps take some. Yes, he had needs, too. He knew he would not be welcome, though. 'Love, I know you're having a bad time, well, we both are. But, look, just only a bit more patience, I swear.' He began to repeat the words of hope: 'I've got boys, good boys – '

'You've got boys, but I haven't got my boy, have I? Where is he this minute? Can you tell me that? Can any of your boys tell me that? Do you know where he slept last night, or the night before? Do you know if someone's messing about with him? Have you thought about that? Have you? Do you know if he's still – ? Do you know if he's all right? Of course you don't.'

'Love, I don't think they'd – '

'Bernie, you got to go to the police.'

'Oh, Christ, please, not that again.'

'Please, listen. Just don't go crazy. Listen to me. Please? I don't love police no more than you do, but they've got a lot of men and helicopters, they got records, Bernie. They're not fools. They might know where to look. They keeps tabs on all sorts, unofficial. That thing they got, you told me.' She waved a hand feebly, unable to find the word today.

'Collator.'

'So, give them a chance. Give us a chance.'

Now Mellick went and sat with her on the other long, heavy-cushioned blue settee. She was folded into a corner, small and tense, like a child who had been beaten. He even risked putting an arm around her shoulders. 'We been through all this so many times, haven't we? You think the police are going to help Bernard Mellick? You really believe that?'

'They got to help, it's what they're there for. And it's not for Bernard Mellick, it's a child, a boy of eleven with the brain of a six-year-old. They're not all rotten. I've heard them on the telly about old ladies being beat up and that saying this is a real evil and cowardly crime and it sounds as if they really wanted to get the people who done it. This is like that, isn't it?'

'Yes, yes, everybody's friend, that's what they are. Christ, you believe that? Jane, love, all they'd think is, This is something

belongs to Tenderness, so who the hell cares? They got all sorts of big scores to settle. They're like that. They like paying back. They haven't been able to put their finger on me for so long. Now, here's the chance. They like saying time is on their side. Well, this is time being on their side, that's what they would say.'

'They couldn't do it. There's some are decent.'

'Police?'

'They got kids themselves.'

'Course they got kids theirselves and they're the ones they look after.'

'Please, Bernie, tell them.' She turned slowly and faced him, her eyes red from crying and sleeplessness.

'You don't understand, Jane.'

'What don't I understand. Am I stupid? All right, some parts of your work I don't understand, and maybe I don't want to. But I understand most of it. I see people who work for you, Ditto and Reg and Len, I know they're not bloody dress designers. I hears them talking. I sees what's strapped to Ditto's shoulder sometimes. I know what a Walther is and it's not somebody with a lisp talking about Sir Walter Raleigh. Anyway, so what even if I don't understand everything about all that, I understand about Graham. There's some bloody thing, some bloody rule, that says people like us or like you don't ever go to the police, you got to sort out everything yourselves. You don't need no police, do you, you're bigger than police. That's what makes you all right, isn't it, a man? A man! It's like kids not telling the teacher. So, who made that rule? Who says so? Maybe it got to be like that about thieving or a hammering, that's private business, always has been. That I do understand. I mean, who's going to tell police about money if we're robbed, where it come from, I see that, it's only sensible. But this is the life of a boy, a retarded boy, Bernie, your son. Who tells you you got to take such risks with him?'

He stroked her face. 'There's risks and risks, love. You don't stop the risks by telling the police. Maybe you make more. How do I know who's paying who? Think, if I was to tell them and the job lands on the desk of someone who been taking a regular drink from Ivor Wright? He looks after his contacts in there. Ivor got Graham, that's almost for sure. Who else? But you see what I mean? These things are tangled up, Jane. Do you see?'

She began to sob and pulled away from him. 'No, I don't

bloody see. They would still have to search, wouldn't they? They can't ignore it. This is a child kidnapped, not even a normal child. If the papers got to hear about that or that *World In Action*, even if it is the son of a – the son of someone the police got a down on. There's people who watch to see they don't dodge their duty, councillors, Members of Parliament. They got inspectors of constabulary, or something like that. All right, I know they're more police, but – well, it can't all be so rotten and bad.'

'They can do what they want, Jane. See, they're police. They runs things. They does it how they wants to do it. Yes, there's councillors, all that, but what do they know? They're only in it for the expenses and the freebies abroad. These police, they're clever, they're around a long time, they know the scene. They can see off a couple of councillors, that sort. Oh, maybe they'd have to make a show that they was looking, but would they be really putting anything in it, if it was someone on Ivor's payroll? Can't you see, love? And then the message goes to Ivor that we're talking to the police, and that could – that might not be very good for Graham.'

'Did they tell you that – no talking to police.'

'They haven't told me a thing, Jane, have they? Nobody been in touch, no whisper since he went. I can try and guess what it's all about, but I don't really know. I can try and guess, but that's all. I even got to guess who got him. I say Ivor, but I don't know it, I couldn't prove it. I would of told you if I knew. Of course I would. But, I'll tell you this, whoever got him won't be happy if we're talking to the police. Yes, whoever got him. We can't find Ivor to ask and we can't find some of his boys – Rick the Intelligent, Bain and Ancient Dave. Ivor got to be near a clinic because he's still not great after them injuries during the late incident, but of course he goes private, so the clinic could be anywhere, it could be abroad. North Africa, Spain, he likes them places. They could all rub a bit of ointment on the scorches for him.'

'Oh, God, Graham could be there, out of Britain? How are we ever going to find him?'

'No, not Graham. Ivor wouldn't handle this sort of job himself. Anyway, he's too convalescent. He got to go quiet. He's not very well.'

She sobbed: 'Burning. Did you have to do that to him, I mean, fire, it's so terrible.'

'Well, he asked for that, Jane. It's terrible, yes, but it was the only way. He had to learn something. Yes, it had to be. There was some things he done before to us. These things got to be settled, haven't they? Ivor was definitely out of order. Jane, there got to be order or business is finished, it can't run without order. Ask anyone in business, the first thing you got to have is proper order. But you don't need to know about all that side of the work. So, don't worry yourself about a turd like Ivor.'

'This turd got my boy. This turd don't go to the police either, even when it's a blowlamp, and he convinces medics it's an accident. An accident – somebody gets his balls nearly burned off and it's an accident, I don't know how. So now he got a frying debt to put right, personal. This turd thinks he knows about order, too.'

'They don't hurt kids.'

'Is that another one of the rules, then?' She was yelling suddenly. 'How d'you know? They never used to take kids away, either, did they?'

'It's just to scare us.'

'Well, it's working bloody great,' she said. She wiped her face and grew quieter. 'I've never been so scared, and since I been with you, Bernie, I been very scared a hell of a lot. Listen now, I said at the start I'd phone the police myself if you wouldn't and I will.' But she did not move from the settee.

He stood up and his voice changed, too. 'I don't want you to do that, Jane. I've told you. I could get so I didn't like you at all if you ever done that, love.' He spoke quietly, the words flat and cold. 'I'd know, even if you done that secretly, or an anon call to them. I'd hear about it. I gets information. That could bring damage to Graham, and if you did that I wouldn't be able to forgive you, Jane, even if I really tried.'

'And what about if – ?'

The telephone rang and for a moment he watched it, as if able to read the worth of the call before answering. Then he crossed the room and picked it up. He listened only for a couple of seconds and said: 'I'll call you back.'

Jane was still hunched in on herself on the settee. 'Something?' she asked wearily, and he saw she could not believe it might be.

'It's possible. I told you, didn't I?' His tone was warm and loving again. 'I'm going to a payphone. I still don't know whether this one has listeners.'

She sat forward and stared at him, attempting to work out how hopeful he really was. 'Bernie, come back and tell me.'

'Yes, of course I will.'

'Whatever it is.'

'Yes, love, of course. But it's going to be good.'

It was good, but he did not have time to go back to Jane. An hour later Mellick was in an Audi with three men. On their tail was a Carlton, with another four in it.

'What Ivor's had is what's known as a relapse, Tenderness,' Ditto Repeato said. He had the front passenger seat and turned to talk to Mellick who was in the back with Len. Reg drove. 'What's known as a relapse,' Ditto said. 'He've gone into this place near Aylesbury where they got top doctors calling and all comforts, he been there before. Near Aylesbury. That's how Vernon got on to it at last, because Ivor been there before. Vernon got this memory, haven't he? Such a memory. He's a new boy and he's young but he knows a lot. Maybe we should of had him in on this sooner, Tenderness, then it wouldn't be eight or nine days to find Ivor. Vernon got this memory and he remembered this place Ivor went to near Aylesbury years ago, not because of the burning, something earlier, it could be a hammering he got when he was younger and was on the street more. It could have been a hammering. So Vernon went down to this place and hangs about outside, it's no good phoning or asking at the desk, they won't tell you who they got in there, it's that sort of place. That's the sort of place it is. They gets poxed up eminences and duke druggies and alcos and topmost characters slipping away with Aids and worried about what they'll say in the deads part of *The Times* if that gets known about, so it got to be confidential. Ivor, he would know about a place like that.'

'Who've we got in this other car?' Mellick asked. 'I wants real people.'

'Vernon's driving and I got you three more real people,' Ditto replied. 'These people will do what you tell them as long as the money's good, and they knows the money's good. They don't mess about. If the money's good they – '

'How much weaponry we got? He could have security at this place.'

32

'Well these three all carry something, this I know, an FN and a couple of Brownings, I think. Yes, Brownings and an FN.'

'You?'

'Yes. The Walther, I like that. The Walther's one I like.'

'I don't want him dead.'

'That been made very clear to everybody, Tenderness, you can rely on that. They knows this boy got to tell us things and even then we don't kill him because it could be wrong, it got to be checked out. What he tells us got to be made authentic. We don't kill him till we got your son back, that's obvious. We don't think he got anyone there with him, and we're sure Graham's not here. I'm sorry to say that, Tenderness, but he's not here. Vernon, he just hung about outside so he could get talking to people coming out of this place because it's the sort of place – '

'They don't tell you anything.'

'Right. You know this place? So, he says to them have they got someone in there, a man about thirty-seven with various burnings including what's known in medical as the genital area, which is the balls, but he didn't say it like that, well, no, on account of this is a medical place. Lucky, Vernon talks pretty rich, he could make Sir Gordon Olivier feel like he come from a work-house, and he got them clothes on, he looks like he really counts. Vernon, he can chat people up real good. These was cleaners coming out, that sort of people, not real medical people, but he didn't want to be saying balls to them, it would likely of made them wonder who he was, because they're used to proper medical talk, like genital area and passing water, even cleaners and that sort. They would of wondered.'

'Wright using his proper name?

'We're close,' Reg said. 'Give them a wave behind.' Leonard turned and signalled to the Carlton.

'No,' Ditto said, 'not his real name. That's how Vernon done so good, giving them a real description, not just the burning and the genital area, but he done it so they could really recognize Ivor and they said he was there, and pretty sick. Vernon really done it good, finding him. I mean, Aylesbury – it's a hell of a way, but Vernon put the finger on him there. They say Vernon's just all clothes and cock-happy, but he done good here. Well, these people Vernon asked said, yes, they had somebody like that, he was in such and such a Wing and room number something.

Vernon got it all. So when it was dark Vernon goes into the gardens and finds the window to this room, it's ground floor, and gets a look in and there's Ivor, lying down like a stone saint in church, getting blood from a drip and not looking great at all. I mean, if it wasn't Ivor you might feel sorry for somebody like that, getting a drip and maybe blood. He's not doing too good. Ground floor, so it's good for us, Tenderness.'

Reg pulled into a lay-by and the Carlton joined them. For a few minutes nobody left the cars.

Ditto said: 'It's about a quarter of a mile on the right. A big drive, but I didn't know if you want to go nearer with the cars. About a quarter of a mile. We going to bring him out, Tenderness, or try to mull over matters with him there?'

'Bring him out.'

'That's what I thought. They got your boy, we got theirs. I can't fault that for thinking. So we got to take the cars close?'

'I need to talk to Vernon, about the geography.'

'He got it good in his head. This memory of his. You may of heard of it. See, that's how Vernon knew about Aylesbury. All right, Vernon got this wanker's accent and talks like Jack Hawkins on the bridge on the telly and that, but he's a real one, Tenderness, he's a real real one.'

'I give him a job, didn't I, for Christ's sake. What you selling him for?'

'Sometimes I think you're not very keen – well, them clothes. But you give him a job, you're right there, Tenderness, I can't say different.'

Mellick left the car and walked back to the Carlton. Vernon climbed out and joined him. 'This got to be quick,' Mellick said. 'We're noticeable.'

'The cars were taken in London only yesterday. No trail to us,' Vernon said.

'I should bloody hope so. You see any security with Ivor when you was here? These people you talked to – anyone mention he had friends with him, that sort of thing?'

'I think he's alone, Tenderness. Out here, so far away, maybe he feels safe. And you know what he's like as I hear it – all that old world spunk and greatness, he could never be bothered with heavies, even now. Touching, really.'

'He's not producing much spunk now. Can you do us a quick map?'

'I have.' Vernon brought out a pad covered in cellophane. He was tall and thin, about twenty-three, wearing the best tapered cords and a cowboy shirt of green silk, with a trailing leather lace at the open neck. Mellick hated to believe anyone dressed like this could be useful, which was why Ditto and sometimes Leonard argued for him so hard. And they had it right: Tenderness knew Vernon was good, even if he did look like a night out in Dude City, and talked as though words had not been invented until he turned up.

Vernon pointed to the map and plan of the clinic. 'It's a late nineteenth-century mansion, Tenderness, good materials, braggart castle architecture, plus modern extensions stuck on to cope with success. Ivor's here, third room along in extension B. Good, big window, so two men could get in at once, but double-glazed. It will have to be smashed if we go that way, which means noise, though that doesn't matter much because there's an alarm and it will be banging away as soon as we break anything. If he's recovered a little and can look after himself, our boys would be soft targets in the window, you could say framed, unless they moved very fast. I'm taking it for granted they can't fire because we want him fit to talk.

'If we use the door it means going in through the main entrance to the original house, here. This time of night, there's a security guard on duty and a porter. The guard has radio contact with his office. If it's the same two as I saw, they're middle-aged and sold on the quiet life. They don't rate as opposition. At about this point, – '

'Can we get a car to the window, close?'

'It's a lawn outside, but yes.'

'Vernon, what about these other rooms? Who's in the two next to him, and down here? You sure none of his protection's there?'

'Virtually certain.'

'What the fuck's that mean? D'you speak English, you portrait? I'm in a hurry. A kid's life is on the line.'

Vernon stayed cool and fluent. 'Of course. Well, I checked as much as I could, Tenderness, without making things too obvious and drawing attention. The security lad patrols the gardens, so I

35

couldn't hang about voyeuring at windows. None of the people I spoke to said he had a crew with him. There's a woman who visits every few days, turns up in what could be Ivor's Scimitar, so it might be Della, I couldn't get much of a description.'

'That don't matter, do it? We just want to know what evil we could meet.'

'Well, I think we're clear.'

'You better have it right-through right, Vernon.' Tenderness stared for a moment up towards where the clinic and Ivor were, the buildings hidden by trees and darkness. 'Here's how it will be, then. You and the people from your car go in at the front door. Deal with whoever has to be dealt with. Just hold them, if it can be done like that. You hear me OK? We don't want no useless blood on the parquet, it's showy. But if it can't be done neat like that, all right, it can't. You have to do – well do what's unavoidable. You tell them boys with you, them people I never met, how it got to be, tell them straight, just a few words and no fucking virtuallies.'

A couple of cars passed and Vernon and Tenderness turned to avoid the headlight beams.

'Me and Ditto will go in at the window,' Mellick said. 'Reg and Len can stay spare in the garden, in case this security guard's around or they get quick help.'

'You really think you ought to go yourself?'

'It's my kid.'

'Yes, but a window entry – '

'Ivor would expect me to do it myself.'

'Yes, of course.' Vernon did not argue any more.

Mellick studied the map. 'Jesus, this sort of operation needs planning real careful, not five minutes in a bleeding lay-by.'

'Yes, I know, Tenderness. Yet these *faute de mieux* things can sometimes work remarkably well.'

Mellick snarled and gazed at him. Then he said: 'So what alarms?'

'First Contact, with local siren and a register at the security base. Break any window or lock and it's in action.'

'We just put up with that.'

'No other way. Move fast. The security base will have a police link. The usual system. But alarms are going off all the time in error. The police don't usually move until there's a confirmation.

We'll be away by then.' He sounded entirely sure. 'You take him in the Audi?' Vernon asked.

'Yes.'

'It's going to be cramped.'

'He's not so big.'

'He was on a drip.'

'Yes.'

'Right. Are you shipping him all the way back to your place, three hours' drive?'

'Christ, no. Ivor in my place? In the Enclave? I don't take work home. You mad or something? You talks Frog but you got any marbles? Just follow us. We'll find some bit of country close and we'll have a meeting of minds in a field. You get a bit of space and some quiet in a field. What you'd call rural, that would be your word.'

Mellick went back to the Audi and chose the heaviest spanner in the boot. Then he climbed into the car and told Reg to drive. Vernon kept very close behind. 'Pretty bright, that Vernon?' Ditto said.

'If he don't fall over his tie.'

The two cars surged up the clinic's long, dark drive. Mellick briefed Ditto and the other two.

'I'd say it's a doddle,' Ditto told him.

'Get the drip gear if he's still on it. Keep the bugger's life-line for a while.'

'Kid glove. We'll be like a couple of nurses with the Queen-fucking-Mother, Tenderness. What we'll be like is a couple of nurses.' He put his hand under his coat, checking the Walther in its holster.

'That only if there's no choice, Ditto, you sure you got it? And not on Ivor. Anyone but Ivor. Even if he got a piece himself. He's useless dead.'

'Tenderness, nothing will go wrong, I know it.'

The trees lining the drive had thinned suddenly. 'Across this lawn, Reg,' Mellick said. The Audi turned off and the Carlton kept going up towards the main house and door. For a second Mellick watched it. 'Christ, I never use people I don't know.'

'These are real people, Tenderness,' Ditto said.

Mellick had the map out. 'Here, Reg.'

The curtains were over in the room, and around the edge Mellick could see a small glow, as if from a night light. The four of them got out very quickly, leaving all the doors wide. Ditto and Reg had pistols in their hands.

'I hope this is right. Hell, they might have have moved him,' Mellick said and struck high at the glass with the spanner. The window shattered and he struck again at the inner layer of glass, then used the spanner twice more, clearing a decent space. An alarm started blaring in the main house as soon as he touched the glass. Mellick hauled himself up, pushed the curtains aside and paused for a second crouched on the sill. 'Greetings, Ivor,' he muttered, then jumped down. Wright was sitting against pillows watching *Newsnight* on television. Although the drip apparatus stood in a corner Ivor was no longer connected. The burn marks on his face and neck had lost some of that first gleaming pinkness but were still a hell of a drawback on the whole even in dim light from a bedside lamp. Della must really like Ivor if she kept coming to see him in this state.

Ballet dancers ponced around the screen. So, Ivor had discovered *Swan Lake*? The only lakes to interest him before were the ones he put people in wearing sinkers. He said something, something long and maybe emotional, looking at the excited way his lips worked, but Tenderness did not hear it over the siren and the music and the commentator, a woman frothing the life story of some foreigner in undersized tights. Mellick jumped down and, as he did, Wright turned and reached under a heap of clothes on a chair near the bed. But he was weak and slow, his hand moving in shaky stages – not a good, direct grab – as if he wasn't sure where it should be going. Mellick cracked down on his wrist with the spanner, then kicked the chair away. A short-nose Bodyguard Airweight revolver flew out and skidded across the floor. Mellick tore the bedclothes off him. He had pyjamas on and looked bulky around the middle, possibly bandages. Perhaps it was the balls burns that had woken up again and started to give him new bother: balls it was well known was complicated and in touch with the soul, nothing like a neck. It could be fresh balls trouble that had really cracked Ivor and made him turn wild and go for Graham. People was very moody about their balls.

Ditto landed in the room, the Walther out. He shoved the muzzle hard against Ivor's head. Mellick grabbed Ivor's shoulder with his free hand and pulled him towards the window. Ditto's eyes were big and sweat drops stood in his moustache. He was yelling non-stop at Ivor, and jabbing him with the gun, trying to help Mellick shift him. They had him out of bed and he stood, bent and rubber-legged, like an old man. He could fall any time. Yes, the balls went right through you, feet, knees, brain, backbone, everything, great for ballet costumes, maybe, but a ruin all the way once they was wrong. Ditto used one hand to grip Ivor's arm and help hold him up.

The door to the corridor was suddenly shoved open hard and Vernon stood there with one of the new boys, both holding pistols. Blood streaked the toe-cap of Vernon's right shoe. The new boy saw this dancer legging it in circles, all suppleness and flashing arse, and with two-handed aim fired into the television screen. Bits of the set flew everywhere and the man started laughing like a fool. Mellick couldn't hear him because of the rest of the din, but it seemed worse like that, madder, this joker's face getting redder, his mouth wide and shoulders shaking.

A fragment of glass or metal from the television hit Ditto high on the side of his head and he put up a hand to feel the damage. Mellick had turned to shout useless curses at the laughing gunman and Vernon, and had half released his hold on Ivor's shoulder. As Ditto's support went, too, Mellick felt Ivor start to go down and desperately tried to take a good grip again, but it was too late. Ivor sagged and then tumbled forward on to the floor, like someone clubbed from behind.

He fell very close to the little Bodyguard Airweight and the new boy saw the revolver there and suddenly stopped laughing. Both Ivor's arms went out in front of him as he hit the ground, and it could have looked as if he had only gone down to reach the gun. Yes, it could have looked like that to somebody half mad. One of Ivor's wrists was red and swelling after the spanner blow. The new boy shouted something panicky and raised the Browning again two-handed. Vernon had his brain going and tried to shove him off balance before he could squeeze the trigger, but Vernon was skinny and light and the new boy a bit of a bull. Although he did shift an inch he was still able to put two bullets into Ivor's back, and might have given him the rest if Ditto hadn't turned and fired in one movement, the gun almost as low as his waist, like someone marine trained. Mellick saw the new boy's big throat torn open, and he was half spun by the impact before folding slowly down near the door. The bullet had gone right through him, smashing one of a picture series on the wall behind showing dogs in trousers and trilby hats playing snooker, the kind of merry, club touch they gave you in private clinics. Vernon kicked him twice with the stained shoe where he lay, so the new boy had blood on his waistcoat as well as on his shirt collar. Some contribution, putting the boot into a corpse.

Two rectangles of blood came through on the back of Ivor's white silk pyjamas, one high, between the shoulders, the other near the waist and to the right. They were spreading fast and would meet soon. Mellick bent close to Ivor's face. His eyes were open and he blinked, though he might not be seeing anything. His lips moved fractionally as he struggled for breath, and Mellick reckoned he would have heard him gasping if the siren stopped. It wasn't going to stop.

Mellick signalled to Ditto and they took an arm each and pulled Ivor upright. He was deadweight now and his head lolled against Mellick's, like a drunk's. They moved him towards the window, his feet trailing through the television debris and making furrows. Len appeared at the window, looking very scared. He liked jobs that were tidy from start to finish and this had turned out a total mess. Vernon went quickly ahead of Mellick and Ditto, climbed out and stood with Len, ready to lift Ivor up over the sill, about four feet above ground level. They leaned in and took an arm each. Mellick and Ditto lifted him from the waist, their hands and sleeves soaked. Now his head hung helplessly back, like someone being hauled drowned from the water. Mellick and Ditto went out through the window after him.

In the grounds, the din from the siren was not so overpowering and Mellick heard Reg rev the Audi before backing it closer.

'I've got to come with you,' Vernon yelled.

Mellick saw what he meant. The dead man with the Browning had two friends waiting in the corridors somewhere. They would want to know what had happened, and might not believe Vernon had done nothing towards his death. For a second, Mellick thought of telling him to sort it out himself with the Carlton boys. If Vernon had handled his job right and looked after that goon with the Browning, there would have been no accident, and Ivor would still be in tidy shape. Then they could have persuaded the information about Graham out of him, most likely.

But he found he could not turn Vernon over to take his chance in the Carlton. Vernon was part of the outfit, and nothing else counted. You had to stand by your people. They made mistakes, but in business you couldn't always avoid mistakes, you had to learn to make the best of things. It was going to add up to five plus Ivor in the Audi.

'Put him in the boot,' Vernon said.

'No. He might not last. He got to talk.' They pushed Ivor into a corner seat and Mellick sat next to him, with Len on the right. Vernon shared the front passenger place with Ditto. Reg had the car moving as the last two climbed aboard.

'What about the others?' Len asked.

'Who?'

'The two new boys.'

'Sod them,' Ditto said. 'Maybe one of them bloody new boys have cost Tenderness his son. We don't know the buggers.'

'If they're taken they'll talk,' Vernon said.

'Yea, we ought to warn them to get out,' Mellick said.

'No time, for God's sake, Tenderness,' Len told him. 'We're deep enough in.'

'No time,' Reg said, and turned the car away from the buildings.

'We saw off the security man,' Vernon muttered. 'His own stupid fault. He wouldn't take it easy. What do they pay those people – enough to persuade them to go in for valour?'

'Ivor,' Mallick said urgently, 'can you hear me? Ivor, it's Tenderness. You're dying, old son. You got to tell me where you got my boy, while there's time. Where's Graham, Ivor?'

'I hear the law,' Len said. More sirens were sounding but Mellick could see nothing yet. Reg took the Audi at eighty down the drive and Mellick had to put his hands on Ivor's chest to keep him on the seat as they hit the rough patches. At the road they turned away from the approaching sound of police cars.

'Ivor, it wasn't one of my boys done this to you, I swear, so don't hold it against me. Look, this is about a helpless kid. Well, you know that. You don't want to see a poor helpless kid hurt, do you, Ivor, it's not like you? We've had some bad differences, I know, but a kid? A kid's different.' Mellick pushed his face close to Ivor again. 'This one a gonner? Please God, no, not yet. Come on, Ivor.'

Ditto turned. 'Ivor, that burning, all right it was bad, of course it was bad, but you was out of order, definitely out of order, you must of expected something like that, and I know Tenderness have had some real regrets about that. It was done in what they calls the heat of the moment, that burning, I'm not trying to be funny, not about something like that, but the heat of the moment. So there isn't no reason when you're going to be finished any minute to keep something like that from Tenderness.'

'He's flooding us out with blood,' Len said. 'It's hopeless. Look at his face. Did you ever see a deader one?'

'Ivor, some of your boys are looking after him somewhere, yes?' Mallick asked. 'Rick the Intelligent and others, maybe. They're good boys. I know they'll look after him good. But they won't know what to do now you're not around to give the orders, Ivor, will they? They could do something you wouldn't want. They could panic if they hears you've gone. And Milton Bain – if he can't get girls, he's liable to . . . You wouldn't want something like that, would you, with a backward kid? So where are they, Ivor? Just whisper it, don't waste your strength, and then we can get you to a medic somewhere. It's never too late, Ivor.'

'Tenderness don't even know what you want, Ivor, why you took the boy,' Ditto complained. 'Tell us where he is, then we can sort out what it is you want. We don't even know what you want at all, Ivor.'

'We got a car behind,' Reg said. 'He's sticking to us.'

Mellick looked back. 'Law?'

'Could be the Carlton.'

'Deep down I always liked you, Ivor,' Mellick said. 'We're two of a kind. All right, we does each other harm intermittent, but that's business, that's just competition. Holding a poor, handicapped kid is very personal, Ivor, no getting away from it. You wouldn't expect me to sit back and just let that go, I know you wouldn't.'

Ditto leaned further over and felt for Ivor's wrist pulse. 'Tenderness, there's nothing.'

'I'm driving a hearse,' Reg said.

42

'There've got to be something,' Mellick screamed. 'He's not hit so bad, not the heart, not the head.'

'He was already bad sick,' Len said.

'No, nothing,' Ditto said, releasing Ivor's wrist.

Mellick looked for twenty or thirty seconds into Ivor's face. He reckoned to know what the eyes of a dead man looked like. Then he said: 'I think he would of helped now if he could of. There was no real rules, but some things – '

'Slow down a minute, Reg,' Len said.

'The Carlton's on our tail.'

'All the same,' Len said.

Reg brought the Audi's speed to about fifteen. Len moved right across the back of the car and crouched in front of Ivor, then opened the door.

'Don't worry, he's proper dead, Tenderness,' Len told him.

'All right, I know.'

Len took Ivor by the front of his pyjama jacket and shoved him out on to the road. The sound as he struck the ground was as if a bale of wet waste paper had fallen from a lorry. Len slammed the door shut and Reg stood on the accelerator.

Ditto said: 'He'd understand, Tenderness.'

'He'd expect it,' Mellick replied.

'In the circumstances,' Ditto said.

'Yes.'

Reg, watching the mirror, said: 'I think the Carlton went over him.'

'For Christ's sake see if there's a couple of rags in the glove compartment to clean up this seat, Ditto, will you?' Len said.

5

Iles, taking his usual lunch of cereals with milk at his desk, said: 'I worry about Hubert, Colin. Our investigator from elsewhere is in the building. You know him? Assistant Chief Adrian Bundy. I don't hear anything usefully bad about him, I'm afraid, and he always buys his round. Thatcherite, only more so. Very bony face. You could trim a hedge with him. He did wonders for traffic in the north somewhere. Bridlington? Hot stuff on roundabouts. Nicknamed Give way to the Right. The Chief likes him, and Lane's not always too bad on people. As far as I know, Adrian's totally clean. I've got a couple of friends asking around in parishes where he's held big rank. Good family life, it appears, though some whiff of fun when he was on Royal protection. I haven't got to the root of that. He certainly doesn't look like somebody to pull the birds. But who can tell? A thousand times I've gazed in the mirror and thought to myself, What woman is going to get into bed with this bleak, unsmouldering relic, and yet now and then a woman will. Well, not so much now, I suppose. More then.

'It's different for you, Harpur. Oh, as a cop you're fatally short of malice and stabbing power, of course, and the creatures of the pit would take over if we were all like you, but there's a very winning liveliness and warmth in your face, though admittedly bogus, and women leap like salmon for any trace of electricity. Good luck Col, I say, it's always been an education working with you. Between us all we can tie up Bundy until he thinks *Paradise Lost*'s a football result, though poor Hubert might be facing very wintery times. Masons don't make anything of martyrs, but Hubert could become one. I've done these inquiries myself, Col. The top people can always put up such a bloody fine brick wall for themselves that no outsider has a chance of getting over or seeing through. But the same wall may stop some nonentity making his getaway, and he's the one the inquiry keelhauls. As we saw, Hubert has inklings. Wouldn't you? Look, Col, in some inquiries I've tried everything to load blame on Chiefs and Deputy Chiefs where they were obviously up to the eyebrows in dirty stuff: part an honest wish to do the job properly, part natural hatred of anyone further ahead than myself. But it never worked. Some sergeant or inspector caught the blast and finished up without a pension pulling pints.

'Bundy will be wanting to see you in due course. I got a glimpse of his schedule. Me, too. Well, these things have to be, but what you and I both have in mind is that this is some silver-buttoned, peaked-cap jerk who's spent his life driving a jam sandwich stalking bald tyres. What the fuck does he know about grey areas, Col – your only habitat, and mine, too, occasionally? Does he know what's necessary to get career villains convicted by a blind, half-soaked, cop-bashing British jury? Does he know how to pull the teeth of rat QCs hired by rat big-timers?'

This was one of those self-answering questions to which Iles nonetheless wanted an answer. So Harpur said: 'Probably not, sir.'

Lane knocked and shambled in.

Iles spoke ecstatically: 'I was just telling Colin how lucky we've been in getting Adrian Bundy for this job, sir, a man who sees things as they are, a resolute, famously balanced Assistant Chief. We can expect nothing but probity.'

'Bundy's godfearing yet subtle,' Lane replied.

'How I'd have put it myself, sir, if I'd thought of the phrasing. Godfearing yet subtle. Yes.'

The Chief sat down. He was in an old navy blazer, with gold buttons and a weighty, lurid badge, perhaps the emblem of a sports club or his university, Warwick, or somewhere up that way. There had been a time when Iles tried to prove that Lane was on the far right in student politics and a racist, even sending Scott to sniff around at the university. It had all been an attempt to stop Lane getting the job as Chief here. Scott had not discovered anything useful, and Lane was appointed. By now, he had established himself pretty well at the top, although Iles still persecuted him when he had a chance.

Lane wore brown carpet slippers around the office, with cream thermal socks, except in high summer. His tie was also old and it, too, looked sporty or academic, a matter of thin purple, red and blue stripes, like merging contusions, Iles had once said. 'Have we been up to see Tenderness about Ivor Wright? Lane asked.'

'Colin himself is going this evening, sir,' Iles replied. 'We're not rushing it, so there'll be no galloping crap about persecution. This is a death in Bucks, nearly two hundred miles away, on another Force's ground, with nothing obvious to tie it to Mellick. We have to be careful.'

'Right. What motive – for doing Ivor now, anyway?' Lane asked.

'They've always warred, sir,' Harpur replied. 'They're both in protection, so each has to be able to guard his clients against the other.

'Yes, but what provokes a crisis at this moment?'

Harpur shrugged.

'I don't know,' Iles said, 'and Colin makes out he doesn't either, but I wouldn't be surprised if he did. He's probably sitting on it, in that engaging little way of his: loyalty to his informants, first, and to us a fortnight later. Wright would want to get back at Mellick for the blow-lamp damage, and then Mellick would have to respond. Something like that, sir.'

'Wright claimed he was hurt in a garage fire, didn't he?' Lane said. 'His sort don't come to us. Officially, we never connected Tenderness with it at all, did we?' Lane asked.

'Officially, they never connected Uncle Joe with the Soviet death camps, sir.'

'Did Hubert Scott have any part in the blowlamp inquiries?' Lane said.

'He was on the case, yes,' Iles replied.

'God,' the Chief said. 'Bundy is – '

'A pontificating prick who thinks all of life should be viewed down the bonnet of a 2.6 Rover,' Iles remarked.

'Don't underestimate him, Desmond.'

'All right, sir: a first-class pontificating prick.'

'I haven't got many whispers on Bundy's line,' the Chief said, 'but one of them could be that Scott was looking after Tenderness somehow – soft-pedalling on the blowlamp inquiries?'

Iles said: 'Don't you fret about Bundy, sir. He doesn't know what he's up against here'

'I want him to get total cooperation, Desmond.'

'That goes without saying, sir,' Iles replied, 'without saying.'

Harpur took Garland with him to visit Tenderness. At the entrance to the Enclave they were stopped by the security firm's barrier and a guard rang through and gave their names.

'Mr Mellick says a visit just now would not be convenient,' the guard announced.

'Oh, grand,' Garland said. 'We couldn't have chosen better.'

The guard smiled apologetically. 'I'm afraid I can't let you in, gentlemen. It would be more than my job – '

Garland left the car, went into the hut and, putting his palm under the guard's chin, shoved him out of the way. He raised the barrier and Harpur drove through and waited for him. 'Nice up here,' Garland said. 'I've always loved leaded lights and coach lamps. Makes me think of pale pink Woolworths Christmas cards people in our street used to deliver by hand, signed "All at number 14"'

'Show me how they'd have got Tenderness's boy away.'

'There's half a dozen paths and lanes through the conifers. You could park at the bottom, pick up the kid from his garden and carry him to the vehicle, never seeing the security.'

'Christ, I fret about him. We know, and do nothing. It's criminal.'

'No, sir, they're the criminals, and they don't want you to do anything.'

'Stuff them. They don't police themselves.'

Garland did not reply.

'No, they bloody don't.'

'Looks like a bit of a function.'

Almost every room in the house was lit up and, as they walked to the front door Harpur heard laughter and music and the buzz of many voices. 'They've found his son? A celebration?'

Harpur rang and Tenderness himself answered, wearing a fine dinner jacket and brilliantly white starched shirt. He looked haggard but bright-eyed, as if he'd dosed himself. Behind, around the big, circular hall people also sporting evening clothes stood in cheerful groups talking and drinking. The music came from an inner room and sounded to Harpur like a Luther Vandross number.

'What is it, Tenderness?' Garland asked. 'A bit early for Burns night, you know.'

'Mr Harpur, Mr Garland,' Mellick replied. 'Can I help you some way? It can't wait? Jane and me, we're giving a party for near neighbours in the Enclave, planned months ago, see? It's not too helpful you got to call tonight.'

'Ah, *Never Too Much*,' Harpur said.

'What?'

'The track you're playing.'

'Yes?'

'Drives the birds crazy?' Harpur asked. 'But they're not birds in the Enclave, are they? Ladies.'

'We've got to come in, Tenderness,' Garland said.

'Look, these are neighbours, I mean, all sorts. Not Tenderness, all right?' He was whispering. 'I got a name. Bernard or Mellick.'

'Of course, Bernard,' Harpur said. 'You're entitled to a name. We can't go around treating you like a recidivist.'

Behind Mellick, some of the guests were trying to make out who had called and was holding their host at the door.

'We've got some rough news for you,' Garland said. 'About an old friend of yours. Well, I call it news.'

'What old friend?'

A woman Harpur did not recognize, beautifully turned out in lilac-coloured silk, came and stood with Tenderness. She looked much worse than he did, and much more heavily juiced.

'Mrs Mellick?' Harpur asked. 'We're sorry to intrude on such a mellow occasion, but it's urgent.'

'What is?' she asked. The stress in her voice and face were painful. 'What's happened? You're police, aren't you? What have you found?'

'We'd better come in, Bernard,' Garland said.

She pulled the door out of Tenderness's grip and motioned the two of them into the hall. 'Please,' she muttered, 'what is it?'

Mellick took her arm. 'Calm down, love,' he said. 'All right? Leave it to me, will you?' He seemed to want to sound consoling and sympathetic, yet it came out like an order.

'What?' For a second she appeared half dazed.

'Leave it to me.'

From somewhere in the hall a man called: 'Any problems, Bernie? Need help?'

'We're fine,' Mellick replied. 'Please, everyone, just carry on, enjoy yourselves. Some private business has come up. Won't take long.'

'No, not long at all,' Harpur said.

Mellick lead him and Garland through the hall towards the wide, circular staircase, with its viva Espana wrought iron balusters. Tenderness had spent well on passable reproduction furniture and large gilt-framed mirrors. A couple of big, restored oil paintings showing good quantities of mud and cows hung one on each side of the double doors to the long rear lounge, where the Vandross l.p. played. The doors were open and Harpur slowed down to look, then turned and walked a few steps into the room, smiling amiably.

'Please,' Tenderness murmured, touching his sleeve, 'there's no need to bother my friends, is there?'

48

A dozen people were dancing enthusiastically, including a snooker star, and the fruit machine distributor that Iles insisted did jewellery hold-ups and chivvied Harpur to nail. Near the long, almost tasteful, mock-mahogany bar stood a small group of what looked to Harpur like City men, some of the Enclave's new commuting immigrants, refugees from London's stress. Every provincial town reasonably near the capital had them now. They could sell their place there, buy a mansion here on the proceeds, or a smart new Enclave villa, and still have enough left over for a turbo Saab to whip them up and down the motorway three times a week. Even after the Exchange crash of 1987 they seemed prosperous enough. Probably they would bring all London's problems here eventually, and then they would move on again, deeper into the country. In fact, the problems had started. Tenderness was one of them. Wright had been another. To cope, a new style of policing had emerged.

'Lordy, this has to be the fuzz,' someone called. 'Have we fallen foul? It's a fair cop.'

'A *blonde* cop,' a woman shrieked.

'Come on, Mr Harpur,' Tenderness pleaded.

They went upstairs to a library stocked with sets of standard works and sat in red leather bucket arm chairs. Jane Mellick would have come in with them, but Harpur saw Tenderness speak to her quietly at the entrance and also saw her break down and begin to weep before Mellick closed the door on her. He brought brandy.

'It's about Ivor, Tenderness,' Garland said.

'Ivor Wright? The scorching? God, I've answered a thousand questions on that.'

'No, he had another accident. It looks as if Ivor might be a wee bit jinxed,' Garland told him. 'He keeps running into rough times.'

'What accident? I would of heard. I mean, through business and that.'

'Well, this happened a long way away, near Aylesbury. Thames Valley police. They play things close.'

'Aylesbury?'

'You've got it.'

'I heard he was away. Medical. But I didn't know there.'

'Aylesbury,' Garland said. It's got a good clinic, with nuns.

49

This place has a worldwide reputation for rebuilding burned balls. You've probably read about it in *The Lancet*.'

'Yes?'

'It's called after a saint, the clinic. St Anselm the Pederast, or something like that.'

'A lot of them are,' Tenderness said.

'Ivor wasn't too good,' Garland replied. 'His balls were fused into one during that garage blaze, like Maltesers if they get hot in your pocket. He went in for a separation job. Cosmetic only, really. He was still functioning perfectly OK, as I understand, one cylinder, yes, but with the force of two. It didn't look right, though, and you know how fussy about appearance Ivor's always been. And Della didn't like it. She felt underprivileged.'

'What happened?'

'Well, he had a tumble from a car. He was in his pyjies.'

'What you telling me, Mr Garland?'

'I don't know, Tenderness. Am I telling you anything at all?'

'What car?'

'An Audi. It was found in a pub car park in Reading. It belongs to a dentist. He was very upset about the blood. You'd think he'd be used to it, wouldn't you – a dentist?'

'He was driving and fell out?'

'Only if he could drive from the rear seat.'

'What's that mean?'

'The blood was in the back.'

'Why blood? And why in his pyjamas? Was he running from the clinic – getting away in a hurry?'

'He was running all over the place. He had two bullets in his back.'

'So he was dead when he fell out?'

'The doctors say no. They think another car hit him and didn't stop. That didn't kill him, either, only broke his legs and knocked him off the road. Thames Valley believe they may have it – a stolen Carlton abandoned at Medmenham, with some damage to the front and bloodstained. Ivor died of exposure and shock three hours later in a ditch. Two little girls going to school found him. Not much of a start to the day for them. I mean, I wouldn't have minded finding him like that, not a bit. I'd have been pleased. But no go for two children.'

'God. I'm glad I asked Jane not to come in. What I'm saying,

Ivor was no friend, stupid to pretend with you boys, but who wants to hear about things like that happening to any bugger? I had fights with him, yes, of course, but I – Well. And them little girls, that's horrible. Jane would be real upset.'

Harpur had stood up and was looking at the backs of some of the books. 'I thought she seemed damned bad already, Tenderness,' he said. 'Some stress? I felt sorry for her.'

'She worried about this do tonight. It's a big thing for us – what I mean, there's a sir in the Enclave, and we didn't know who would show. He's a lovely man, sir for exports, that sort of thing, no side, but we didn't know if he would come, and it was very important to Jane. We didn't know if any bugger would come. But it's all right, they're all here and it's great, but she worries about things to do with fitting in, that sort of thing, you know? She wants everything right. That's why I bought them paintings, they're genuine.'

'Genuine what?' Garland said.

'What do you do with your son when you throw a big party, Tenderness?' Harpur asked. 'He's on your profile. Called Graham?'

'He's away with some friends. He often goes. He likes that.'

'Anything wrong there?' Harpur asked.

'Wrong?'

'Why Jane looked bad.'

'No. What you getting at, Mr Harpur? He's a bit backward, like, you know that, I suppose. But he's a happy kid, that's what counts.'

Garland said: 'Thames Valley have a witness sighting of the Audi near the clinic about 11.10pm. It was loaded, probably all men. There's a description of one that could be Ditto Repeato.'

'Last night? Ditto? At Aylesbury? No way, Mr Garland. Ditto was – .' He held up a hand and smiled weakly. 'Wait a minute, now: you trying to tie me or my boys to this what happened to Ivor?'

'Two bullet wounds, a couple of broken legs and a cracked wrist, as if he might have been going for a piece in the clinic and someone banged him. They found a little Airweight, the sort of thing Ivor would take along with the barley water for his bedside cabinet.'

'Am I going to drive all the way to bloody where was it – ?'

'Aylesbury, still,' Garland said.

'All that way if I wanted to do him some damage, on strange ground, when I could see him any time I wanted to here?'

'Unless there was some sort of crisis,' Harpur said, 'with time short.'

'What crisis?'

'Something putting you under pressure', Harpur replied.

'Like?'

'There's a security guard kicked to death at the clinic and a porter knocked about, tied up and blindfolded, almost suffocated, poor old soul,' Garland said. 'This was quite an operation. Upwards of six men. Thames Valley found only one of them, a bit of hired rough from the Elephant and Castle. Half his throat gone. The porter thinks one of the others was from that way, too. He heard him talk. The dead was knocked over by a shell from a Walther, and we don't need the magic computer to tell us that Ditto's into Walthers. And how are all the rest of your lads, Tenderness – Len and Reg? Does Reg fancy Audis? And then the apprentice kid in the razzle-dazzle gear, Vernon. He OK? Don't leave him alone with any birds you value, will you, He's very thrustful.'

'You got your fucking minds made up already, haven't you, before you come, even?' Mellick said. 'Ivor Wright is given the treatment so it got to be Tenderness. Listen, Wright got a heap of enemies. He never took no care about offending. I could give you names of five people who wanted Ivor dead, and that includes some who worked for him.'

Garland said: 'I told you, this was an operation. It would take someone of prime calibre to put it together. That's why we're here, Tenderness. We admire your organizational ability.'

Mellick stood. He was thin and quite tall, with prominent, big, front teeth and a feeble, yellowish moustache. It was hard to think of him as dangerous until you read his papers. 'I got a solicitor coming to the party. I don't say no more till he arrives. Now I got to get back to my guests. I'm out of order neglecting them like this. Jane's going to be real angry with me.'

'*Your* solicitor? Sandicott?' Garland asked.

'Yes.'

'He doesn't live in the Enclave. I thought it was neighbours. Why Sandicott, Tenderness? Were you expecting us?'

52

'I always works close with my solicitor. He's more like a friend.'

'Sweet.'

Harpur said: 'Which friends does your lad go to, Tenderness? Where are they?'

'My lad? Graham? Why? Leave him alone, Harpur. He don't come into this, do he?'

'I don't know, Tenderness, does he?'

'Thames Valley say the dead they found in Ivor's room at the clinic was a ripe head-banger, Peregrine Proctor-Dye, known always as Frenzy. Mr Harpur and I both told them he wasn't the kind of material you would normally be seen dead with, as it were . . . We think of you as being very fussy about personnel: one or two of your boys will probably get the OBE before they're finished, and Ditto's for the Order of Merit, I should think. Would you like to tell us where you were last night, Tenderness?'

'Didn't I just say, I don't talk without Harry Sandicott?'

'Thames Valley could take you there for their quizzing,' Garland said. 'They can be deeply thorough. They're very fair with people and it takes a long time to be really fair. Lads disappear into their system for days, no trace. We've had a couple of cases where – '

'Look, I don't give a fuck about them or you. You got nothing to say to me, and I certainly got nothing to say to you, so I want you out of my house, now. Now,' Tenderness bellowed. He walked to the library door and was about to pull it open, but turned around to speak. 'It's like usual, one big bluff and bullshit. I wouldn't be surprised you heard we was having this important party, trying to get to know people proper, and you decided to come up just to put me down in front of my neighbours and make me look dirty. That's real police thinking.'

'You're on edge, Tenderness, and I don't blame you in the least,' Garland said.

'You don't see me off like you and that Iles saw off Cliff Jamieson and Favard, and especially that Iles.'

'What are you getting at, Tenderness?' Garland said.

'You know what I'm getting at. Just don't come no heavy stuff here, that's all. I seen it all before.'

'Tenderness, we know you've seen it all before. Isn't that why we're here? Look, we honestly dislike bringing bad news, especially to such a lovely home and on a charming social oc-

53

casion. You must believe that,' Garland said. 'Myself, I'd be willing to bet you genuinely believed Ivor was dead when you pitched him out of the Audi under the Carlton. To you, it was just like one of those solemn, touching burials at sea, but without the union jack: We commit his body to the road until the ditch shall give up its dead. Do you think it's a pleasure to destroy that fragment of consolation? Are we monsters, for God's sake? We know you run things with a certain decency and consideration. You're not one to get out of order.

'I'd say you were damned horrified when Ivor took those bullets in the back. We know they came from Frenzy Proctor-Dye's Browning. Well, of course. That's not your style. And, as we see it, Ditto Repeato did him in retaliation. It's so easy to understand. But what you have to ask, I'm afraid, is, will Thames Valley be open-minded? See it from their point of view, Tenderness: they've got bullets flying, malicious kicking and damage to decent property in what's really a very refined piece of their patch. Tory MP, I should think, liable to do a lot of effective stirring. If a police force can't look after blameless nursing sisters – you see my point? You should talk to us. We're like kith and kin, if that's not presumptuous of me.'

'Just get out. This I don't need.' He was still shouting. 'I got powerful people downstairs, I don't mean just Harry Sandicott, but big people with capital, owners of factories, who knows how to make a complaint, influence, so it reaches that councillor Tobin and some others. This Enclave, we're people who have made it, all in different ways, maybe, but we made it, and we didn't make it by no accident. We're determined, we knows how to look after ourselves, we knows how to get good advice and we can pay for it and we got skills.'

Garland said: 'Definitely. The snooker man knows how to pot balls, you know how to burn them.'

'You want trouble, Harpur, you can have trouble. You're not dealing with a clueless yob off of the street. I could say a few things myself about that Iles, and you. Yes, and you. You ought to watch yourself.'

'Who located Ivor for you, Tenderness, so far away in Aylesbury?' Garland asked. 'That was pretty sharp work. He must have thought he was so safe, poor suffering sod. "You have some

54

visitors, Mr Wright," and in come Tenderness, Ditto and half the scum of London blazing away.'

Mellick opened the library door and stood there, waiting for them to go. Below, they had changed the period and some sweet 'twenties jazz climbed lazily up the staircase. 'You remind me of Gatsby, Tenderness,' Garland said.

Harpur prepared to leave. Jane Mellick must have been waiting right outside and she hurried forward at once and spoke to Tenderness. 'What was it? Why have they come?' She would be nearing forty, almost as tall as her husband, with dark hair and a long, angular face, handsome enough in its way even now, after the weeping, and set off sweetly by her lilac outfit. She would look pretty good, no matter what the company. Half the country's aristocratic women could be taken for molls these days, anyway.

'Routine,' Tenderness replied.

'What routine?'

'Routine menaces,' he said. 'My name come up on the computer for a bit of arm twisting.'

'But what did they say? Oh, please.' She looked from his face to Harpur's and then to Garland's, urgently trying to read what had happened between them.

Whatever sedator they had her on was no longer doing much of a job and Harpur feared she might start crying again. She seemed to have done nothing to restore her face after the last bout. 'Mrs Mellick, Jane, if you need help, you know where I am,' he told her.

'What help's she ever going to need from you?' Tenderness said.

They went down the stairs, Mellick leading. Among guests spilling out from the main room into the hall, Garland turned and said grandly: 'No, Bernard, it's nice of you, but we really can't stop. There are pleasure domes and there are paths of duty and regretfully we are committed tonight to the second. But we'll take a raincheck, certainly.'

Mellick came out alone with them to the car to make sure they left. 'Yes, I know how to shift you bastards, Harpur. You don't like to hear about Tobin, do you, and you're frightened white if someone says they might start blowing the whistle on how you and Iles runs things there, and especially now you got this inquiry, this Adrian Bundy. He don't take no shit, is what I heard. You boys got worries.'

'He's not wrong,' Harpur said as he and Garland drove away.

'Has Hubert Scott been keeping him informed?'

'Some bugger has.'

As they went out of the Enclave, Garland gazed back at the house. 'A very select affair. *Nouveau* is a damn sight better than never, which is our prospect. But he's hard. I thought he might crack if I said Ivor was alive when he hit the tarmac.'

'A bit of fiction's OK now and then, Francis, but, the trouble is, he'd expect us to lie about something like that.'

6

The boy knew something was wrong. The men had become suddenly frightened and angry and they shouted a lot. He did not like it or understand. They shouted at one another and at him. Many times they used that word which his mother said was not needed.

And there was another word they shouted. It was 'dead.' He knew the word well enough because he had often heard it on television. The men did not have a television in the farm house, only a radio. Rick listened to it upstairs nearly all the time. He had a quiet voice, yet he was the one who began shouting first, yelling the word 'dead.' He came running down the stairs to the other two.

They were playing cards, but they stopped when they heard him and stood up and stared at Rick. Graham was in a corner of the room trying to build a fort for the plumed soldiers with Lego pieces.

Dave said: 'What do you mean, fucking dead?'

Rick said he heard it on the News, dead on the road. The boy wanted to ask who was dead, but he knew he must not. He sensed that what had happened was not favourable for him and he kept his eyes on the fort, while he listened and tried to understand.

But, suddenly, Milton turned around and kicked the fort so that pieces flew everywhere in the room. The few walls and towers the boy had finished were shattered. To Graham it seemed that Milton was very upset because he heard that word, 'dead.'

They began to shout a name, but it was not one he had heard before. They said Ivor used to be in a clinic, but now he was dead. The boy knew about clinics. He went to one sometimes with his mother and father to see a doctor.

When Milton, Dave and Rick were shouting and moving about they bumped into the table and everything fell to the floor. Because he wanted them to like him, Graham began picking up the cards and money so they could play again. Some coins rolled across the room and he was glad of that. It meant he could put distance between him and them while they were angry. Some- times Dave laughed a lot but he was not laughing now. The word dead did not make him laugh, it made him upset.

Then Dave said: 'You know who did this?'

Graham did not know the answer, but he became more afraid. He could tell that there was someone Dave did not like.

Milton said, 'Of course'.

Then they all said it was Tenderness, but he had never heard a name like that, or like Ivor. Tenderness was what his mother called it when he was little and wet down his leg and went out in the wind. She put ointment on his leg to stop it hurting.

He knew that they all hated Tenderness because Ivor was dead in the road. He wanted to keep on picking up the money and cards, so he could still stay away from them because when they were angry about Tenderness they seemed angry about him, as well. He tried to keep his eyes on the cards and coins, but he knew all the same that they were looking at him. To make the job last longer, he secretly put some of the cards he had picked up back on the floor.

Dave said: 'This is your fucking dad, Podge.' He was looking down at him and pointing. Before, when Dave called him Podge it had comforted him. Sometimes when Dave said Podge he laughed, and it did not seem to matter any more about the biting, but now when he used that name the boy could tell it was not because Dave liked him, and he was not laughing. Graham saw it was not because of the biting, it was because of Ivor and Tender-

57

ness, and he could not understand why Dave was angry with him about that. He did not know Tenderness and Ivor. His father was called dad and he was called Mr Mellick and his mother called him Bernie, but he was not called Tenderness, that was not a name.

He put the cards and the money on the table for them but they did not notice and they did not say thank you. They were all looking at him.

Rick said: 'What do we do now?'

Milton said: 'We got to watch.'

Rick said: 'What about him?'

When Rick said that, Graham knew Rick meant him. Rick did not look at him when he said that and he did not point like Dave did but the boy knew. Rick spoke as quietly as he always did, except when he ran downstairs shouting 'fucking dead' and 'Ivor' and 'on the road'. Milton went to look out from the downstairs window. He said: 'We got to watch very careful now.'

Dave said: 'Yes.' Then Dave said something else that Graham could not understand. 'They would not kill Ivor until he talked.'

The boy tried to think about it. He knew kill. It was like dead. It was like hitting a fly with a book until it was dead. He could not get beyond that, though.

'Yes. They'll be here,' Milton said. Graham thought it was not really like saying, it was more like screaming, like a girl called Tracy at school did one day. 'I'm going upstairs. I can see further.'

As Milton hurried to the stairs he knocked the table right over and all the cards and money fell again. This time, Graham did not pick them up. He knew they did not want to play cards. They were frightened.

Rick said: 'What about him?' He spoke very quietly again, as if he did not want Graham to hear, but he did.

7

When she could get a few hours away from the house Ruth and Harpur sometimes went to a cheap, reasonably spruce, local, side-street hotel. They could be happy there, or almost happy. He hoped the staff did not recognize him, but he could not be sure: the job meant his face came up on television sometimes, and there were pictures in the papers. At least they had the grace to pretend they did not know him. He and Ruth made love there as if there was no tomorrow, which there might not be, and they both realized it. They talked a little, but only a little, because talk always led them into dead-ends, and agonizing guesses about the future. Sometimes he thought of it as nothing but escapism, and sometimes as more than that. Whichever it was, he knew he had to settle for it.

Hurrying from the hotel tonight, so Ruth could reach home as if from an evening class, they met Hubert Scott waiting outside in the porch. For a fragment of a moment Harpur thought it might be an accident and was about to try some yarn on him. Then he saw Hubert's face and his mind started to operate properly again. Hubert stopped the street door from swinging shut on its self-lock. 'I wanted a quiet word, sir.' He glanced about. 'Perhaps it's not suitable here, though. The room's yours for the whole night, isn't it? We can talk up there. Get some more of your money's worth. It won't take long. I know you both have commitments. How are the children and Robert, Mrs Cotton?'

Harpur said: 'Look Hubert, I – Christ, you tailed us here?' Suddenly he saw himself sucked into Scott's rough troubles.

'Your routine's not hard to discover, sir. I'm a detective. Was. Remember?'

'Ruth has to – '

'Very brief, sir.'

She had begun shaking, part rage, part shock. 'Hubert, what the hell are you doing? We were friends. This bloody awful snooping.' She whispered, though there was nobody near in the street or the hotel porch.

Scott put a hand up and momentarily covered part of his face, as if miserably embarrassed. He seemed about to reply but then spoke to Harpur. 'Let's go inside, sir. This really is conspicuous.'

At once Ruth said, desperately: 'Colin no, please. Don't let him in there.'

Scott gave a small, almost sad, smile. 'I do understand. It becomes your place for a little while, your only real place, and you don't want some soiled heavy in there talking dark.' He pushed the hotel door open wider. 'But it's secure, Ruth. After all, that's why you chose it.' He led the way and stood in the hall.

Harpur was about to follow but Ruth held his arm. 'Tell him to get lost,' she said.

'It'll be all right, love.'

'In God's name, what's going on?'

Through the glass door he could see Scott waiting for them. Harpur spoke quietly to Ruth: 'He's leaning on me – wants a deal. It happens. Iles tried the same once, didn't he?'

She frowned in thought. 'Iles gave him the idea now?'

'They're great mates. They look after each other. It's a kind of duty.'

'What deal?'

'Who shops who to Bundy. I've got to humour him. He's not safe, Ruth, not predictable. You've seen as much as I have of that.'

Harpur went ahead up the stairs and opened the room. The others followed. Ruth stepped quickly to the bed and pulled the eiderdown back up, reminding Harpur of a woman hurriedly covering her nakedness. Then she walked to the window and stood looking out. The room was poorly lit. Harpur and Scott sat on each side of the bed in straight wooden chairs, like hospital visitors around an unconscious patient with only a night light.

'I know what Ruth said just now, but please, both of you, don't think there's anything dirty or sinister about the way I'm making contact tonight,' Scott told them.

'We understand,' Harpur said. The sod could make what he liked of that.

'I wanted to talk to the two of you. How else do I do it, Mr Harpur? I looked around for somewhere discreet. As she said, we've been friends or colleagues all these years. Am I going to play vicious with such people for God's sake? What are your private lives to me?'

'Hubert, Ruth has to get home.'

Again he gave that small, comforting smile. 'Of course. It's this, Mr Harpur: I thought we all ought to make one or two preparations for Bundy. That's only common sense.' The smile opened out momentarily into a laugh. 'I'm past the stage of

60

clobbering people with golf clubs. And I don't want to start my retirement doing protective solitary.'

'I've always thought of you as a great copper,' Harpur said. 'And I'd say so to any inquiry.'

'Thank you. Thank you very much, sir. That's one reason I decided to come to you for advice now. I knew I could rely on your good will. It doesn't matter a bugger you're not in the Lodge. We've been through a lot, a lot, yes, just as coppers together, that's what counts, ultimately.'

'Yes.' Ultimately was a location Harpur always tried to skirt.

Ruth had turned to look at the two men. When her eyes were on Scott, her face filled with a mixture of hatred and pity, but mostly pity. Ruth did not know much about hating. Harpur saw she was urgently trying to understand what Hubert's words were really saying, behind the greasy politesse. He spoke earnestly, as if packaging bits of contradictory doctrine for divinity students.

'Mr Harpur, I've used some pretty ripe contacts and come to some pretty shady arrangements in my time, with all sorts of crooked bastards. I don't deny it. To you, I mean, I don't deny it. Why should I? The point is, you've done the same thing – I know you're still doing it. How do we get information otherwise? How do we convict? Oh, sure it's dangerous ground, bloody dangerous. That's how it has to be, though. We have to win, haven't we? If we don't, the slime takes over.'

Harpur nodded, but did not speak, waiting for whatever came after the declarations of buddydom.

'You and Jack Lamb, for instance,' Scott said. He paused, in mock apology. 'You're shocked, offended? Lamb is supposed to be one hundred per cent secret, I know. There's no such thing. People like you and me, we've got this trained nosiness about others haven't we, including our own colleagues, especially a very successful colleague like yourself? We want to know how it's done, don't we? I'll say this for you, you've been bloody careful – meetings in car parks, the old gun emplacement at the Valencia, and even Billy Graham! Great, that. You've really looked after him a treat, and I know he's sure to be grateful. But, then, he's looked after you, too, hasn't he? The old, worn face was alight with admiration for Harpur's methods. Scott wiped his moustache, as after a meal: Harpur's arrangement with Lamb seemed to give Scott almost sensual pleasure.

Harpur's gloom grew, and so did the sense of being roped into a jinxed partnership with this fading, unhinged man. 'You've had an eye, have you, Hubert? You're not the first to spot him, but you've done well, all the same. Never had sight or smell of you.'

Scott became blank-faced. 'Well, you wouldn't, would you, sir? I know my trade.' Then he grew expansive again suddenly and sat back more comfortably in the uncomfortable chair. 'His name's safe with me, sir. Need I say it? This was just a private investigation of mine. Nobody else need ever know about you and Lamb, not from me. I hope you'll believe that, sir.'

Harpur said: 'Thanks, Hubert, thanks.'

'Take it absolutely for granted, sir.'

'Thanks.'

'Ruth, I wonder if you realize how this kind of thing works? An officer is fed tips about crimes and villains by someone not too clean and in return arranges a little protection for the informant. Jack Lamb – well, he's into all sorts, but Mr Harpur looks after him beautifully, because he's simply a supreme source. Of course, it's a damn dangerous life for Lamb, even with the protection. If one or two of the hard men found they were being shopped, well – '

'Does Ruth really have to be here, Hubert? It's getting late.'

'She's not going to think any less of you because you use a nark, sir,' he said, chuckling man-to-man. 'She's a police wife, twice, as well as a police mistress. I'm sure she realized pretty well before this how we operate. She knows it's not all point duty and visiting schools. I'm only giving the details.'

'What the hell is it you want, Hubert?' she asked, her voice shaking. Harpur's fear had reached her.

'Why don't you sit down,' Scott said, getting up from his chair and offering it. 'I can use the bed.' She did not move and in a moment he sat on the chair again. 'What I'm saying, I suppose, is that we're in the same boat, Mr Harpur and I. Ruth, you might not realize how important it is to get that established first. You see, in the kind of shit-dig Mr Bundy is going to mount there's always a big danger that the people at the top come out all right and some poor old expendable footstool like me catches all the shrapnel. Think of that Lieutenant Colonel North in the States. Covered from head to foot in blame, while Reagan is up there smirking behind a free Thanksgiving turkey. I can't tell you how often I've seen it happen in the police, and so I'm quite keen it shouldn't now.'

Harpur said: 'I'm told Bundy is – '

'Fair? Honest? Bundy's a copper, has been for twenty-five years, sir, and he knows what's expected of him: boats are not to be rocked, and if you chuck some bugger over the side, make sure he's a lightweight so the trim's not disturbed.'

Ruth said: 'Surely, he will – '

'My equivalent to Mr Harpur's Jack Lamb is Tenderness Mellick. That's really the guts of it all,' Scott said gently. 'I've had a long and useful contact with him. For a good while it remained private. I was as careful as you, Mr Harpur. But, like I said, there's no perfect secret among police. People never stop sniffing. Now, the rumours are around, and so Mr Bundy shows up.'

'I heard them,' Ruth said. 'But if Bundy's been a policeman for twenty-five years he'll know what's normal for a detective, won't he?'

'He might. He's not CID. We're a different species. And he's from a different part of the country. Local customs change.'

She hesitated for a second. 'The rumours I heard said more than what you've – '

'Of course, ducks. They make out I'm on the take.'

At once Harpur said: 'Nobody who knows you will believe that.'

'Bundy doesn't know me. Why they bring in an outside officer, isn't it, sir?'

'People will tell him about you – we'll convince him. Mr Iles, the Chief, myself.'

'Perhaps. Who knows what people say when they're alone with an inquiring officer? They think of their own arses first, second and twenty-fifth.' He repeated that gesture of putting a hand up and covering part of his face. 'Anyway, what does it mean, "On the take"? Mr Harpur, are you going to tell me you never had a *petit cadeau* in any form from Jack Lamb? This is a lad who must have made thousands he couldn't have without your help. Am I supposed to believe there was no cut, no fee?'

Ruth took a step towards Harpur. 'Oh, my God, tell him,

Colin. Please, tell him.' She did not sound too confident that he could. Maybe that's what it did to a woman being twice a police wife and once a police mistress.

'No cut,' Harpur said.

'Never?' Scott asked. 'Never?'

'Never.'

'Understand?' Ruth demanded.

'I hear what he says,' Scott replied.

'Colin wouldn't – '

'All right, perhaps I believe that. Perhaps,' Scott said.

'You've got to bloody believe it,' she told him.

'All right, say I do. But, so what? The real question is, will Mr Bundy believe it? One thing about me, another about Mr Harpur?'

'But Bundy doesn't know about Lamb, does he?' Ruth asked.

'Not Yet,' Harpur said.

She studied his face. 'Christ, I see. I'm being stupid. Someone might tell him.'

'Yes, someone might,' Harpur muttered. 'So, what's your proposition, Hubert?' The room was getting cold. The wooden light-fitting in the centre of the ceiling had holders for three bulbs, but, for as long as Harpur could remember only one functioned, and it gave a feeble, yellow glow which left the corners of the room shadowed. Yet, it was a room Harpur had always found delightful, because of their love meetings here. Now, it seemed bleak and touched by absurdity: wasn't it farcical to be discussing these things with Scott across the used-looking bed? Ruth's instinct that it was wrong to let him in here had been spot on. An artist could have made something of this scene now, the gloomy light, the bed and the three stiff, mysterious figures, acting out a crisis.

'You've said you'd put in a word for me, sir.'

'Of course.'

'I really am grateful, Mr Harpur.' It sounded like someone saying thanks for a genuine pewter tankard when he'd been hoping for a Jaguar. 'This is a big boost.'

'So, what else, Hubert?'

'As I see it, sir, it's got to be something specific. You know the police mind, especially the high-up police mind: it can only cope with exactitudes, because of years of contact with those truth-mangling turds in wigs.'

'So, what else, Hubert?'

'Yes. Well, sir, it's not too difficult, I think. What I'd like is for you to say I was under confidential orders, yours, to infiltrate Mellick's operation and take his shilling if it was offered, because I was supposedly on their staff.' He stared through the dim light at Harpur to see his reaction. Scott's tough, blunt face was drained and tense, like a priest's lusting in a confessional.

'Hubert, that's not – '

'The thing is, we've done that kind of penetration in the past, so it would be quite credible. Of course we have, often – sometimes no other way to nail these people. Even a Woodentop like Bundy will have heard of such operations. After all, we had Ray Street who got into Jamieson's outfit, answering only to yourself and his name known only to you, in case of leaks. It's standard in that kind of work, isn't it, sir? If you said it, Bundy can't dispute it.'

'Hubert, you've been a cop on this patch all your life. You're known. Pictures in the paper, for God's sake. Street was a new kid. Bundy would never believe you could pass yourself off. And he'd never believe I'd allow you to try.'

'I've thought of that. Yes, it makes things difficult. But it's my only chance, Mr Harpur. They'll dig out the bank accounts, won't they, and there's money I can't explain. So, I say betting wins? Is he more likely to believe that old crap?'

'No, I can't do it, Hubert. It would be suicide, double suicide.' No wonder he never got past sergeant.

Scott did not seem to be listening. 'I've taken this bloody dogsbody's job in the poly to make it look as if I'm hard up, but once they glance at the statements – '

'I'm sorry, Hubert.'

'You can't ask this,' Ruth snarled. 'Not even you.'

'Mr Harpur,' he said genially, 'I can do very big damage. It's not what I want, but it's touch and go for me, isn't it? And I don't want Jess to see me crucified. I've given her a shock or two, acting that way at the presentation, and a few other things, but she mustn't be hurt any more.'

'Are you threatening Colin?' Ruth yelled.

Scott put his finger to his lips and looked towards the door.

'They'll think we've got an orgy going in here. Well, of course I'm threatening him, you dumb cow. Mr Harpur would expect that, in the circumstances. You don't understand, girl – there's a lot of bargaining goes on. It's a professional thing. We call it reciprocity.'

'So two of you sink, instead of one?' Ruth said.

That silenced Scott for a second. If he had thought she would make things easier for him he must be regretting asking her to stay. But then he said: 'Let me tell you the whole picture, Ruth, will you, love? Honestly, I didn't want to go into all this, I mean spell everything out, but I'm sorry to see you don't really understand. There's more to it than Jack Lamb and this regular, irregular bedding of you, the wife of one of Mr Harpur's subordinates and widow of another. On top of that – '

Ruth strode across the room suddenly and hit Scott twice across the face, a right-to-left-and-back-again sweeping movement, one blow with the palm, the next with the knuckles. She remained standing near him, glaring waiting to see what he would do. Scott did not move – stayed sitting and had made no attempt to defend himself, or even to ride the impact. It was as if he thought he deserved it.

Harpur stood up and went around the bed to Ruth. Putting his arm across her shoulders, he directed her gently back to the chair he had been occupying. She sat down, her shoulders hunched forward, and began to cry. Scott looked across the bed at her. 'I know it's hard for you, Ruth. It's hard for all of us. There's going to be muck flying everywhere. A lot of people will be trying to look after themselves, and that always means peril. We're dealing with some very fierce people, on both sides, people who've learned a long time ago how to get out of a mess, no matter who's damaged in the process.'

'You said there was something else,' Harpur reminded him. 'Is it about Mellick's boy?'

'Sharp, sir.' Patches of red had come up on his face from Ruth's fingers.

She raised her head a little. 'What boy?'

Scott did not explain. 'You've done nothing about him, Mr Harpur, although the signs are you knew days ago. The Billy Graham meeting? Lamb had a tip from someone on Mellick's side or Wright's, I don't know and don't pretend to, but I'd say it must be Lamb who told you. It's top quality information, and only somebody with top quality contacts is going to get it. The question is, What would Bundy make of this? Any time now that kid's body might be found, and you're still sitting tight.'

'Is this right, Col?'

Scott went on: 'As I see it, you had this tip, yes, probably from Lamb, but he said you couldn't do anything yet, because it would point to him, or his source. Didn't Lamb have a run out with Wright's present woman, Della Maine a long time ago? There might still be contact, and perhaps she draws the line at kidnapping a handicapped kid. If it's Della, it's obvious she would be scared the finger could point at her. She might just have told Lamb to get it off her chest. Women do things like that. So Lamb gives it to you and makes you promise not to move yet. It's crazy, but we've all had situations like that. So, you held fire. Ruth, this is a helpless, eleven-year-old, retarded boy we're talking about. God knows what's happened to him. And we're waiting for the nod from a nark before we can act. Think if the papers got hold of the story. They'd slaughter us.'

'Col, please, is this right? Why haven't you done anything?' She was sitting up straight, staring at him.

'It's not simple, love,' he replied.

'The boy was snatched by another protection racketeer on our patch, Ruth, one of Mellick's business rivals,' Scott said. 'I don't have to tell you, this bit of the world's become very prosperous. It's not just people retreating from the Great Wen, it's the efficiency of the motorways in speeding them back there when they need to go, to pick up the cheques or take someone over, or look for bargains in the share slide. This is happening in provincial patches all over Britain. They're becoming very hairy.'

'Can we skip the sociology?' she replied. 'Yes, I've heard it before. Just tell me about the child.'

He smiled. 'OK. Probably the idea was to lure Tenderness somewhere alone, without guards, by promising to return his son. This is after they'd driven the Mellicks half mad by silence. There were big scores to settle, you see, and these people always settle, in their own way. It's part of the rules, it's in the folklore. But Wright has been killed. And the kid is probably dead, as well. Or he's being held by three yobs, frantic with panic, and liable to do anything, now their boss is gone.'

Harpur said: 'Christ, Hubert, you must know Mellick didn't want a search, wouldn't even confirm the disappearance. What could I do?'

'Would Bundy accept that as a defence, sir? Of course he wouldn't, nor should he. No, you were looking after your informant, first law of the jungle for a detective, and generally fair enough, no question. But is some ACC who's spent his life flapping white gloves at Minis going to understand this, when there's a dead kid about and the headlines are getting bigger and nastier every day? We're looking at disaster here.'

Ruth picked up Scott's word. 'Is it a defence, Col?' It did not sound as if she thought so. Perhaps Scott had known what he was doing after all when he asked her to stay.

Hubert stood again. 'Don't answer at once, sir. Think about it.' He made for the door, then paused. 'You'll ask, how could I be sure you'd spin the tale to Bundy, if we had an agreement. The answer to that is that I'd trust you. Aren't we long-time colleagues, for heaven's sake? Haven't we come through enough troubles together? If it's not presumptuous, we're friends.'

On his way home later, Harpur found himself ceaselessly watching the mirror, but he spotted no tail. Megan and the girls were playing Trivial Pursuit, and he joined them. It was a game he often won, as long as he could keep clear of literature and art questions. When the telephone rang his younger daughter, Jill, went to answer and returned saying it was for him. 'Somebody sinister again. Why can't they ring you at work, dad? Hazel and I hate talking to them. Slimy.'

It was Lamb. 'Col, Ivor Wright's warrior, Richard Percival Penton, also known as Rick the Intelligent, has been seen buying a hell of a lot of food in the local Spar at Georgeboon. You know it? A big village, hardly a town. Lots of remote farms that way. This doesn't seem to me a likely setting for Rick. As far as I know he's got no country property and he's not a rambler, either . . . It would make a good lie-low location, though. Was that your babe who answered? Always sounds so friendly and pleasant on the phone, Col, a credit to you.'

'That's funny, she just said, "It's the man with the lovely, warm voice."'

'That's nice. Yes. I suppose what she really said is, "It's your regular big mouth." At that age they don't miss much, do they?

68

But they don't know how the world runs, and let them stay that way for as long as possible, Col. I like youthful values. Go very gingerly up around Georgeboon, won't you? There'll be armament. Well, I don't have to tell you. None of the buggers are shots, but they can squeeze a trigger, and bullets find their way by accident into the tenderest places.'

'What sort of food?'

'You mean, was there some for a boy of eleven? I don't know. This information comes very round about. I can't tell you if the lad's alive.'

'Who's the source?'

'I didn't hear that. The line broke up.'

'Yes, all right.' It had been the unpermitted question. Now and then Harpur felt he had to try it. Jack never answered. He wouldn't be the great informant he was if he did. The craft had delicate and complex rules. 'I'll take a solo look first.'

'I'd think that was wise, but play it any way you like, Col. I'm not asking you keep it close from now on. This is a kid's life, even if it is a Mellick kid.'

'Was it Ivor's Della who told you about the boy, Jack?'

He ignored that, too, but Harpur liked to show him occasionally that there were other good tipsters about. 'A battalion might panic them, Colin. Milton Bain, Rick himself – they're edgy people. Ancient Dave's all right, but he's keen on keeping out of jail and a big posse could disturb even him.'

Jill opened the door to the hall and called him back to the game. She held her nose and pulled an imaginary lavatory chain with the other hand. Harpur closed the door. 'Jack, go rather carefully yourself. Your name's in circulation.'

'Again?'

'Tenderness might have it.'

'Your friend Scott?'

'Eyes open. How's your mother? How's the new girl.'

'Cheerful, grateful, respectively.'

8

Harpur drove himself to the area around Georgeboon first thing next day. The search for a possible hideout near there was the kind of work he understood best, systematic, trial-and-error effort and needing a bit of luck, a big bit.

And he loved going out on his own. On this sort of operation he could even feel for a moment that he took on a fraction of worthwhile symbolism as the law's lone man against conspiring forces of darkness. It was only for a moment. Always he swiftly did to death the idea of himself as a shining knight. Christ, it was lunatic not to take account of the wide and widening areas of darkness in himself, and nothing could have made him spell out such self-inflation to others, especially not to his children or his wife or Desmond Iles. 'Lone', for fuck's sake. He must have got that deadbeat touch of drama from BBC News.

The notion of himself as the cleanser never totally disappeared, though, and occasionally it could grow overpoweringly strong: Ruth's dismay that he had done nothing about Mellick's son helped shove him into hurried action now, action that might counter the delays . . . And it had to be solitary. He needed to put his image right with her, and to put himself right with himself. He should not have delayed over Mellick's son, not even for the sake of Jack Lamb's skin, and Jack's source's skin. It was not the first time that Harpur had been driven by a chewy sense of guilt.

He was unarmed. It would have been impossible to tell the issuing officer why he needed a pistol. That was a drawback he had to accept if he wanted to do this solo. Even pre Waldorf and Cherry Groce, he had never felt happy with guns, anyway, either being pointed at or pointing. Iles had said once that this showed an extremely nice nature, an extremely nice old woman's nature, and ought to stop him for ever from getting top rank. 'If there's one thing that makes my flesh creep,' Iles had gone on, 'it's a squeamish cop.' But even Iles could show a weakness now and then.

Harpur's liking for the methodical side of a search like this, the old-fashioned plod, sometimes surprised him. After all, he was a police college whiz kid and could make a bright showing on the philosophy of law enforcement and the uses and limitations of the computer. But he did believe, too, in door knocking and foot slogging. It always made Harpur feel he was really working, and that soothed something in him. Deep in his lineage there must have been a mixed Puritan and Catholic marriage, to produce reverence for work plus a taste for guilt.

He had come to agree with Lamb that a remote farm was the most likely spot and on the ordnance survey he drew a circle around Georgeboon, with a radius representing about two miles. There were rock hills to the north and west and no farms. To the east, Georgeboon straggled out with a few small factories and a council estate, until it reached the beginning of a reservoir; again, no farms. Harpur decided he must concentrate to the south for his first tries. He picked out four farms there, lying inside his limit.

The approaches would be difficult. He could not drive too close or occupants would be alerted; so, park out of sight and walk the last stage, using the cover of hedges and outbuildings when he could. Just the same, he would feel very exposed, very helpless. Yes, this lone cop did have symbolic stature, after all. What he stood for was cock-up and bad preparation and crazy, pious self-blame.

Unless he found the hideout early, supposing there was a hideout, the hiking across fields meant his search could take a long time. And he did not find it early. The first two calls he made turned out to be normal, working farms. Luckily, he could tell this without going near enough to be seen; at both he watched people he did not recognize busy about the yard, and obviously the real thing.

It was late in the morning before he reached the third. This was the most difficult so far to approach unobserved. Set on rising ground, it would have a view from upstairs over miles of fields, obviously one reason they had picked it, if they were here. He parked behind a copse and then sat in the car for a few minutes trying to work out tactics. In fact, there were no tactics, except the ones he had already followed at the other farms – to hoof the last bit and hope for the best. He left the car and went forward, keeping his head down as much as he could. Years ago he had questioned Rick the Intelligent about some offence, possibly arrested him, so Harpur would be remembered. Even without that, there were few villains on his ground who did not know what he looked like. Not that all this mattered much because the people holding Tenderness's child would regard every approaching stranger as an enemy, someone to be coped with.

Occasionally, when the house came clearly into view through breaks in the hedges, he did lift his eyes and tried to spot any movement at the windows, hoping that panic might make them careless. He saw nothing, though. Nor did he see people working. And there was something else: at both the other farms, dogs had come out and challenged him, making it quite tricky to watch unobserved. Here there seemed to be none. Harpur began to think he could have it right this time. Suddenly, he decided that it might actually be safer if they did know who he was. With any luck, they would imagine that, with his rank, he must have back-up close, and they might take it easy with him. That is, if they didn't go bananas. He put his head back, walked upright, and smiled like Bill Bailey coming home, sure of a grand welcome.

He made his way through mud along the edge of a field, climbing all the time, a dangerously slow advance, and he had to work hard to keep the smile alight. Reaching a gate eventually, he climbed over. In a moment he would be at the yard around the house. He passed what might once have been a cowshed, stone-walled and with no windows. A heavy, gleaming new hasp and staple had been fitted to the door and the padlock holding it shut was also shining new. Something bright-coloured lay on the ground a few yards from the door and, without stopping, he went closer and saw a plumed Lego knight on a horse that had been snapped across, as if by a kick from some creature of a different scale. Yes, shining knights would not have much hope these days, and he did not really want to be one. You had to know how to kick first, and harder.

Harpur opened a small gate to the kitchen garden around the house and went up the path to the front door, looking cheerful, he hoped, and feeling like a target. He glanced in through a downstairs window and saw a barely furnished room, with what looked like more Lego scattered around the floor. Amid this shambles a couple of grey model fortress turrets remained partially intact, like walls left standing in pictures of war shattered Berlin. This glimpse changed his mind. Until now he had intended knocking the door and announcing himself when they opened it, the proper, formal procedure. But these sad traces of a child's games somehow enraged Harpur and unbearably sharpened his worries about the boy. He had to get into this house quickly and look all over it. To wait on the doorstep and play friendly would be mad.

He gripped the door knob and turned, but it did not give. Rocking back a couple of times he aimed his shoulder at the spot where the lock bar would be and then crashed against the door. On the second attempt it burst open. Perhaps he ought to shout 'Unarmed police', an appeal to their sense of fair play. Or, then again, perhaps not.

He was in a stone-floored hall or passage. The only furniture was a chair on which stood a washing-up bowl half full of greasy water. In it floated an empty take-away curry carton and a couple of small, yellow apples, like some grubby variation of the Halloween ritual. He stood for a second, taking whatever messages the house would give him and waiting for reactions to his entry. There were no sounds, beyond what seemed to be a window upstairs rattling in the wind, but he could smell burning. That, too, seemed to come from upstairs. To his right was the closed door of what must be the room he had seen from outside. Was the place empty?

He opened the door and pushed it wide with his foot, remaining in the hall. The drill said you swept the room with your eyes and your gun followed your eyes, as long as you had one, so he made do with his eyes. He saw nobody and went in, crunching on sections of Lego wall and more warriors and horses. There was a small table and a couple of chairs at the top end of the room, out of sight from the window. On the table he found only a folded *Daily Telegraph*. Beneath the table was a three of diamonds but no sign of the rest of the pack. The newspaper was the previous day's. The crossword had been completed except for one word. Iles could have dealt with that.

Harpur stood still again, listening. In a corner, behind the ruins of the toy fort, were some model lorries and cars and a television detector van. A couple of rush mats covered the floor and on one

73

of them, near the towers of the fort, was a cushion, as if the boy might have sat there assembling the pieces. Any child who could put a Lego fort together was not all that dim. Perhaps he'd had help. It sometimes happened in these cases that one of the gang became fond of the hostage. Rick the Intelligent probably wasn't the man. As Harpur recalled him, he would be too centred on himself and his heavy bits of hand jewellery. They said Milton would turn to boys if there were no women about, so some sort of relationship could have started there. He did not want to think about that. He preferred to hope simply that one or other of them had a humane streak. Harpur would not count on its being applied to himself, though. Were they waiting for him somewhere in the house?

He moved gingerly towards the kitchen and found a couple more empty curry cartons, some Marmite and jam, three-quarters of a loaf, more apples and a dozen tins of unopened meat – corned beef, ham and tongue. A set of body-building weights and their lifting bar stood near the draining board and a shirt and a pair of white socks hung on a makeshift line and dripped slowly on to the floor. Half a dozen empty cider and beer flagons lay strewn about and he took one of them in case he needed a weapon. Then he went quickly up the stairs.

There were three bedrooms and a combined lavatory and bathroom. Swiftly and carefully he searched each and found them all empty. He put down his flagon in the bath. In the last of the bedrooms he discovered what had been causing the smell of burning. Papers and large photographs had been set alight in the grate but the fire had almost died leaving several large pieces intact. Some of the material still weakly smouldered, Harpur pulled a few of the biggest items out of the grate and made sure they were no longer burning. Three were fragments of photographs, and one was half a sheet of A4 paper with handwriting on it. The photographs seemed to be of Tenderness's house in the Enclave and his dark-windowed Mercedes. It looked as if only a small part of the written notes had escaped the fire but they were obviously a description of the security at Elms Enclave and the layout of Tenderness's garden. Small pieces of Sellotape fluttered on the wall in a draught from the rattling window, and he guessed that the pictures and notes had been stuck around the room for memorizing before the boy was snatched, and taken

74

down only very recently, before the team suddenly baled out. It would be when they heard of Ivor's death, probably. They would fear he had talked and that Tenderness was on the way. That looked to be wrong.

In the big front bay window of the main bedroom stood a kitchen chair, and it would have been from there that someone kept watch over the chief approach roads. Each bedroom contained a camp bed and some straight-backed wooden chairs. That was all the upstairs furniture. If there were three men, as Garland's inquiries suggested, where did the boy sleep? Harpur's anxieties switched abruptly from the house to the outbuilding in the yard. It had worried him as soon as he saw the new lock and fittings, and the ruptured piece of Lego. Now, he worried more. Returning to the kitchen, he looked in the drawers of the sink unit and a cutlery cupboard for a key, but did not find one. Slowly and full of fear he crossed the yard and stood near the locked door. 'Graham,' he called, 'are you in there? This is a friend of your dad. I've come to take you home. Everything's fine.'

There was no answer. He repeated the call twice and still heard nothing. Leaving the yard, he returned over the fields to his car, taking the piece of scorched paper and photographs, and then drove right up to the farm and stopped near the outbuilding. In the boot he always kept a crowbar and working with feverish energy he tore the hasp out and shoved the door open wide. He saw a wheelbarrow, a grey, metal feeding-manger plus some other farm equipment, and in the middle of the floor a sleeping bag. He felt half relieved, half disappointed. There had been a chance that the men had grown scared and fled, leaving the boy – and leaving him alive. Why should they endanger themselves if this had been Ivor's personal revenge operation? Ivor was not bothered about revenge or anything else now.

He went inside. The place smelled clean enough and had obviously been done out with disinfectant. Perhaps they had prepared it specially to hold the child. He returned to the car and swung it around to point into the outbuilding, then switched on his headlights. Kneeling at the sleeping bag he examined it very carefully. Near the top were what looked to him like small patches of dried blood. They did not seem new to him, but he was no expert. Urgently, he began to shift the larger pieces of farm equipment so he could look behind at any space capable of concealing the body of a kid of eleven. While moving the wheel-barrow aside he noticed on one of its corners another stain that could also be dried blood. Harpur grew very alarmed now and went faster in his search.

The manger was covered by a tarpaulin which had been tied underneath. He undid the knots. As he pulled the sheet away, he recalled the many times in morgues when attendants had made a similar movement, so Harpur could identify a body or look at injuries. The resemblance did not end there. When the tarpaulin shifted, it exposed first the far side of the manger and Harpur suddenly saw the hand of someone who was lying in it, the fingers straight and spread out along the grey metal edge. Harpur was so appalled that for a second he felt paralysed and stopped tugging the sheet. Then, he realized this could not be the hand of an eleven-year-old boy. It was too big, and decorated with a fortune in rings, like a statement on the vanity of riches in death. And this dead man was in a manger. Someone could probably have hatched a sermon on that, too, though Harpur did not see exactly how it would go.

Drawing the tarpaulin right off, Harpur bent over to look closely at Rick the Intelligent. He lay on his back, head slightly turned to the left. They had not closed his mouth or his eyes, and it was as if he were gazing at the hand that rested on the edge. He might have been trying to pull himself upright and then found he had lost all strength from his fingers. He had a long, sensitive and very thoughtful face, and even though he was now a corpse in a trough with his mouth gaping, anyone could see how he might have gained the nickname. It was probably Rick's crossword, with one clue unsolved. As Harpur remembered him, he was the sort who always got there, almost. But then, if he had been someone who successfully completed what he started, perhaps he could not also have been found stretched out dead in one of the Christian world's best known emblems of life and hope.

Rick had on jeans and a navy roll-topped sweater, which was heavily bloodstained, torn and scorched on the chest, as if a medium calibre handgun had been held with the muzzle actually touching the fabric and fired, fired at least twice, Harpur thought, going by the damage. It meant he must have been held or was helpless through sleep or unconsciousness when shot. There appeared to have been no attempt to take the rings from his right hand, either, and at a rough count Harpur reckoned he was showing on both about four thousand pounds' worth of diamonds, amethysts and gold. It might have upset him to know his colleagues thought nothing of his treasures. In the side pockets of his jeans, Harpur found a couple of tenners and some change. There was nothing else. He put the money back. Then, taking the body by the right shoulder he turned it half over so he could search the back pockets, too.

As Harpur would have expected, there were bullet exit holes near the shoulder blades and it became clear now that he had been shot three times, not twice. In the rear pockets he found only a Spar bill and a packet of four french letters. Someone should let the DHSS know that their Aids publicity was getting through to all sorts.

9

'Tenderness, we got the biter.'

'What? Who is it? I'm listening.'

'Of course you are.'

'Don't ring off. You in a box? You going to run out of money? Can I call you back?'

'Some fucking joke. Don't worry. It's on a pay card. Now, listen, you been to the police? What about this phone? A tap – a trace?'

'No, no police, I swear. They don't know a thing.'

'That better be right, Tenderness.'

'Would I go to them about this?'

'Would you? You got a missus, haven't you?'

'She knows we don't go to – '

'The thing about a missus, you never know what they can do, especially when it's a kid. They gets worked up and they don't know, do they, they don't know how the game's played?'

'Jane isn't – '

'Where is she now?'

'Jane?'

'Come on, who else? Where is she? She in the room with you?'

'No. Upstairs.'

'You got an extension? She listening? Well, it don't matter.'

'No. She's sleeping. She been taking something. Look, who is this? Is this – '

'Don't say no names. Don't ever say no names. Only dead names, that can't hurt. Ivor can't hurt, can he? Let's just say we're the boys who got the biter, that's all.'

'Yes, I understand.'

'Of course you do. You was surprised we wasn't there, wasn't you?'

'What? Where? What you talking about, for God's sake?'

'When you went up there.'

'Up where. I don't know what you mean.'

'Not much you don't.'

'Is Graham all right? Look, I know he bites sometimes but he don't really mean no harm. It's only he gets a bit frightened.'

'When you went up the farm. You was shocked we was gone, yes? We're not so dim. Are we going to wait for you to call? That really what you thought, Tenderness.'

'What farm?'

'Come on. The farm. The one Ivor told you about before you done him.'

'I don't know any farm.'

'The farm you went up to looking, only there was nobody left there. Well, nobody alive left there.'

'No, I don't know what you're talking about. For Christ's sake, what d'you mean, nobody alive there? What farm?'

Mellick felt he might lose control of his mind, he was so confused and defeated by what the voice said. He recognized it as Ancient Dave's, but he did not understand what was meant about the farm. All he did understand was that Dave and the others had Graham. But he had known that pretty well, anyway. 'It wasn't us that done Ivor, you got to believe that. That's not down to me, no way. I heard about that. But I had a respect for Ivor, in a way.'

'Am I bloody stupid? You think I'm stupid?'

'No, no, but I swear – '

'Of course you done Ivor. Of course he said the farm. You know how to make it rough for people, and hot, don't you Tenderness? You know how to make them cough. Of course you

78

do. You're an artist. Sometimes I calls the kid the biter, sometimes Podge.'

'Is he all right?'

Jane came into the room and stood near the door, her face
frantic with interest and dread, her body arched forward and
tense. God, she looked old. Mellick signalled silence with a finger
to his lips.

'Yes, he's all right, Tenderness. He might not of been, but we
dealt with that.'

'I don't know what you mean.'

'What I was saying about the farm. You didn't find nothing up
there? Well, not everybody in the outfit thought we should take
the boy, you understand? That become a very difficult matter. We
had to settle that, didn't we?'

'Settle?'

'Yea, you know.'

'Well, I'm glad.'

'Yea, you ought to be glad.'

'Thanks. I want to thank you with all my heart.'

'That's it. You'll have a real good chance to say thanks. I'm
going to tell you about that, Tenderness.'

'What?' Jane whispered.

Mellick shook his head and covered the mouthpiece.

'You got someone there with you, Tenderness?'

'No, I told you, I swear.'

'This sort of case, the police moves in with people. I heard of
that. You fucking me about, Tenderness?' He suddenly began to
scream. 'You better think, you really better think. This kid of
yours, sometimes he's nothing but a pain and a nuisance. He
makes it a peril for us, don't he? He bit me in the face. I'm marked,
marked, you got it? All my life I spent with rough buggers, but I
never been marked before. Now, some kid, so I'm not very fond
of that kid. There was some book in school with a kid who was a
biter, I always remember that. Biting's not nice, Tenderness. But I
keeps patient with him, I wants you to believe that. So far, I keeps
very patient with him.'

'Honest, no police. They can't help.'

'Too right.'

'But, the boy – '

'Ivor, all he was interested in was a bit of get even. Well, you can understand. You ever been scorched, Tenderness, fire down below? Hard to forgive and forget. But revenge is real childish, if you think. Where's the percentage? I got other ideas now. What I say, we got the boy so make use.'

'Yes, I understand.'

'I know you do. How much do you understand, Tenderness?'

'A price?'

'That's right, a price.'

'What you thinking of?'

'There's two of us, was three. And that kid, your Podge, no wonder I calls him Podge, he can eat. People he bites and food he bites, plenty. All that costs. Every couple of days we're down that Spar at Georgeboon for grub. I said no names didn't I, but what do it matter, you knows that name and the High Hill farm from Ivor and you been there, I know. Well, we was gone a long time, so up you. Someone got to pay for all that Spar grub, Tenderness, bloody Marmite and cakes. There's nothing coming from Ivor now, is there, except cremation dust one day? Think he's getting to fancy fire? You give him a taste for it?' He had a laugh at this.

'Well, say a figure. What I want to be is reasonable. I always tries to be reasonable in business, you got to be. It's great, real great, the way you're looking after him. I'm well, grateful. We wants to show it good.'

Jane sat down, crouched again in the corner of the settee. She held her head in her hands and stared at the carpet.

'This is what's known as a preliminary call, Tenderness – just to put your mind at rest, like, and so you can think about things, if you know what I mean, so you can think peaceful now you know the kid is all right and getting fed.'

'Yes, but don't ring off. Please, don't ring off.' He saw Jane turn to stare at him as his voice rose, her hands still gripping her head. 'We can talk terms now, can't we. I – '

'You keeping me on here so your friends the police can do a trace, yes, Tenderness?'

'No. No that, not that. But I don't want to lose you, Dave.'

'Didn't I say no names? What you playing at? Who says it's Dave?'

'I'm sorry, it just come out.'

'Cash.'

'Yes, of course.'

'I want you to start taking cash out now. Not all at once. Them banks – they talks to the police, the police looks at accounts when there's something like this going. Take out bits, so it's gradual, but big bits.'

'Yes.'

'I'm going to ring you again, later. I won't say when. You know what it's like, phone boxes vandalized, disgusting, really. Destructive people everywhere, no respect. I don't know when I'll be able to get through.'

'A hundred grand.'

'I'm going to say right away, you're in the right direction, Tenderness. Definitely promising. You keep having a think on them lines. See what else you can do, yes? I'll come back.'

'Give me some guidance, what you want.'

'You keep working on it, Tenderness, keep going up. Think to yourself, This is my boy I'm making bids for. See it like that, Tenderness. It will make the money come easier.'

'One two five. Please, don't – '. He heard the receiver go down. 'Ring off,' he finished. For a moment later he remained with the phone to his ear, then replaced it.

Jane said: 'What?'

'He's all right.'

'Who says?'

'It was Ancient Dave.'

'How do you know he's all right?'

'I could tell he wasn't lying.'

'How?'

'I could feel it.'

'Oh, God. Why did you only say 125 grand?'

'Jane, to Ancient that's big money.'

'So he rang off.'

'He's coming back.'

'When?'

'He'll come back. He've learned from Ivor – how to make us stew. We got to be patient, love, that's all.'

Her head still in her hands, she rocked slowly forward and back on the settee, moaning gently. Then she said: 'If we had the police, they could of traced that call, couldn't they? They can do all sorts. They can go real quick on them calls.'

'Don't start that again, love.'

81

'Couldn't they, though?'

'Maybe. Then what? They send an army and frighten them so much they – '

'They got a way of dealing with this sort of thing. They seen it all before. What I mean, they got a drill, Bernie. They does it step by step, they've tried it all before, and they knows what works, what don't.'

'No, it don't always work. You heard of the Black Panther?'

'They finds out about the way these people's minds work, and then they makes their move.' She began to moan and rock again. In a moment she said: 'Does your way work, Bernie? Does it?'

'He's still alive.'

'They say.'

When once more she started to moan and rock, he yelled: 'Stop that, stop it, for God's sake. You think you're the only one who cares, the only one who suffers?' He took a couple of steps towards Jane as if about to attack her.

She looked up and said: 'No, I know you suffer, love. I wish I could help you. I don't know how.'

'Well, we must just help each other,' he told her gently. He took a few more paces and bent and kissed her on the forehead. 'I shouldn't of shouted, Jane. Do whatever makes you feel better.'

But she did not resume the noise and the rocking and in a minute left the room. As he dialled Ditto he heard her begin to wash some pots and dishes.

Because of what Dave had disclosed on the telephone, he and Ditto took Reg and Vernon and drove to High Hill farm, leaving Leonard to stay with Jane and handle any calls. Mellick would have preferred to take Leonard and leave Vernon, because he was bright and good with words and would be able to handle any talk with Dave better. But that was the trouble. Vernon could spiel – and he was young and he was dressy. Mellick found he didn't like leaving him with Jane now. The girls went for Vernon, because he had the looks and the money and the clothes and the toughness, and he could talk, as well. Something might happen with Jane in that state, desperate for comfort. Before this, he never considered that she might look at someone else, but now there were times when he felt he didn't really know her, and times when he felt she was losing belief in him. Vernon was much younger than Jane, yes, but she still had a body and, before all this strain got at her, she had a face, too. Enough of it was still there for a ram like Vernon, most probably.

Tenderness told Reg and Vernon to carry something and he brought a Magnum himself. Ditto took the Walther. Dave had said they were gone and it was probably true, but maybe not. They drove straight into the farm yard and sat for a few seconds gazing at the house and outbuildings. 'Look at them doors,' Ditto said. 'Them doors been opened violent, both. The house and that cowshed, both opened violent.'

'Police?' Vernon said.

'How can it be police?' Mellick snarled at him. 'The police don't know nothing.'

'Police wouldn't leave it open, doors swinging loose,' Reg said.

'So, it's some other crew who want your kid, Tenderness?' Vernon asked. 'How would they know he was here? Why'd they want him?'

'That a sleeping bag on the floor in the cowshed?' Ditto said. 'Yes, a sleeping bag. Who the hell sleeps in a cowshed? No windows, nothing. Not a window.'

Mellick got out of the car and walked towards the outbuilding. Ditto followed him. 'Tell the others to search the house,' Mellick said. For a while, he stood at the door of the cowshed staring at the sleeping bag on the floor, fearing to go in because of what he might find.

'Smells clean, anyway,' Ditto said. 'Smells like a hospital.'

Tenderness walked slowly towards the sleeping bag and bent down to look at it. 'Is that blood?'

Ditto looked. 'Yes, could be blood.'

'The bastards would lock a kid in a place like this?'

'It smells clean, though.'

'All this sodding stuff here.' Tenderness started to move pieces of farm equipment very gingerly, so he could look behind them.

Vernon appeared in the doorway. 'Nobody in the house. It looks like a rapid exit – toys all over the place. I'd say myself someone else has been here since they made their run.'

'What someone else? How do you know that? Kids? Thieves?' Mellick asked.

'I doubt it. Someone seems to have taken charred stuff from the grate. There's a trail.' Vernon came inside. 'Have you looked under the tarpaulin?'

'No. No, not yet.' Tenderness found he was whispering, unable to manage a real voice.

'You want me too?' Vernon said.

Mellick hesitated for a second. Then he answered, 'Yes, why not,' and turned away.

Vernon pulled the sheet off the manger.

'That's Rick the Intelligent,' Ditto said. 'Funny, he used to wear a lot of rings, was a great one for rings, Rick the Intelligent. Where they gone? I mean, real stuff, not something you gets out of a cracker, diamonds, them others, I forgets the name. He really knew about rings.'

'They've been pulled off. You can see the marks,' Vernon told them, bent over the left hand. 'You think Milton and Dave took them? Jesus, that's a bit dark, even for them. Or, as I said, someone's been here since. A collector: charred paper and rings. Who? Someone after evidence?'

'Yes, well they'd be worth a packet, them rings,' Ditto said. 'Nothing cheap.'

'Dave sort of mentioned all this,' Tenderness said. 'So, he was telling the truth, thank God.'

Ditto searched the body. 'Not a lot here. It wouldn't make sense for them boys to leave the rings. He's not Pharoah and he's not going to be buried with all his gear. No, not Pharoah, but he used to go to a lot of night classes so he could be intelligent. Night classes such as Spanish, not just woodwork and looking after cars. Hello, who was he knocking off these days? Yes, Spanish, he was a trier. He could do more than "Olée" and "Por fabor", much more.'

When they returned to Mellick's place in the Enclave Leonard was there alone, looking pretty sweaty. 'Jane went to the bank,' he said. 'I tried to persuade her to wait, but she wouldn't have it, Tenderness. What am I supposed to do?'

'There was another call?' Mellick asked.

'Yes. They wants two hundred and fifty grand, fast. He's going to let you know where and how. And no police, he said.'

'You told Jane?'

'She was here, in the room, Tenderness. What am I going to say to her?'

'So she's gone down the bank looking for a quarter of a million.'

'You got that sort of money in the bank?' Ditto asked. 'That's a lot to keep in a bank.'

'Of course I haven't.'

'She doesn't know?' Vernon asked. 'Is the account joint?'

'No. She never bothered about all that. She thinks money grows on trees. I didn't mind. It's nice for a woman to be like that. They're going to have a big giggle at her.'

'How could I stop her, Tenderness? I mean, did you want me to get heavy with your wife?'

'Get down there now, Reg and you, Len, see if you can stop her. Stop her any way you can and bring her back, the silly little cow,' Mellick said. 'She's going to make me look a fucking berk.' When they had left, Mellick went on: 'Two hundred and fifty, Jesus.'

'You could raise plenty on this lovely house and the furniture,' Ditto said. 'It's better than executive, it's select development, much better than executive.'

'All debt. The bank's screwing me.'

'Are you going to pay Dave and Milton?' Vernon asked.

'What else?'

'Pay it all? No bargaining?'

'I'm dealing with wild men. Can I mess about with my kid's life?' He had begun to shout. 'These are scum who take the rings off a mate's body.'

'They'll crack,' Vernon said. 'They're without leadership. They're just making it up as they go along. Ancient Dave, Milton, they're nobodies.'

'It don't take a somebody to kill a kid, you spouting ponce,' Mellick screamed at him.

'We'll get the money, Tenderness, and we'll get it back after,' Ditto said. 'Get the money, get Graham, then get the money back again. This is Ancient Dave and Milton? Yes, they're wild, yes they're a bit strong now because of your boy, but we can see to them, no trouble, after.' He spread his arms, signalling that a very big idea had arrived. 'Push the payments from the casinos

85

up and from the bars. We tells them they got to pay a year's cover now, instead of a week's, and then no more till 1989? If we talk real intimate to them, I mean, mention Molotovs in the casinos and personal home visiting, they'd get the merit of it. They're given a sort of season ticket. We could make them see the beauty of it if we took a real emphatic approach.'

'They couldn't do it,' Vernon said. 'This is two-fifty grand. This is not Whitsun Treat money. They can't build that sort of cash in time, even these boys, even in these glitter days.'

'Christ, whose side you on, Vernon? How did you get so sodding clever?' Ditto asked. 'You want Tenderness's boy back? How come you got all the answers and none of them's any good, then?'

'He's right, Ditto. They wouldn't have it. No, we can't do it from the collections.'

'It will have to be a job,' Vernon said. 'If you're going to pay.'

'Haven't I told you?' Mellick said. 'I – '

'We'll line something up,' Vernon told him. 'It will have to be a bit swift and hurried, but it can be done.'

Ditto fixed on to the enthusiasm and forgot his anger. 'Yes, of course we can. Something from the bars and casinos and something big from a job. It will add up. We can – '

Jane came into the room, with Reg and Leonard behind her. She had a cut over one eye and blood had run down her cheek and on to the shoulder of her denim jacket. The sleeve of the jacket was smeared with dirt and what looked like white wash, as if she had been thrown hard against a wall.

'Did she get there?' Mellick asked.

'No,' Reg said. 'We reasoned with her and told her it was stupid, and after a while she agreed with us.'

'Come on, love, sit down,' Mellick said to her. 'Let me clean you up, and I'll get you a drink.'

'What you need's a drink, Jane,' Ditto told her.

Mellick went forward and put an arm around her shoulders. She did nothing, simply stood inert. After a moment she said: 'Bernie, these two reckon there's no money in the bank.'

He did not reply.

'It's right, is it? So what kind of cunt am I married to? Anyone want to tell me that? Vernon?'

10

Graham hated the new house. Except for one soldier on his horse, he had been forced to leave all the toys at the farm. When they were going from there, he managed to pick up two of the horse soldiers but found that one of them had been broken across the middle by Milton's kicking. As they passed the cowshed on their way to the car he threw that one away.

The other he kept now in his pocket. The trooper had a coloured helmet and Milton had told him in the farmhouse that on a real soldier those colours would be feathers. He liked colours. In the farmhouse he could look out at a lot of fields when he was upstairs and some of them were green and there were trees. In this house he could not look out because the curtains were together all the time. There were two colours on the soldier's hat. Someone used to teach him about counting, but he could not remember who it was now.

He kept the soldier out of sight in his pocket, sure the two men would be angry if they saw it. They seemed to dislike the other house and the farm now, though he did not understand why, and he sensed that they would not be pleased to find he'd brought something from there. He reasoned that he could produce the soldier and play with it one day when they were not angry.

For now, when Dave or Milton seemed excited and were shouting he would put his hand in his pocket and catch hold of the soldier and his horse. They had come to seem like his secret friends. He had no real friends in this house or in the other one. When he caught hold of the soldier and the horse in his pocket he felt less frightened. Now and then, when he was very scared, he would squeeze the soldier in his pocket until it hurt his hand, and that made him feel better, a little bit.

Because of the shouting he sometimes thought Dave and Milton would fight. In school boys and girls used to fight, but he had seen men fighting only once, apart from on television. That had been in the farmhouse. It had made him very upset.

He could remember that there used to be three men in the farmhouse, not two, and he could just recall the missing man's name, Rick. After Rick came running down the stairs saying 'Dead' that day the three of them began to shout at each other, and it was then the fighting began.

Rick was the one who took him to go to sleep in the cowshed. But in this house now he did not go out of the house when it was time to sleep. In this house he slept on the floor in a room with Dave and Milton and he was cold. He did not have a sleeping bag because they had left it at the other house. They had blankets but not a pillow and the floor was without a carpet. It was boards. It was not like a bed, it was hard, and he could smell dirt.

They said he must never pull the curtains back. They shouted this at him, the two of them, and Milton said he would fucking blow his head off if he did. He did not ask where Rick was, but now and then he heard Dave and Milton talk about him. They did not seem to like him any longer and they might not want him in this house.

They had brought Rick's radio from the other house and they listened to it all the time, but not music, talking. He was frightened in this house when Dave and Milton shouted at each other, but in the farmhouse he was more frightened by the three men that day. He was sitting on the floor then by the toys and near where the fort's walls and towers had been until Milton kicked them over. A lot of what they yelled and snarled at each other had gone from his memory now but he could still recall some of the words. They were 'dangerous' and 'Tenderness' and 'pay', Dave had said. 'Tenderness will pay.' Rick kept saying 'dangerous', and 'too dangerous.' Dave said some numbers, very big numbers which Graham did not understand. They were bigger numbers than four.

But Rick kept on saying 'dangerous' and then Dave said he was 'Fucking yellow'. The boy knew yellow to be a colour, but he could not remember which one it was on the snooker table. He looked at Rick's face but saw no new colour.

While he was staring at Rick's face the fighting began. Rick had become very angry and he said to Dave and Milton: 'Too dangerous to hold him. We finish him and leave him.'

Graham feared those words. Rick did not shout them, he was very quiet again and he did not look at Graham, but the boy knew they were about him. He used to like Rick because he did not shout, and because he used to take him to breakfast, but now he was afraid of him.

Then Dave said to Rick: 'It's you that's fucking finished.' Dave yelled these words and they were so loud that they seemed to the boy to be still inside his head now. He could hear them, and they continued to terrify him.

He had continued gazing at Rick to see if he was yellow and he saw him move his hand very fast towards his shoulder, inside his coat. When he moved his hand like that it was pretty, like a lot of colours rushing through the air, because the light shone on the rings and made a sparkling line.

The boy had known that Rick moved his hand so fast to reach a gun under his coat. He knew about guns, and had often seen them on television. Sometimes in the farmhouse, Rick had taken his coat off and Graham saw the gun. It was in a thing like a cowboy had but was held on by straps on his chest, not at the top of his trousers. Once, in the room upstairs where the picture of Sam was on the wall, Rick and Milton had played with their guns, seeing who was fastest in pointing them. They were laughing then.

Now, Rick was not playing and none of them was laughing. Milton was standing behind Rick and did not try to get his gun out fast but caught hold of him from behind with his arm around his neck, and he was pulling Rick's head back very hard. Rick stopped trying to reach his gun then and with his two hands struggled to get free.

Then, suddenly, Graham saw that Dave had a small gun in his hand and he was pointing it at Rick. He put it against Rick's chest and held it there. Dave shouted to Rick to keep still and then he put his hand under Rick's coat and pulled out the gun. He held both of them against Rick's chest and shouted to him again to keep still.

After a while, the boy saw that Rick was growing tired and he no longer fought to break Milton's hold on his neck. Milton kept his arm there but he was not pulling back so hard now. Dave did not take the guns off his chest but he was not shouting any more.

Then they made Rick stand up and Milton pulled his gun out as

89

well. Milton turned and said to Graham that they were going outside and he must stay in the room or there would be trouble. Dave went first, he was walking backwards with the two guns against Rick's head. Rick was next to him and Milton was behind Rick, his gun against Rick's back. They went very slowly, out through the door. The boy saw that Rick did not want to go, but Milton pushed him with his gun and shouted at him to make him walk.

When they were outside Graham could see them through the window. They were in the yard and going towards the cowshed. Dave spotted him looking through the window and started shouting at him to sit down, and Milton shouted at him as well, but Milton did not turn round to look at him, he was looking at the back of Rick all the time and pushing him with the gun.

When they had gone out the boy thought about running to the back of the house, opening the kitchen door and making his way through the little rear garden into the fields. The men might not be able to find him there. But then, in his way, Graham began to worry, and he hesitated. If he was in the fields his mother and father would not be able to find him because they would be in a car. He would be in the fields by himself with the animals and he did not like that, it frightened him. If he was running in fields he might come to some cows. They were big and they were always chewing and they had thick strings of spit hanging from their mouths.

But then he thought that if he was in fields and his mother and father did not find him he would shout a lot and somebody might come to help him. Sometimes there were shepherds in fields, he knew that because he sang about it when it was Christmas. They were in the fields in the night. It would be night soon. If he shouted and a shepherd came he would say his name and his mother's name, he knew that, it was Mrs Mellick. If he told the shepherds this they would be able to take him home.

But then he had more doubts. If he was in the fields shouting, Dave and Milton might hear him and they would hit him and make him come back. Sitting in the room then, Graham had begun to cry. He wanted to ask someone what to do, but there was nobody.

Then, while he was sitting there, confused, he heard what

sounded to him like fireworks or like guns on television. Milton came back and then Dave. They no longer had the guns in their hands and they began getting ready to leave. They were hurrying. They told him to get ready as well and bring his toothbrush and the clothes they had bought him, but they said they would leave the sleeping bag, it was not needed. They told him he could not bring the toys, there was not time, but when they were looking the other way he picked up the two mounted troopers, but then he threw one away because it was broken.

When he went upstairs to get his toothbrush and some clothes he could hear them, they had started shouting again. It was about the rings on Rick's hands. He put the clothes and the toothbrush in a case they gave him and when he came downstairs they were still shouting, and he was afraid they would fight. Milton said to get the rings and take them with them and Dave said No, it wasn't right, he would not have it.

So, then Milton said he would leave the rings and they stopped shouting and took him out to the car. He saw it was a different one, not the green van they had when they came to bring him from the garden. He saw the big door of the cowshed where he used to sleep and it was locked. Milton drove out of the yard to the road and then they went fast. He was in the back with Dave and they did not stop, only to get some petrol.

They came to this new house. When they arrived he was very hungry, and there was no cooker in this house and no fridge, but Milton went to a shop and brought some hot food, meat and rice and big white crisps. The meat burned his throat and his tongue and he wanted to throw it away but they shouted at him to eat it, so he did.

This house was not like the farmhouse. Through the curtains, he could hear cars outside all the time and people talking. He wanted to shout to them and say his name, but he was afraid to. If he ran away from this house he thought there would be streets outside and his father and mother might be able to find him with the car.

But it would be hard to run away here because Dave and Milton were with him all the time, except when Milton went to a shop. And sometimes Dave went out. He said he was going to the telephone, because there wasn't one in the house. Dave did not tell him who he was ringing up but he said it was to ask somebody for a nice present. That puzzled Graham. He knew it was not Christmas because there were no trees in the shops when they came past in the car to this house and no decorations, but it might be Dave's birthday. He was old, but old people still had birthdays, so perhaps he needed a present.

11

Mellick and Ditto Repeato waited in the street opposite Hubert Scott's house. They had the car near but stood in a shop doorway so they could get to Scott quickly if he came out. In the old days, when Mellick was seeing him pretty regularly, Scott generally took a walk to a pub on the corner late in the evening, and Mellick would sometimes intercept him, especially when, to push his price up, Hubert was playing hard to get. There had been times, too, when Scott wanted to end the partnership altogether, and it had been important to reach him somehow and let him know they were tied together for keeps. That would happen sometimes with police. A man might take and take and take and then one day he would decide he was going to finish with all that, and would come along and tell you so sadly that the arrangement had to end. It was a bit of a laugh, really. It never took long to persuade them it couldn't end, ever.

Mellick sensed that Ditto was becoming edgy, and Mellick's own anxiety and impatience had grown almost unbearable. He would be crawling to Hubert, and he loathed it. Above all he loathed it because he feared that nothing Hubert could do or say would help get Graham back. Hubert was the last hope, and a bloody bad one. Tenderness Mellick, the patient schemer and planner was pinned in panic corner and liable to take a very bad beating, and he knew his people saw it and were sickened. Things could come apart, and all because of two luxury-model thicks like Ancient Dave and Milton.

'We could go in and see him,' Ditto said, 'not hang about out here. What's wrong with knocking on his door, then?'

Mellick did not answer.

'We could go in and see him.'

'His wife.'

'She can't give no trouble.'

'He acts up when she's around.'

'What you mean?'

'Gets all brave and difficult.'

'Well, we can change that. That's easy to change.'

'Not so easy. He got guts.'

'Yea, I know that, Hubert's no patsy, but – Well, I mean, he's not going to piss us about, Tenderness, if we're chipping slices off of his missus, is he? He got to be a gent then and cooperate. A gent thinks of the women first and Hubert can't ignore it if his wife's being give anguish in detail. Hubert's a gent. Don't he belong to a golf club? He wears white collars, very white.'

'I don't want no noise. Screaming.'

'Well, cushions.'

'I don't want no violence, unless it absolutely got to be.'

'Of course not, Tenderness. But if they asks for it, what can you do? Of course nobody wants to hurt nobody, that's just like animals, but if they acts out of order – Well, if they acts out of order. I mean, it's your boy. We got absolutely no time to mess about, no time at all, have we?'

'No. I got to have his help.'

'Of course, but – '

'Frighten him, yes. Pressure, like. Talk about his wife and what could happen to both of them. If it can be done talking, I – '

'So right. If. Yes, if. That's the word. Confrontation? Unpleasantness? we can do without it. What are we, for Christ's sake, Arthur Scargill? Are we Scargill? It's only if they don't understand a gentle, kind voice, Tenderness. There's some like that, it's bloody regrettable, they think they can do what they like if they sees a bit of gentleness and kindness. This doorway fucking stinks. We going to stay all night? I thought we was in a hurry.'

'It's going to be tricky,' Mellick said. 'There won't be no hearty welcome. He got trouble, brass brought in from outside poking around. Hubert's the star, they'll have his backbone out. Police can get real rough with mates. It won't be straight, it's police, but someone's in for a parcel of pain.' God, he must sound feeble to Ditto.

'All the more reason. We got to encourage him to help, yes? He got to be give a good chance to see our point of view.'

'I don't know if them sods are watching him now, I mean if there's this inquiry. They could be doing surveillance on him. If they turn on him they'll do the job thorough. You keeping an eye open?'

'Bloody cars parked all the way along, and half the street lights out, you can't see who could be in them. No Escorts there, but the buggers use all sorts these days, and girls, not just heavies. You want me to walk down and have a good look? They can send a heavy and a plain clothes girl and then they can pretend to be on the job if they think they're spotted. Well, half the time they *are* on the job, but sometimes they're pretending, what they call cover. That's what's called their cover, pretending nooky. That's why they gets so many girls joining, and equal pay for it, it's a picnic.'

'No, they'd recognize you. It's drawing attention. We got to chance it.'

'Why they give up Escorts, probably – no room for a heavy and a girl to spread theirselves. Hello.'

'Here we go.'

Scott left the house and began to walk swiftly along the pavement on the opposite side of the street. The speed of it, the cockiness, angered Mellick. That taking bastard had no lost kid to drive him half mad. He thought he could just walk away and fill himself with scotch and water. Then as Mellick was watching him with hatred Scott suddenly turned around and began to walk back even faster.

'He's seen us,' Mellick said.

'Of course he has, he's a fucking cop.' Ditto ran hard from the doorway across the street trying to intercept Scott before he could disappear into his house. Mellick followed. When he reached them Ditto was barring the front gate to Scott's garden and talking to him urgently. Scott looked bad now, not cocky at all.

'A bit of info is all we wants, Hubert. This won't take two seconds. It's important for Tenderness, real vital. I mean, life and death – life and death of someone so close to him, I won't say no more than that. I know you got such a lot to be grateful to Tenderness for, many a boost to your standard of living, you

94

deserved it, you always been a gem, Hubert. But you don't want to see Tenderness suffer now, that's obvious.'

'I can't,' Scott said, 'it's too – '

'We got the car close,' Ditto told him. 'A spin. No time at all.'

'We wouldn't have come if it wasn't real bad, Hubert,' Mellick said. 'I got consideration, believe me.'

'Hubert don't doubt that. He don't doubt that, Tenderness.'

'I'm no good to you now, anyway,' Hubert said. 'I'm retired. You know it. I'm not hearing things any longer.'

'You still got good friends,' Ditto said. 'Someone like you, Hubert, you don't lose all your pals just because you stops working. You can pick up a phone and on the end there's a fine colleague who's still glad to hear from you, talk about old times, chewing the fat, talking about what's going on now, because you're still interested. Of course you are. That was your life, they knows that. They're real pleased you called. That's the kind you are. You got a hold on people, it's in your nature. That's what I mean, a gem.'

'I'm poison down there. Can't you understand? People are scared to talk to me.'

It could be true. He did not look too good when you were close. His eyes were red, and his face seemed thin and the skin grey. Mellick was getting to recognize the signs of deep stress.

'That's bloody disgraceful,' Ditto said. 'I never heard anything so disgraceful. Cutting you off? Ashamed of you? But they're not all like that, Hubert. Can't be. Just talk confidential to someone, someone who owes you, there got to be plenty.'

'What info, for God's sake?'

Mellick saw he wanted to get out of the street. There was a lamp near them and light from a downstairs room at the front of his house, making them very obvious. 'Thanks, Hubert. Ditto, go and get the car.'

Mellick and Scott moved along a little, into the shadows, while they waited. Scott said: 'I would hate to find myself so weighed down by dum-dums in my gut that I lose my balance and fall out of this bloody vehicle, Tenderness, like Ivor Wright. If anything in that category happens, Harpur and a few others will know where to look, and they'll come after you, you'd better believe it.

Harpur's got a blind eye, yes, but the other one's sharp, and he can become very wounding.'

'Don't be crazy, Hubert. This is an S.O.S. I'm desperate.'

'Harpur wouldn't give a shit about Ivor, but if something happened to me – All right, I'm ex and I'm stained, but he'd never let it go. We've worked together. He'd take it personally. That's how it is with us, regardless.'

'You got this all wrong, I swear. Ivor? That's not down to me and even if it was, well, you're something else. Haven't we been friends? I feels very close to you. I've met your lovely wife, Jessie. When I thinks of you, I thinks of you like being part of the same team as me. But maybe you don't like to hear that.'

The car arrived.

'You say where you want to sit,' Mellick told him. 'This is just a talk, that's all.'

Scott climbed into the back and Mellick followed. Ditto drove gently out into the countryside.

'What info?' Scott asked.   ·

'We need a target,' Mellick said. 'Fast.'

'What the hell are you talking about, a target?'

'I got to raise some funds.' He could think of nothing but how crazy this mission was and what a waste of time.

'So, what's happened to the collections?' Hubert asked. 'The casinos getting difficult? I can't do a thing about that now, Tenderness. If I go near I'm finished. Look, I've already had one very sweaty day with this Mr Clean, the fucking outside brass and – '

'The casinos are paying fine. Everybody is. But that's chicken feed.'

'What we got to have is two-fifty grand,' Ditto said, over his shoulder. 'We got to buy his kid back from Ancient Dave.'

Scott was silent for a moment. Then he said: 'Christ, where's that sort of money?'

'You tell us,' Ditto replied.

'We got a couple of days,' Mellick said.

'We think we got a couple of days,' Ditto added.

Scott laughed. 'Am I going to know where's there's two-fifty grand tomorrow or the day after? Look, I'm sorry about the boy, but – '

'Of course you're sorry about my boy, Hubert. There's a very nice, feeling side to you, to all cops.'

'It's amazing, but we was discussing that not long ago, Tenderness and me, the feeling side of cops, the heart side, Hubert. It's a side they're not give enough credit for, that was what we decided at the end of the discussion. Not enough credit.'

'Any luck at all, we'll get these funds back, once we've rescued Graham,' Mellick said. 'We hand it over and then we takes it back, the way the police does it in kidnappings. It's only Dave and Milton. While they got the boy they're strong because they're so bloody twitchy and mad, they might do anything, they got to be handled so careful. They know it. They're just about clever enough to know that. They're strong because they're so bloody weak, if you see what I mean. But as soon as the boy's safe they're just Ancient Dave and Milton, a couple of Chernobyls, real disasters, and we'll take them to bits, too easy. What I want to say is these funds would be spare once we got the boy back, and you'd definitely be in on the split, Hubert. This is a very nice sum we're talking about, a lot of chalet time at Butlins.'

'Well, thanks, but – '

'You could get on the blower to someone and see whether there's any big cash movements, banks, wages, in the next couple of days,' Ditto told him. He parked the car on a remote hillside lay-by and they looked down on the lights of the city.

'Wages? Who pays cash these days?' Scott replied.

'That's it, Hubert. You're thinking now, Mellick said.'

Scott muttered: 'An operation like that – '

'It needs planning for weeks,' Mellick said. 'I know. Ditto knows. It's not even our sort of joust. But what can I do, Hubert?' Once, years ago, he had been in on a bank job, not running it, just waving a sawn-off and helping with the sacks. Always he had said he would not look at anything like it again, too much strain on the heart.

'And a meaty plus in it for your colleague, of course, your informant,' Ditto said. 'That would be for you to sort out with him personal, but very meaty, it's worth it to us, especially to Tenderness.'

'I can't say to you, like I usually would, Think about it, Hubert. Not like the old days. We got no time. This boy been gone nearly a couple of weeks. All sorts have happened – that death of Ivor. Something like that makes people edgy and ratty. I got to be ready. When Dave rings up next time I got to be able to say the money will be coming.'

'Such a long shot, Tenderness,' Scott answered. 'There might not be any bank taking that sort of loot in the next few days. And they don't always notify the police.'

'Yea, I know. It's chancy. But tell me what else I'm supposed to do.' Christ, he was yelling. Sometimes he thought he was already in bits, a wreck. All he could talk about was how far down he'd gone. 'Look, I got my wife looking at me like I'm a murderer of my own kid. She wants the police in. No, disrespect, about mates, Hubert, but – Well, she don't understand, the police would never split no guts looking for Tenderness Mellick's boy.'

'They'd look,' Scott told him.

'Oh, yes, they'd look, but would they really look, get all the stops out, would they balls? So, I got Jane thinking I'm King Shit.'

'His wife's a very lovely woman, a fine woman,' Ditto said, 'but there's stress there. Well, can't you understand it? This is a woman who've seen stress and there's certain effects, Hubert, it's regrettable.'

'We got to move out of the house because she hates it now, and I'll tell you something else, Hubert, I wouldn't tell nobody else this. No.'

'What's that, Tenderness?' Ditto asked.

'Hubert, she's looking at one of my people. You know what I mean, looking at him? This is a mature woman, looking at a kid. It's Vernon, the thin twat in fashion boots who's talking about art when he says a Constable.'

Ditto stared at him. 'Oh, no, Tenderness, I just can't believe – '

'And the big laugh is, I got to leave him there with her for the phone, because the other buggers can't handle the situation right. This is a woman in a big worked-up state, you see what I'm getting at, looking for comfort? So you can see I'm in a hurry, Hubert. While we're talking here now – '

'No, Tenderness,' Ditto said, 'I just can't believe – '

'It's a mess, I can see that,' Scott told Mellick, 'and I'd really like to help, but – '

'Tenderness been so delicate about all this you know, Hubert. I said, Come down and see you in your property, but Tenderness didn't want that, what he wouldn't have was any what they calls intrusion into your domestics, the household. He got a real respect for that. What he worried about primary, you know what he worried about primary? – it was the worry it might give your wife if we was to come to your place this time of night and raise matters so serious, tramping all over the carpets and that, and maybe talking loud. This was what really give Tenderness anxiety, he didn't want your wife give trouble of any sort, any sort. Well, he got a wife, a lovely wife, and he knows how a wife can suffer, they really feel pain. I don't mean pain in the body, nothing like that, of course not, but pain in the feelings and so on. That's where they really feel it, it can be very sad. So we hangs about in some chemist's doorway where the world have pissed and puked since Moses come for his tablets. That kind of consideration – well, I know you'll agree that's not usual, it shows friendship that most people would really think was great. I mean they would try to respond in a really full manner.'

'When he's talking about your wife, Ditto don't mean no harm, no harm at all, Hubert. I don't want no threats, nothing like that. This is about my kid, for God's sake, my family. Am I going to turn rough on the family of someone else? Would that make sense?'

'Of course not,' Ditto said. 'Didn't I make that clear? I want to make it very clear. When you're talking about family you're talking about something fucking sacred, that's a fact, fucking sacred.'

Scott said: 'All I can think about is this inquiry with Bundy. If he gets me, Tenderness, he gets you, as well, you realize that? It's worse for me, I'm an ex cop, but it would be bad for you too, passing bribes. I have to be so careful.'

'I know that. I trust you, Hubert. You can beat the sod.'

'You want to tie me in deeper through this, to make sure I keep quiet?'

'I said I trust you. I know you wouldn't shop us, not yourself or us, Hubert. You just keep giving him a brick wall, what can he do? There isn't no cheques, nothing traceable, how's he going to prove it? You got false name bank accounts?'

'Of course, but they know about these things. They're dealing with them all the time, Tenderness.'

'You'll be all right. I know it.'

Ditto had been talking to them through the gap between the front seats and suddenly reached back and grabbed Scott by his jacket and shirt and dragged him forward. 'You open your mouth to that sod and you better get some asbestos pants, Hubert, because we'll have your balls with the blowlamp. And your wife will earn some free suntan treatment to her face, you got it? It's hard to tell her face from her arse, but I think I got it sorted out. Christ, I don't know why we're wasting time with you, treating you like a duchess, I'd see to you and dump you here, you're no use to us, you're a soaring peril.'

Scott had been surprised by the speed of it but now pulled away violently and at the same time put a short, fast punch between the seats, catching Ditto in the mouth and nose, a heavy, useful punch, and Ditto went back hard against the steering wheel, half stunned.

'You had that coming,' Mellick shouted at him. 'I told you, didn't I, nothing like that? You all right, Hubert?'

'That champ slopper-out, do you think he's ever going to hurt me?'

Mellick left the back of the car quickly, opened the driving door and pulled Ditto's Walther from his pocket before he was properly recovered. 'Any more of that and I open your chest, Ditto. Have you forgot what we're here for, you jerk? We're here to make a deal, a proper business arrangement, not – Hubert's a friend, a long-time friend, a colleague for God's sake. He's going to help me.' He rejoined Scott in the back. 'I'm sorry, Hubert. Ditto's under strain, like all of us.'

'Yes, under strain,' Ditto said. He was wiping blood from his face. 'That don't mean a thing, what I said, Hubert, well you know that, and unforgivable about your missus, I want you to forget it. For her age she's a very lovely woman, if you know what I mean, I don't mean she looks old, nothing like that, she's a charmer through and through, a charmer, and always so loyal to you, it's a treat to watch. We got no intentions against her at all, not at all, Hubert, nor against you. None against either of you. I don't know what I was saying. I know you're going to see us all right. I feel that. Christ, my lip's doing a balloon. Well, like you said, Tenderness, I had it coming, I forgot about Hubert's left, he's no has-been.' He offered his hand and Scott shook it, looking away.

'So, you might be able to do something for me and my boy, Hubert? My feeling is, if your wife knew about this, she'd want you to help. She would understand how we're feeling, Jane and me.'

Ditto drove Scott back and put him down near his house.

'Hear from you soon,' Mellick said through the window. 'I mean, not more than twenty-four hours. That's how it got to be. Now, look, Hubert, you forget about all that violence and Ditto's talk, it was just his way, his stupid way, you know him. He's good all through, but he can get things round the wrong way a bit now and then. I trust you, Hubert, I know you want to help, and there's a packet in this for you and a friend, that's all you got to keep in mind. Real decent money.'

On the way to the Enclave, Ditto said: 'Was he listening, Tenderness? He's bloody hard.'

'Yes, he was listening. He thinks a lot of his wife. That's the thing about a marriage and a family, it's a funny thing, it gets to people. You ever noticed that?'

Ditto did not reply until they were near Mellick's house. 'Marriage? Yes. It goes deep, sometimes. Tenderness, not speaking out of turn, but – about Jane, that come as a shock, what you said to him, that was a real shock. Did you mean that, or was you just – ? No, of course you didn't mean it, about Jane and Vernon. No, Jane and you, well you're a pair, a real pair. It was a gambit, was it Tenderness? It was a bit of extra to help get that bugger with us?'

'You can't tell what they'll do when they're steamed up.' He returned Ditto's Walther.

'No. That what's known as hormones, Tenderness?' They came to the security bar. When they were through Ditto asked: 'Listen, you want me to park down the street from the house, so Jane and Vernon don't hear us coming and we might – '

'I thought of that.'

'We could really get – '

'But what the neighbours going to make of it, leaving the car the two of us and walking? They might put two and two together. I don't want these snooty sods thinking I can't trust my woman and having to sneak up. That would be all round, fast. They don't know what to make of us, already. There's a sir on the Enclave, you know, and others. They're keeping an eye to see how we goes on, see if we're all right. They'd love that, they lives on gossip and dirt. No, I don't think so.'

'Yea, neighbours in a place like this, you got to think of that, you got to act acceptable, in keeping. I should of thought of it.'

At the house when they arrived, Vernon was sitting near the telephone reading a book about wine that he must have brought with him. 'Jane's upstairs, I think,' he said. 'No calls, Tenderness.'

12

A routine car patrol reported discovery of a body with gunshot wounds at High Hill farm, near Georgeboon and Harpur drove out there with Desmond Iles. The call said the dead man might be Richard Penton, also known as Rick the Intelligent, one of Ivor Wright's cabinet. Harpur knew Iles loved attending in person when a butchered villain was on show and had informed him at once of the find. Such rare sights seemed to convince the Assistant Chief for a moment that the battle could be won, and he would often grow mellow and exultant viewing a really top-flight criminal's corpse, particularly if wounds were obvious. Rick the Intelligent was not top-flight by any stretch, but still a long-time pain in the arse, and the call spoke of gunshot injuries. Rick would do for today. The officer reporting the discovery was sergeant Robert Cotton, Ruth's second husband, and Harpur could have wished for someone else.

On the way, Iles talked of one of his abiding concerns, the fading of beauty through age. 'For myself, I tell you frankly, Col, I find it damn difficult to come to terms with. I've gathered rosebuds while I might, but could I have gathered more? I almost envy people like Lane or yourself, lucky enough to have little to lose. If anything, age will improve you. Faces that from babyhood look as if they've been badly knocked about, or display quaint features like the Chief's adam's apple, poor sod, can take on a kind of weathered quality later in life, and attract sympathy from women – as good a way as any of getting their legs apart. But can you understand how it is for me when I look in a mirror now and think back to what I would see not long ago? Please, I'd hate this to sound like vanity, one vice I hope I can plead not guilty to. No, what I'm talking about is the insult that time offers to a few, the special malice it seems to reserve for some of us. Simone Signoret or dear Anthony Eden.'

'How's Sarah, sir?'

For a minute or two he seemed to think about this and might have considered answering. There were times when he obviously liked discussing his wife, and would even invite advice. Now, though, he let his head sink forward, and it was as if he were taking a nap or inventorying sadnesses. In a while he said: 'I was able to manage a swift look at that ponce Bundy's papers on the inquiry so far while he was out of the building. That's one advantage of having him operate from headquarters – we've got keys. As you'd expect, there's what appears to be an exhaustive collection of Hubert's bank statements.' Iles produced a small notebook. 'He has deposits here, in Leeds, Wales, and London – two. No regular pattern in the payments – well, the bugger's a pro – and they're not round figures, naturally.' Iles read: 'Four hundred and twenty three pounds and twelve pence, three hundred and thirty seven pounds, one thousand and seven pounds and eighty six pence. Like that, all through. They add up to about thirty four grand over two years.'

'Any indication of how Hubert's trying to explain himself?'

'No, I did look, but I couldn't give the room a decent turn-over, could I? This is a very senior colleague and guest. Anyway, that might be on tapes gone for typing up. Col, are you bothered?'

'Hubert knows how to fight dirty. It wouldn't be nice for him inside. He's looking at ten, twelve years among people he's hurt.'

Again Iles seemed to lapse into himself. They entered the farmyard. As they were leaving the car, he said: 'Yes, I'd like to do something for him, if it's possible, which I doubt. Not just on account of the Lodge. Christ, he's a cop since the Creation. Because he's into a bit of stain, are we supposed to forget that?'

This was another of those questions which sounded as if it needed no answer, but with Iles it did. 'I was always happy to work with Hubert.'

'Oh, you generous, large spirited, mealy-mouthed gent.' Cotton approached. 'Does this one suspect you're making his wife happy?'

'Possibly, sir.'

'This is a grand piece of work, sergeant,' Iles declared.

'Thank you, sir.'

'Do we know what's behind it?'

'Some sort of internal squabble?'

'Where is he, Rob, in the house?' Harpur asked.

'No. This outbuilding. In a manger.'

He spoke as though resenting the need to answer Harpur and wanting to spend as few words as possible. There must have been a time when Cotton used to call him 'sir', but Harpur could not remember it.

'Yes, he does know,' Iles muttered as Cotton went a few yards ahead of them, towards the outbuilding. 'So what sort of Force is this, for God's sake – a chief super flagrantly entwined with a sergeant's wife?'

'A loving Force, sir?'

'Do you realize what Bundy – ?'

'We can deal with Bundy, sir.'

'Of course we can. All the same – '

Cotton turned and said: 'Here's Rick.' The body lay as Harpur had last seen it.

Iles eagerly approached the manger and gazed down silently for a few seconds. Then he announced: 'Death can do things for people. He looks full of creativity, wouldn't you say? Inspired? Who was it spoke about "sane and sacred death"?'

'Some idiot poet I should think,' Harpur replied.

'Well, half right. The first half. It was Whitman. Where are the rings, though?'

'Rings, sir?' Cotton said.

'Don't I recall from the dossier that he was a collector of jewellery?'

'Yes, I do believe he was,' Harpur replied.

Iles walked around the manger and had a look at Rick's hand, peering at the places from which the rings had obviously been removed. He put out his own hand and seemed about to take hold of Rick's, then stopped. Once, Harpur had seen him flick a dead villain's arm up into the air, making it appear for a moment that the man was still able to move. It had reminded Harpur of a cat tossing a dead mouse to try and make it run again, pleased about the kill, yet grieved there would be no more sport. Today, Iles drew back, no doubt realizing that Rick would be too stiff for anything like that. Instead, he simply stared at marks on the fingers where Rick's rings had been. 'They've stripped him. I wouldn't have believed it, not even of that crew.'

'There could have been others up here, sir,' Cotton said. 'Kids, vagrants.'

Iles went to examine the sleeping bag. 'He slept in here? Did they have Rick as a prisoner or something?'

'Could be. There's a new lock and fitment,' Cotton said. 'You'll see blood on the bag, sir. Possibly they surprised him, while he was blotto.'

'So why would they turn against him?'

'Who knows, sir?' Cotton replied.

'Colin?', Iles replied.

'What about the house?' Harpur asked.

'Looks like three or four people lived there, possibly a kid.'

'How do we know that?'

'Toys.'

'What kid?' Iles asked. 'The others would be Ancient Dave and Milton, yes? Have they or Rick got children?'

'Not that we know, sir,' Harpur said.

'We'll need to put out a call for Dave and Milton,' Iles said.

'I've done that, sir,' Cotton replied.

He had handled this pretty well, given that he started from total ignorance of the background. In fact, almost everything Harpur heard about him these days was a plus, from Ruth as well as colleagues. That helped explain why Harpur hated meeting him. Cotton was popular and capable, and Ruth said he had quickly won over her two sons, even though they used to idolize Brian, her first husband. Harpur did not begrudge him the credit, not very much.

Cotton looked good, too: lean and nimble, with bright blue eyes that always seemed alight with enthusiasm for what he was doing; or, at least, always seemed alight with enthusiasm until they met Harpur's. Anyone would be able to understand why Ruth had chosen to marry him following Brian Avery's murder. Would anyone understand, though, why she chose to revive the relationship with Harpur so soon after she became Mrs Cotton? Did Harpur understand it himself? All he understood was that he and Ruth had something solid and that so far and somehow it survived – survived her marriage and his own. Or, you could put it the other way: their marriages so far had somehow survived the love affair. It was the children who saw to that.

He went through the house with Iles. 'We assume a boy child?' the Assistant Chief said.

'I should think so.'

'Perhaps they brought women up here. One of them might have a son.'

'That could be it, sir. I'll check on their floozies.'

Iles half opened a discarded take-away carton. 'Are you hiding some fucking thing, in your usual sweet way, Harpur?

'No. Why do you ask, sir?'

'I get a feel for these things. It's why I'm the one with gold leaf on my hat and you're not.' They went into the living-room and he began to reconstruct a ruined Lego tower. 'Hasn't Tenderness got a son?'

'I think he has, sir.'

'Might it make sense for Ivor's people to snatch him – in revenge for the scorching?'

'And you believe they might have been holding him here?'

'Something you never thought of, naturally.'

'It's certainly an angle, sir. I'll look at it.'

'Yes, do that. As I told the Chief, I suppose you've been sitting on something, to protect an informant.'

That was not a question, so Harpur did not feel required to answer.

As they were driving back to headquarters, Iles said: 'So kind of you to ask, Col: Sarah's well enough.'

'Grand.'

'She's got something going somewhere.'

'Oh?'

'This time I've no idea who. It's not like when she was interlocked with your friend, Francis Garland. She more or less proclaimed that, like an Olympic Gold. Now, discretion, of a sort.'

'Well, perhaps you're being unjust to her, sir. There might be nothing. A lot of married women like to go out by themselves, just to be alone. That's what I've heard.'

'Yes? Now and then I run my tongue around a cup she's been using.'

'A cup? What sort of cup?'

'Come on now, Col. You know what a cup is, don't you? Thing you put on a saucer. You've never done that?'

'No, I don't think I ever have, sir, I don't know why.'

'She'll come in late and make tea.'

'It's a sedative, sir. I do it myself. You like to be close to something she's touched with her mouth? I think that's quite moving, sir.'

'Taste of cock where her lips have been on the rim.'

Harpur drove for a while in silence.

Iles said: 'All right, you're going to say you wouldn't recognize it.'

'I don't want to get sanctimonious about this, sir.'

'I suppose I come out of this looking pretty quaint.'

'Does she – ?'

'Know? See me do it? Do I tell her? Of course not. Tonguing crockery? What the hell do you take me for? Listen, one day I'm meeting royalty at receptions, making small talk about Mahler or our new leisure centre, and the next I – I mean, how would it look?'

'Well, you must think a lot of Sarah.'

'In my way, I think I do. In my way.'

'I don't think anyone can say better than that, sir.'

'Kind.'

'I still maintain you could be mistaken about her, though.'

'You're saying they've brought out a specially flavoured tea bag for frustrated women?'

13

Mellick took another phone call at home.

'Tenderness, you putting them funds together then, I mean, urgent?'

'Yes, urgent, yes, I swear.'

'You know what urgent means, Tenderness, I mean, real urgent?'

'Yes, I'm doing it, I swear.'

'Last time I rung, you wasn't even there, was you? Did he tell you, the one you left behind?'

'Yes. Look, I was out getting the funds together, wasn't I? That sort of money, I don't keep it in the house. It's not something you just rings up the bank about. This is seeing people, making arrangements. It's going along nice. It won't be no time now. You got no worries at all.'

'Well, I hope that's what you was out for, not doing something stupid like looking for us. You're not going to find us. I knows what you thinks – that we're dumbos, can't run something like this without Ivor. Don't believe it.'

'No, I – '

'You'll see different. This is a real operation. We knows how to lie low. We got patience. We're not going to stick our heads in no trap, so forget it, Tenderness.'

'Yes, I know, I can see that.'

'Out getting the funds? All right. That's what he said, the one you left behind. What he said, that you was out doing the catering. That's what his words was, cheeky sod. Ponce voice. That Vernon, the one with the shirts and that and the aftershave? I heard he was on your payroll these days.'

'Yes, Vernon, that's right. He's useful.'

'You leaves someone like that in the house with your missus on her own? You're a big truster, Tenderness. Your missus, she's still a great looking girl, you know, Tenderness. I'll tell you something, he sounded a bit breathless. Do you think they might of been playing Pat-a-cake, pat-a-cake? Your problem. So when's it going to be, when you going to have this nice package together?'

'Soon.'

'Soon? What's that mean? I mean, that don't mean a thing. Soon is just some time. You got to get exact. Tenderness, you sure you got this sort of money? Some of you people, living up the Enclave and all that, all show and debt, red hat and no knickers. You messing me about? That's how it looks sometimes, you know that? Listen, I'm getting edgy, real edgy, I got to tell you that – well, it's natural.'

'Yes, I've got it. Of course. No probs. But it got to be what's called realized, some of it.'

'Like it's bonds and shares?'

'That's it.'

'You going to get a good price? I mean, shares, that's not shiny like real cash, especially not now.'

'It's going to be all right. Look, can I meet you? This phoning, waiting for a call, it's hard, it don't seem so, like, close. In business I always like the personal contact.'

'Of course you do, as long as you got the blowlamp. Yes you can meet me. Why not? Yes, when you got the money. What use before? What we going to talk about? The political situation?'

'But I – '

'I wants you to think urgent about something. Do you know what real urgent is? Yes? I suppose you been out to that farm I told you about. Maybe Ivor told you about it before, well, of course he did. But it don't matter, yes or no. You seen what was there. That's what matters. Well, someone's going to find that pretty soon, bound to, and when they do they're going to dial nine-nine-fucking-nine, no hanging about. And the law will see how it all is and they'll really start looking for me and the other one. They knows our scene, who works with who, and that, so they'll come looking and not just a bobby on a bike. When that happens it's going to be real tough for us, you see what I mean? I mean, getting out from where we are now to collect from you, or even to come out here and make a call like this, because they'll have people looking for us, really looking, serious. So you got to move fast, Tenderness. You're not taking this serious enough, that's your trouble. Sometimes I don't think you're a real family man. Sometimes I don't think you care so very much about this boy. A real family man – is he going to leave his wife in the house by herself with a lover boy like Vernon? I don't know what sort of man I got to deal with here, that's a fact, Tenderness.'

'Yes, I care, of course I care. The boy's my life, I swear.'

'Maybe I ought to speak to your missus, not you. You seem a cold one. You don't seem – not urgent enough about it, you hear me? I'm crazy talking away like this, that's what you makes me do, take risks like this, because you're so cold and you mess me about. You sure you got not police in on this, no tracing? If I sees silver buttons doing 80 mph, Tenderness, it's got to be so bad for Graham.'

109

'You know I wouldn't. You knows I hate them. Would I trust them with the life of my boy?'

'All right, all right, I think I believe you. You're cold, but you're not stupid. So, listen, let me talk to your wife. She's there, yes?'

Jane was sitting in the room with Ditto and Vernon, all of them watching Mellick.

'My wife? No, she's not here now.' Jane stood up.

'Didn't I say don't mess me about, Tenderness. I got no time. I'm standing here on show in a box with glass walls, like a wreath in a plastic bag. Tenderness, just get her, yes? I got something important, just for her. Where the hell would she be if she's not there? You tell me she'd go out, when there might be a call?'

'Well, she's – '

Jane walked not too steadily towards him. Vernon stood up, too, and seemed about to help her, but she turned her head for a moment and glanced at him, and he remained where he was, on his feet. When she reached Mellick she stood close, in front of him, and stretched out her hand for the receiver. She said nothing.

'I'll give you ten seconds to get her on the line, Tenderness, and that's it.'

Mellick handed her the telephone.

'Yes?' she said. 'Please, tell me about Graham.' Her voice was weak, but clear enough.

Mellick watched her face as she listened. Yes, as the voice had said, she was still a lovely woman and he still wanted her to be his and only his. Occasionally he could hear a word from the other end but too few to make out the sense: 'funds', 'urgent', 'Tenderness', 'stupid stalling', 'boy'. Anyway, he knew what the message would be.

A couple of times as he watched, her face broke up and she began to cry silently, the tears dropping from her cheeks on to the carpet with a tiny sound, like light rain falling from a leaf. He felt grieved and enraged and wanted to put his arm around her to strengthen and comfort her, and perhaps take the phone back and shout defiance into it. But he remained still. How could he risk offending Ancient Dave, or whoever it was? They had all the cards. There was something else: he found himself unable to embrace Jane and try to console her because of Vernon standing there, tense and protective, as if all the responsibility for her was his, not Mellick's – and because of the way she had turned to look at Vernon a minute ago, obviously able to reach him without speaking.

'Yes,' she said into the receiver. 'Yes, I understand. The two of us – we understand.'

She was quiet again and Mellick heard the voice at the other end clatter away at her: 'urgent', 'money', 'get the money', 'police', 'careless', 'police.'

'No, I promise, no police. No, I don't want police, either. They can't help.' Mellick watched her listen for a while and then grow more frightened looking. 'No, it's not true, I never wanted them, police, what good would they be? They would only pretend to help. Do they really care what happens to a Mellick? Bernard don't want them, I don't want them. I wouldn't ever try to persuade Bernard, never, not about police. It don't make sense. All we wants is our boy, he's a bit backward, you know, so don't get angry with him or anything like that, will you? He tries to do his best but, well, he's backward. He got a lovely nature, he's very loving, if you could just be a bit extra patient with him. You know what I mean?'

She was still weeping and stumbled on many of the words. Once more she listened, gripping the receiver so hard that her knuckles shone white. 'Yes,' she said, 'yes, of course we can get the money. There's plenty. It's just – '

Suddenly, she seemed to grow confused and frightened. 'No, don't ring off,' she said, 'please. Oh, please. Are you there? What? What have you seen?' For a few more seconds she kept the receiver to her ear, then turned and spoke to Mellick without putting it down, as if afraid to break the link from this end, even if the call seemed over. Hoarsely, she muttered, 'He's gone. Why? Bernie, what happened?'

'What did he say? Did you hear anything, any noise at all, behind his voice?'

'Behind his voice? No. But just before he went he said there was someone coming. I couldn't make it out properly. He was whispering. He seemed scared. Bernard, what is it?' She was shaking and her voice had grown desperately high and thin. 'Have you told the police? Have you?' She sounded as if she would blame him if he had, despite all her earlier pleas for him to do that. It was hard to keep up with her fears and hopes.

'No, love, no police.'

'If he panics—'

'He's all edgy, Jane, he said so. He's imagining things.'

'When they're in a panic, people like that, they could do anything. He – '

'By now he's found there's nothing to sweat about, love. And he'll be OK.'

'Yes, I know it, Jane,' Ditto told her. 'He'll be OK by now.'

'He said you're not trying hard enough to get the cash, Tenderness. What he said – you think more about your money than about Graham. I know it's not true, Bernie, but that's what he said. You're going to get the money somehow, somehow you'll get it, won't you, Bernie? It's risks, I know that, but you wouldn't think about that if it was Graham's life, would you Bernie, I know you wouldn't?' She was staring at him across the telephone table.

'Of course he wouldn't, Jane, love,' Ditto said.

'Why don't you come and sit down?' Vernon asked her.

'He said I better have a word with you, Bernie. He said I better tell you how urgent it is.'

She sounded like a child reporting a message, slowly and carefully, as if she really believed he was stalling.

'It's all fixed up,' Mellick told her. 'The cash is on its way. We got nothing to worry about. It's like money in the bank. Yes, just like that.'

'He don't believe it. That's what we got to worry about.'

'He's putting the screw on, that's all, Jane,' Ditto told her. 'Shouting away like that, getting so steamy, it's putting the screw on. That's why he had to talk to you, isn't it, love? He knows he can put the screw on easier with you than with Tenderness, if you don't mind me saying it. I mean, being a woman, being Graham's mother. In a way it's nice, it's feelings, a woman. I don't mean Tenderness haven't got no feelings, not at all, he got real feelings, Tenderness, but a woman, he knows it's easier with a woman, don't he, that's why he's putting the screw on. You was very good with him, you was calm, you was talking to him brave. Very calm and brave. He don't know you was crying, Jane. He'll be good to your boy, you asked him real calm and brave.'

112

For a second or two she gazed at Ditto without speaking, and Mellick saw him shift his feet a fraction, obviously troubled by her stare. Then she said: 'Thanks, Ditto. You wants to help, I know. You're trying to be kind. I wish I could believe you, that's all. But this one, the one who was talking, he's just a villain, isn't he? He don't care if I'm calm, if I'm brave. All he cares about is getting the money and keeping himself safe. If he thinks he's not safe, my boy is not safe, either. Who did he see? Can you tell me that? Where is he now? Where's my boy now?'

'In a minute there'll be another call, you'll see,' Ditto told her. 'He's getting jumpy, that's all.'

'Yes, he's getting jumpy,' she said. 'So what's the use me being calm and brave if he's getting jumpy?'

The phone rang.

'Didn't I say?' Ditto cried. 'You listen to Ditto.'

Mellick picked up the receiver. A voice he recognized as Hubert Scott's said: 'Can we meet?'

'Information?'

'Yes'

'Is it good?'

'Good enough. You'll have to move fast.'

'Well, of course. That's how it has to be.'

'Where we used to meet? The little street? Say ten tonight?'

'Great.' He put the phone down.

'Him again?' Jill asked.

'No, about the funds. It's all laid on. Just a matter of collecting.'

She tried to smile. 'All of it?'

'All we need, love. I told you it would come all right, didn't I?'

'Really, all of it? Who'd do that for us, Bernie?'

'We got a lot of good friends, when there's big trouble. People who owe me.'

She stepped close and kissed him briefly on the mouth. 'Yes, it's wonderful, wonderful to have friends,' she said.

14

Graham knew that word. Dave said it. He was looking out of the window upstairs from around the side of the curtain and the boy heard him whisper, 'Pigs.'

Milton went to look and they were very quiet. Dave said: 'Pigs all over. I saw some in the street when I was at the phone box.'

Once more Graham was baffled. He knew about pigs from school, but pigs ought to live on a farm. This house was in a street, like where his mother and father lived, and pigs did not go in streets. He thought that this might be why Dave and Milton were staring. He wanted to see the pigs for himself but when he went near the curtain Milton pushed him away hard and he fell down and hurt himself again, but not very much. Milton whispered at him: 'You make a fucking sound, you're dead.' Then Milton asked Dave if the pigs were coming to the house and Dave said he didn't know.

Graham considered that. Would a pig be able to ring the door bell of a house? When he thought of this he tried to stop himself making a noise laughing about it but couldn't, and Milton turned and came over to him very fast and hit him across the face. The blow knocked him to the floor once more and he began to cry. Dave was still looking around the side of the curtains and told Milton, 'Shut him up, for God's sake. The pigs will hear.'

As the boy tried to stand, Milton caught hold of him hard and put his hand right over Graham's face, covering his nose and mouth, and he could hardly breathe. Graham knew it was so he could not make a noise, in case the pigs heard. He struggled to get away and Milton said: 'Keep still you little sod.'

The boy did not know that word, though he knew one like it, 'God'. God made the world and the daffodils in the jar at the Sunday school. But Milton did not say God, he said sod. The boy did know the word 'little' and he hated it. If he was not little he would be big, and Milton could not hold him and keep his hand over his mouth. Because he was little he could not get away from Milton by fighting and kicking, so, instead, he bit Milton's hand to make him let go. He had worked out a long time ago that if you were little you could not be strong, but you could bite.

Sometimes if he bit people they would shout because it hurt so much. He could remember that Dave shouted when he bit him at the green van. Milton gasped now and made only a small sound, but Dave turned around with a finger on his lips to tell him to keep quiet.

Then Graham felt Milton catch hold of his hair with his other hand and start pulling it very hard, trying to force the boy's teeth apart. Although Milton was hurting him, Graham did not let go and he could taste blood and felt something in Milton's hand like string near his tongue, or like a piece of the meat at dinner which was too hard to chew. Dave came away laughing from the window and said, 'This bloody biter, he done me, too, when we took him from his house.'

Then Dave reached out and caught hold of his neck with two hands and began pressing and Graham found again that he could not breathe. 'Let go, you little sod,' Dave said. He was still laughing.

And Graham had to open his mouth so Dave would stop it and let him breathe. The room had begun to grow very dark. He did not understand it. There was a light on but he could not see properly. He could see Dave's laughing face just in front of him and his arms because they were so close, but he could not make out the other side of the room or the door.

Milton pulled his hand away fast and Dave let go of Graham's neck. The boy's legs were shaky and he sat down carefully on the floor. After a while he began to feel better and the room was not so dark now. He saw Milton sitting on a chair drinking something from a bottle. It looked like the colour of tea, but did not smell like tea. Milton held the bottle in the hand that was not hurt and kept the other on his lap in front of him. Graham saw it was bleeding and marking Milton's trousers, but he did not move it. Then, when he had finished drinking, Milton poured some of the stuff with the funny smell over the bite. Graham saw it was hurting and Milton made a big noise when he breathed, but he did not shout.

Graham was afraid they would be angry with him because of the biting, and he wanted somebody to help him. But he did not know who it could be. Dave went back to the window and was looking out again for pigs, around the side of the curtain, and the boy began to wonder whether pigs could help him. He did not really think they helped people, they were just on a farm. But these pigs were not on a farm and Dave and Milton seemed afraid of them. They worried in case the pigs heard him and came into the house. Did Dave and Milton know that the pigs wanted to help him?

It seemed to him that if he called them they might come. He did
not know if pigs went in houses or if they could go upstairs. He
did not think so. They were not really like Miss Piggy on television. But he did not know anybody else who would come, so he
tried to call them. He found it was not very loud because Dave
had made his neck sore and it hurt when he tried to shout. He
called, 'Pigs. Pigs.'

Milton said: 'Christ, the – '

Dave began laughing again. 'It's all right,' he said. 'They've
gone. They've missed us.' He went on laughing. Pigs, pigs,' he
said. 'They'd come running to that, wouldn't they?'

But Graham did not know what he meant. He stopped calling
the pigs, though. If they were gone they could not hear him.

15

Harpur and Iles stood in Mellick's roomy, stained–glass porch
and Iles rang the bell, which played some bars of *The Bells of St
Mary's*. He beamed appreciatively and beat time with a gloved
finger. As soon as the tune finished he rang again and smiled with
even more pleasure on the re-hearing. It was a long time since
Harpur had seen him looking so cheerful and malicious. When
Mellick opened the door, Iles nodded amiably to him and said:
'Lovely neighbourhood, Tenderness, an assembly of like minds
and brilliant careers, and a lovely property. So much more than
bijou, yet not grossly baronial. I would always have relied on you
to choose sensitively, and my faith is gloriously vindicated in –
what's its name again – Ankle Iron? But I jest: Moorings. Nice.
Can we come in and have a talk and perhaps meet Mrs Tenderness and some of your friends? I think I glimpsed them through
the port hole.'

'This is getting close to harassment, you know that, Mr Iles? I
mean, it's no time at all since Mr Harpur – '

'Was here. Yes. But this is a real matter of import, I can safely
say that,' Iles replied and walked past him into the house. Harpur
followed. Iles opened the door to the right, where Harpur had
seen party guests on his last visit. 'Ah,' Iles said, gazing in, 'your

gorgeous wife and Ditto and someone I don't know. Col, do you recognize this svelte item of dress sense?'

'Vernon Pitt.'

'Is he in our memory bank?'

'He's got a bit of form. Nothing grand.'

'Yet. Tenderness, do you know, I was going to let Colin make this call alone and then I thought, Why shouldn't I see for myself how you're shaping as a home-maker? And I'm so glad I came. It's cosy here, and yet a distinguished touch, too – the pictures; by mail order from that warehouse in Yeovil? I do love art, don't you?' He gazed about and then said, 'I know about Ditto, but what does Vernon do for the company, Tenderness?'

'One of my associates.'

'Grand. He doesn't take his eye off the phone. Are you expecting a big business call? It's damned exciting to be here at the heart of your operation, you know that? I'd bet some very significant decisions have been taken over that instrument, real money-bags decisions.'

'Mr Harpur, please, what's it all about?' Mellick asked.

Iles held up a hand. He had removed his gloves now. 'I know, I know, Tenderness, you feel easier talking to Col, don't you? Yes, Harpur's really hot stuff on the common touch. It's central to his charm. And he doesn't have to put it on, that's the beauty of things. Totally natural to him. The fact is, he's jumped up from nowhere himself, so he mixes readily with the lowly. Myself, some people find me a trifle polished, rather St James's Palace. It makes them shy and I'll tell you, it can be a pain in the . . . well, because of Mrs Mellick, I'll say in the kidneys. Yes, in the fucking kidneys. So, not to beat about the what-you-call it, we found a dead.'

Jane Mellick gasped and whispered: 'What? What are you saying?'

'But why are we all standing?' Iles replied. 'I always like to be off my feet when I'm talking about the deceased. Why should they get all the rest?'

'Who?' she asked.

Iles lowered himself into an armchair and passed his hand approvingly over the upholstery. 'Who? I don't want you to fret, Mrs Mellick. Not your boy. We've got men out looking for him, really beating the streets, but no luck yet.'

'What the hell you talking about, Iles?' Mellick asked. 'Men out looking for Graham. Why?'

Harpur remained standing and so did the other four.

'We found he body of Richard Penton and put two and two together,' Iles replied.

'What two and two?' Mellick said.

'Rick the Intelligent dead?' Ditto asked. 'This is a surprise, the Intelligent dead. How did it happen? I know he was sickly. Them brainy ones.'

'Mr Harpur and I are here to see whether you're going to help us find your son, Tenderness,' Iles said. 'Tenderness and Mrs Tenderness.'

'What's my son got to do with this, I mean with Rick?' Mellick asked.

'Do you know what he's got to do with it, Mrs Mellick?' Iles said.

She did not answer immediately. Then she seemed to make up her mind and said, 'No.' When Harpur had seen her last here there had been a terrible feverishness in her features, and in all of her behaviour. Today, he sensed something closer to despair. That fine, long face seemed to have grown longer and become more angular. There were times now when she looked old enough to be Vernon's mother, and she probably was old enough, but he suspected the relationship was different. Although she had become so gaunt he could see why she might still attract even a pretty boy like Vernon. Anyway, wasn't that sort of age difference fashionable? The sugar mum was in.

'So, where is Graham?' Harpur asked.

'With some friends, a holiday. Haven't I said all this?' Mellick replied.

'Which friends? Where?' Harpur asked.

'We don't want our boy brought into it,' Mellick replied. 'You people – trying to tie him to a corpse. You're not normal. I don't have to tell you where he is. We won't, will we, Jane?'

'You're not thinking of paying out, I hope, Tenderness,' Iles said. 'We don't care for that.'

'Paying out what? Who to? What for?'

'It would be crazy,' Harpur said. 'You know it. Once they've got the cash – '

'How the hell can you be so sure?' Jane Mellick cried. 'If we – '.

Harpur saw it dawn on her suddenly that she was saying too much. She put an arm across her chest and gripped her shoulder and the top of her other arm, massaging herself gently in a nervous spasm.

'Oh, why can't you leave Bernie alone?' she said softly. 'Please. Perhaps you really wants to help, but you would help us most if you just went away. I don't want to be rude, but can't you just leave us alone?' She glanced for a moment at Vernon Pitt and then stared down at the floor, like a reproached child.

Pitt said to Iles and Harpur: 'You're doing a grand job here. Is all this necessary?'

Iles gazed at Mellick's wife from the chair. 'Mrs Mellick, Jane, my dear – may I? – yes, you're right, we're here to help you, and, more to the point, to help your boy. We're already trying. This is a full-scale search we're running. I don't know whether you realize the sort of come-back I'm risking by ordering that. I've no hard information to go on, have I? I've parents who insist the child is not missing. I'm acting largely on intuition. I think Harpur here has had a tip, but he's quite secretive, I'm afraid, where inform- ants are concerned. It's the way people in his side of the business operate.' He shrugged. 'We'll press on. But, you see, Jane, I'd have thought you'd want to give us every assistance you can. Perhaps you do want to, or perhaps you did, but Tenderness here has convinced you otherwise. These cases, they're very, very delicate, we all know that. It's crucial that nobody makes a wrong move. Of course, that's what worries you, and worries Tender- ness more. He can't believe we'd handle this sort of job properly, and especially when it's the child of Tenderness Mellick. Listen, love, I'm certainly not going to say we're infallible in kidnap cases. These things are full of uncertainties. What I would say, though – '

The telephone rang. Harpur saw Jane Mellick's body quiver and her face momentarily lose its despair and grow all at once appallingly tense again, almost hopeful. Vernon, too, became agitated, and stepped towards the instrument. He stopped when Mellick turned for a moment and glanced at him. Mellick and Ditto remained rock calm and it was only after a few seconds that Mellick moved to pick up the receiver. He gave the number and then listened. In a few minutes he said: 'Yes, that sounds good.' He smiled, as if the conversation was one of the most pleasant and comfortable he had enjoyed for months. 'I can say we would be interested.' He listened again. 'Yes, that's right. Yes. All right. Yes.'

He put the phone down.

'Important?' Jane asked.

'Yes, it's important. A business matter, that's all.' He was still entirely in control.

She was trying to read his face. 'Yes, but – '

'Oh, Basil Maine-Thomas, the broker, about some shares, love. Lot of cheapies about since the October '87 massacre.'

'Shares?' Vernon said.

'That's it,' Mellick replied, not looking at him. 'You heard of shares, I suppose, like in companies?'

Iles stood up. 'Very decent show, Tenderness. Give him an Oscar, someone. He picked up from your voice we were here, did he, whoever it was? That won't help things.' He moved a couple of steps towards the door. 'You're sure you've got nothing to say to us, Jane?'

There was another pause and then she said, 'No,' this time at full voice.

'Of course she hasn't,' Mellick added.

'Not a thing,' Vernon said.

16

Harpur decided he was being tailed. It took a while to know for certain, but, once the doubts had gone, his top wish was to get his two daughters out of the car and to safety. At first, he thought about hitting the pedal and driving home or to the nearest nick. But either would mean keeping the girls with him for longer than if he dropped them as planned at the Esplanade Leisure Centre. In any case, he worried that a change of routine might unsettle the tail and make him more dangerous. Him, or maybe them.

He was driving his daughters from the house to karate class, a chore he handled every Tuesday he was available; anyone who did a bit of research could know about it. Tailing him must be a doddle – starting point, destination and route all standard: just the sort of stupid, patterned behaviour he was constantly warning other people about.

The car behind kept its distance, not allowing the gap to lengthen or shrink much, even when Harpur changed speed. It was getting dark and for most of the time he could make out little more than headlights in the mirror, though occasionally he thought he identified a silhouette of perhaps an old Princess. He had no idea how many people were in it.

To suggest calm, he began talking to the girls about an l.p. that had impressed him, by an Irish girl called Mary Coghlan.

'So, what's wrong, dad?' Jill, the younger one, asked.

'Wrong?'

'You seem a bit sweaty.'

'I don't think so.'

'You'll be wearing out that mirror.'

'Something stalking us?' Hazel said, looking back.

Jill looked, too: 'It's what Mr Kinnock says: our streets are not safe. I see it as a gross failure by police.'

'Who is it, dad? A vengeance posse?' Hazel asked, smacking her lips.

'Obviously heavies working for some baron,' Jill said. 'Have you been disturbing one of their rackets, dad? That's not fair. It makes them angry – I mean, they're used to being left to do what they like on your patch, aren't they?'

'Don't take any notice of her,' Hazel told him. 'She's into that "out of the mouths of babes and sucklings" crap and thinks she has to say something all-seeing every time she speaks, like Holden Caulfield.'

'Is he a boy at the Centre?' Harpur replied. 'Here we are, then.'

'Oh, Dad,' Jill said, 'she's read a book, that's all. How do you manage to keep so ignorant?'

The tail must have pulled in somewhere and was waiting. When the girls left the car Harpur got out as if helping them with their gear and looked back, but spotted nothing. The girls stared, too.

Jill grew suddenly anxious. 'Dad – no fooling now – is it safe? Why don't you phone from here for some help?'

'Perhaps he's gone,' Harpur replied.

'So there *was* somebody.'

'I didn't say that. What are you, a cop, or something?'

121

When he drove away, the headlights reappeared almost at once in his mirror, and, on a stretch of road around abandoned docks near Valencia Esplanade, a brown Princess came suddenly abreast of him and stayed there. Crazily, Harpur's mind went to the scene in *Bad Day At Black Rock* when Ernest Borgnine in his big heap tries to push Spencer Tracy in his small one off the mountain road and over the precipice. There was no precipice but a steep drop on the left into what had been the dock. Harpur thought of accelerating away and out of trouble, and was just about to try it when he looked across to the other car and saw Hubert Scott alone inside and signalling with repeated nods for Harpur to pull over. When he did, Scott drew in behind and came to join Harpur in his car.

'Well, you can see I've been studying your life, Mr Harpur. It seemed reasonable.'

'Where the hell did you get that crate?'

'I need something a bit anon these days. I'm living dangerously.'

He was slewed around in the passenger seat to face Harpur, looking happy and pleased with himself, looking old, too, maybe, but still as tough as ever, still no grey in the heavy moustache, as far as Harpur could see in this light. Scott seemed to radiate triumph, and it was hard to think of him as the man who had fallen apart at his presentation. When he spoke his voice boomed, full of confidence and friendliness: 'Mr Harpur, I hope you'll believe it when I say I felt ashamed about the way I talked to you last time, and the circumstances. I had real regrets. Coming to the love hotel like that and upsetting Mrs Cotton. It wasn't necessary, nor the threats about you and Jack Lamb and so on. Crude. Christ, behaviour like that could give detection a greasy name. And none of it would work with a man of your sort, don't I know that, for God's sake?'

'What's the message, Hubert?'

'You're going to love it, Mr Harpur. Look, how would it be if I called you Colin? I'm retired now, so it's no insubordination.'

'What's the message, Hubert?'

'Well, thanks Colin, I appreciate it. It's this: I can tell you how to take Tenderness Mellick on a bank break. Play it right and it's infallible.'

'A bank? That's not Tenderness.'

'I know. Not usually. This time, yes, Colin.'

'Tenderness couldn't – '

'He's going to try. No shadow of a doubt.'

'With his own boys? What do any of them know about banks? They're all PhDs in extortion.'

'Believe it. Look, Jack Lamb's given you one or two fat whispers about bank raids in his time, hasn't he, and you eternally look after him as a result? This is better than anything he ever offered. Now, be fair – isn't that a fact, Col? Think how long you've been trying to nail Tenderness, not just for the scorching and Ivor's death, but a ton of stuff before. Well, here he is, on toast.'

'Sounds sweet.'

'It *is* sweet.'

'How do you come by it, Hubert?' Harpur thought he saw the real answer to that, but was interested in Scott's version. He did not get it right away.

Hubert sat back in the seat and some of his good spirits left for a while. He was looking out through the windscreen as he spoke now, not at Harpur. 'This inquisitor, Bundy, will give me a hard time. He's got bank statements. Well, you know that.'

'I do?'

'I've had a word with Desmond Iles. We consult. It's no secret. Anyway, wouldn't you expect statements? Routine on this sort of thing. We're still at the general, polite stage, Bundy and I, but when we get to the statements he'll just keep on hammering away, hammering away. Attrition. You know the technique. We both do. That's why half the villains in Parkhurst are there.'

'And you're going to tell him I ordered you into Tenderness's outfit, and you had to take the cash because you were supposed to have turned and joined his staff?'

Scott was beaming again. 'Well, I'll hardly need to tell him that, will I? Don't you see, Col?'

'Perhaps.'

'Of course you do. It's irresistible.'

'If you give us Tenderness – '

'If I give you Tenderness, I'm delivering, aren't I? Even after I've retired, I'm still looking after you, using my inside knowledge. This is the vindication of all my undercover work as part of Tenderness's outfit. This was what it was all about, what we've been waiting for.' The docks road was a well-known shortcut and vehicles went by regularly. Still beaming, Scott gazed about. 'Don't like it here much, but I had to get to talk to you somewhere reasonably quiet, and it's not suitable for the telephone. Where do you meet narks like Jack Lamb, Col – I mean, besides at Billy Graham?'

'I don't, these days.'

'Oh, I thought at the Tesco car park sometimes. But maybe I'm wrong.'

Whatever anyone said about Hubert, he was a bloody high-class detective.

'So, when you confirm my story to Bundy there'll be no risk to you at all, Col. You'll have Tenderness inside to prove it, or dead. And his boys. They'll all be on this. Ditto, Reg, everyone. You'll need a good team. God, I wish I could be with you.'

And that would be true, not bullshit from a hidey-hole. Scott loved an outing, the rougher the sweeter.

'You haven't got long,' Hubert said. 'This is for the day after tomorrow.'

'What? He'll rush into a job like that in forty-eight hours – something he knows bugger all about – and hope to get away with it?'

'He's had a tip there'll be big money there for one day. So he can't wait.'

'A tip from where?'

'Would I know, Col?'

'Is the money really there?'

'As I said, that's his information.' Scott grew restless. 'We must move. Col, I had a word with Desmond Iles about this whole business, and he agrees it's going to make things much easier for you with Bundy. I'm damned relieved. I don't need to consider any of that unpleasant stuff we were discussing; spreading it to Bundy about you and Ruth Cotton, or about the delay on the kid for Jack Lamb's protection.'

'But, of course, you've got all that still there if necessary.'

'Col, it won't be, can't be. And I really am pleased.' He leaned across and for a moment Harpur thought he was going to shake his hand. But then Scott obviously realized this would not be wise and pulled away.

Harpur said: 'He wants this money to buy back his kid.'

'Yes, so I gather.'

'That's the real reason for the rush, and for trying something he knows nothing about?'

'Part of the reason.'

'What happens to the boy if those two holding him hear we've stopped the cash flow?'

'I've thought about it, believe me, Col. I've thought about it a hell of a lot. It's tricky. But can you sit back and allow a robbery?'

Harpur saw he was beautifully sewn up. Scott beamed more widely still as he exercised all the intricacies of the trap.

'He asked you for a bank where there was big cash, did he, Hubert?'

'Something like that.'

'He's got reason to think he can call on you for help, has he?'

'I don't like that question. Do you want Bundy's job, then?' Scott asked, his voice hardening. 'Aren't we on the same side?'

'And *is* there big cash at the bank?'

'Does it matter, Col? You're going to take him.'

'You just gave him the name of the first bank you thought of?'

'Not at all. I'm not sloppy. I picked the one where it's easiest for you to lay an ambush. I'm part of this operation, even if I can't come on it. I want to contribute everything possible.'

Harpur thought for a moment. What was there to think about, though? 'All right. Where and when? Guns?'

17

Mellick took Ditto and Vernon with him to look at the bank, with Reg driving. As planning it was a joke – everything to be covered in a couple of hours. Probably professionals on this kind of job would think and watch for weeks. Graham did not have weeks. Accepting the rush and the risk had become a sort of test for Mellick; he had to prove to Jane that he would do anything to get the boy back, even turn fool. The madness of it had become almost a plus; it proclaimed how far he would go for her.

Sometimes, he could not believe he was behaving like this. But he wanted her, and he wanted her at any price. He wanted his son back, too, at any price. Above all, though, he had to hold on to Jane. The way to hold on to her was to get Graham back, and the only way he might get Graham back was to do this bank, and do it now. He was in a trap, without choices, the kind of situation he had been avoiding since he was a kid, but not any longer; not at the clinic in Aylesbury and not here.

They could view outside easily enough from a parked car. The interior was more important, though, and to get some familiarity there meant risk. It would be mad to go in together. Three men doing no business but idling and staring would be remembered behind the counter, or by a guard; no point grabbing hundreds of grand here if the bank could find where to call half an hour later and grab it back. Mellick said they must go in separately, when there were plenty of customers about, and see what they could. Afterwards, they would put it all together. Vernon was pretty useful with a sketch pad and could get it down, outside and in. He had a sackful of talents, not just all those words.

Four of them sat in the car while Vernon did quick drawings of the frontage and the buildings next to it. They could not hang about; a lot of people knew Mellick, and particularly a lot of police. A lot of people and a lot of police knew Ditto and Reg, too. Vernon, less so; that was another of his bright assets. But, in any case, a car parked near a bank with four men aboard was always going to get attention.

Mellick did not like the look of it, and he could sense the fears of the others, though nothing had been said. The bank was a big grey stone place standing between two office blocks in a square which had only one way out, a narrow street leading in opposite the bank and connecting from a main road. Anyone could spot the perils. If you hit that bank and were not away in minutes you never would be. They would wipe you off the granite next time the road cleaners came round. A simple road block in Degree Street and you were finished, penned like sheep. It wouldn't need police. Any bugger whose hobby was collecting letters of thanks from the Chief Constable could do it with his Metro. You'd never see a better spot for an ambush.

Most of their outside observations they managed in the evening when the square was quiet. But they had to come down in the day, too, because that was when the job would be done, and they needed to know about traffic, and whether they could get their vehicle right in front of the bank doors. That seemed on. State Square had double yellows all the way around, and the only time anything stood for more than a few seconds outside the bank was when Securicor called. They were on double yellows now, watching, with the engine running. Vernon, sitting alongside Mellick in the back, was doing a close-up drawing of the bank's pair of swing doors. He hummed to himself, like everything was so rosy. At the wheel, Reg had begun to grow edgy again. One of these days, he might have to let Reg go. One of these days? Were there going to be many more days?

Vernon said: 'We'll want someone on the doors, Tenderness. A guard could lock us in. We don't want the hostage game, do we?'

'We get it and get out very fast.'

Reg said: 'I'm going to move, Tenderness. There's a warden.'

'Yes, I'm OK,' Vernon told him.

They pulled out, but an office equipment van was delivering to insurance offices and they could not get around him. 'Christ,' Reg said, 'this would be all we needed.'

'Tomorrow's another day,' Mellick replied. He knew Reg was right, though.

'Yes, another day,' Ditto said.

'Worse?' Reg asked.

Mellick could not answer that one. 'Pull up when we're a decent distance out of the square. I'll walk back first and do the inside. Then Ditto, then Vernon.'

And, for a moment, as soon as he had left the car and was on his feet Mellick felt like running for it – longed to ditch Reg and all of them and disappear. No, not just for a moment; for a stack of terrifying moments the idea took fierce hold. He kept going towards the bank, walking as if he meant it, because he knew they would be watching, but during all that time the idea was in his mind to melt away and forget everything as soon as he went out of sight around a corner. With the boys in the car, and before that, he had found himself almost overcome by dark certainty that this raid would be a disaster. Panic had closed down his brain and there had been a couple of minutes when he would even have found it impossible to speak. Never had he known such a collapse before. There had been bad times, very bad times, but he had always been able to think his way out of them, or battle his way out of them, or burn his way out of them. Although he was not proud of some of the things he had done to get back from the depths, he did not know how he could have survived otherwise, and at least he hadn't crumbled. Now, he was crumbling? Did any of those three spot it? Vernon had the brain, but Ditto was the one who knew him best and picked up signs.

What did they care, though? Why should they worry if he did not come back? None of them was in love with this job. Vernon said he had done a bank raid once, but all any of the rest knew about such outings was what they read in the papers. And Vernon might be just bullshitting. He had make-believe coming out of his eyeballs, that one, and if you said you were going to screw protection payments from Margaret Thatcher he'd say he did it when he was a schoolboy. The truth was, all of them would be as scared of this as Mellick himself. Already it showed in Reg.

They could not even be sure of picking up good gains if things went well, because the takings were needed for Graham, the only reason for going into this. All right, they might collect more funds than Ancient Dave had named, and there would be some left over for a share-out. They might; Scott said he was not sure how much would be here, except that it would be at least a quarter of a million. He knew what was needed and swore the take would not be less. Mellick had to believe him. That might be another part of the stupidity and risk. Of course, it was possible they would get twice, three times two-fifty grand, which would leave a nice bit of salary for the boys. Nobody was betting on it, though. And if Dave found out in time how they raised the money and that they had a surplus he was going to jack up the price to whatever they took. Business was business.

Mellick did not run or melt away. Christ, how could he? His son's life and his marriage depended on what he did today and tomorrow, especially tomorrow. He turned into Degree Street. At this time of morning the pavements were crowded with classily dressed people busying about, getting rich, or trying to look as if they were getting rich, and he was glad of that, could mix in and make himself inconspicuous; he had put on a good, dark suit himself. All the same, he felt now like an animal again, not a penned sheep any longer but some wild creature entering the passage to a cage, where the bait had been laid. At home, once, they had caught a grey squirrel like that with bits of apple when it moved into their roof space. What came of living near fucking trees. You were supposed to drop the trap into a deep bath of water to drown the pest, but Graham had cried when he saw the squirrel going frantic and banging its face bloody on the bars, so they took it into the country and let it go. Afterwards, Mellick was glad they'd done that. One of his happiest memories was the sight of that stand-up tail scooting off free into the distance. If they were blocked in tomorrow nobody would give them that sort of chance. He looked around at all the high, hard grey stone frontages that walled State Square and felt panic threatening to gut him again. It was like being in a well. If there was bait, who had put it out? Could he trust that bastard, Scott?

They had bought him for fine money a long time ago and he had been worth it. But a cop was always a cop, even when he took, and even when he retired. The buggers really believed they were different and, if people believed that enough, they *were* different. You never knew when they might turn again and stoke up their burned-out love of the law. They thought they had responsibilities, and it did not matter who got hurt as long as they did their bit of duty. Anyway, Scott might be in trouble now and looking for a way out, and one man's escape could be another one's trap. Mellick knew that Vernon wondered about Scott, and wondered a fat bit more when he saw where this bank was. But Vernon had no kid missing. He did not need to grab whatever speck of hope showed, even if it did look as shaky as hell.

He went in at the doors that Vernon had been drawing and found himself in an outer hallway with a big circular staircase leading to architects' offices on the upper floors. The bank was through another swing door on the left. He studied a killed in action plaque while taking the feel of the building and especially of the hallway. 'They shall not grow old,' the plaque said. You couldn't argue. The hallway was square and, while Mellick stood there, always had a few people in it, either going to or from the architects, or bank customers. Vernon was right: this area and the doors would need at least one man on them, and anyone in the hall would have to be forced into the bank and kept there. Len must handle that, and on his own. It would take himself, Ditto and Vernon to go into the bank, and Reg would be outside in the car. He could have done with more help. That he had known from the beginning, but he had known, too, that there was no time to get it. All the thinking and all the attempts to plan came back to the fact that his child was held by nobody villains who might crack and turn wild any moment. And to another fact; the one that said his wife had begun to think of him as useless and under-capitalized – which was the same as useless – and uncaring about Graham, and might turn in despair to a man who wore leather ties and was young enough to be another of her sons. The thought that he might lose her dragged him down. He had never fully realized until now how much she mattered to him. Of course, he could have sent Vernon away, or he could have had him taken out altogether, nothing simpler. Ditto would see to that with a smile. Was it going to do Mellick any good with Jane, though? She would know what had happened and hate him. He didn't believe she hated him yet, only saw him as a failure, and that could still be put right. He was here to put it right.

He entered the bank through a second swing door. The counter was an L. Staff worked behind shatter proof glass which reached the ceiling and bars to head height. There was a wooden door for customers visiting the manager, and they would have to blast the lock, or threaten to kill someone through a grille if it was not opened. The door looked a standard, veneer and ply job, but it could be that the ply covered steel. Christ, he wished he knew more about banks.

As Mellick crossed to the corner of the L, where a collection of investment brochures were on offer, he could see the open strong room set well back from the counter and big enough to walk into. He picked up a leaflet about special deposit rates and pretended to study it, while he counted the clerks and managers and tried to work out where it would be best to stand to cover the lot, and make sure nobody reached an alarm. There were about fifteen, mostly girls. It was true he did not know anything about banks or bank staff but he did know that you could never tell by looking at people, men or women, which would turn out brave enough to risk their lives when they did not need to. He had been studying Reg's face a bit lately, too.

Nobody seemed to notice Mellick as he set his memory to work on the layout, measuring distances as best he could, and noting where desks and cabinets might be obstructions. If things went wrong, desks and cabinets might also turn out to be cover, but he switched off that idea. It had become a habit of his these last few days, to push out of sight any thought that might stop him going ahead with this raid. He knew he was doing it and knew it was not like him, but he went on. He did not want a choice.

When Mellick was back in the car, Ditto asked: 'How does it look?'

'Not impossible, not easy.'

'That's the sort of answer I like,' Ditto said. 'Not impossible, not easy. That's the answer from somebody who knows he can win, but who can see the problems, too, and see them in plenty of time.'

'We've got to win.'

'Shall I go now, Tenderness?' Vernon asked.

'Try not to be memorable.'

Vernon had some sense and was wearing a dark jacket and a decent tie today in place of his rodeo gear. 'I have this gift of physical self-effacement,' he said. 'It really is a gift. I don't know how I do it, but I do. I can stand in a crowded room and I seem able to will people into not seeing me, though I make no effort to do that.'

'Yes, never mind your will, just fuck off now so *we* don't see you here for ten minutes,' Mellick told him.

'Anyone looking like plain clothes in the bank?' Vernon asked, as he was about to leave the car.

'Plain clothes? What the – ?'

'Like they were there to watch for us. You see, Tenderness, I don't know about Hubert.'

'He wouldn't – '

'Hubert wouldn't,' Ditto said. 'Not Hubert. He've always played square.'

'If they had plain clothes, it could be a girl among the clerks or some yuppie asking about his overdraft,' Vernon added. 'They're not going to use heavies you'd recognise.'

'All the same, I would of picked that up, that's for sure, Mellick replied. 'I'm not a kid.'

'Of course you would of, Tenderness,' Ditto said. 'Of course he bloody would of. Is he a kid, for God's sake?'

18

Once, when Dave and Milton were fighting, the boy managed to get downstairs and look at the front door. Normally, they made him stay in the bedrooms. It was an all wood door, so he could see nothing through it, though he heard cars and voices. It had a bolt at the top, too high for him to reach. That upset him.

While he was near the door Dave came downstairs and became very angry when he saw him. He told him to get back upstairs, but did not hit him. He said: 'It's all right, Podge, he won't touch you now.' The boy knew he meant Milton.

He could tell that Dave thought he might run away. But he did not know how to or where to go. If he opened the door and went out to the street, he would be lost. But he did not want to stay in this house. He did not like it when Milton touched his trousers and he did not like it when Dave and Milton were shouting at each other and fighting. When Milton touched his trousers he said: 'I want some fun with you.'

Graham knew fun. Fun was a game or going on the climbing frame or the slide in the park. It was not fun when Milton put his hand on his trousers like that. Sometimes Milton caught hold of his hand and made him touch Milton's trousers and told him to keep his hand there. A teacher at the school touched some boys like that and made them touch him in the coats cupboard.

Dave came into the room and saw what Milton was doing and they started shouting and fighting. Dave shouted: 'Dirty sod, dirty sod.'

And Milton pulled up his zip very fast and said: 'Never no fucking girls here. What am I supposed to do?'

And Dave said: 'Dirty sod.'

The boy hated the sound when Dave's fist hit Milton in the face. It made him think of when a girl threw clay against the wall in school and it stuck. While they were fighting, Graham ran out of the room and downstairs, because he was afraid and felt upset by the noise and blood. He went to look at the door, but then

Dave came down and said to go back up. He was angry with him but not very angry. Dave had some blood on his hand and on his shirt. When the boy went upstairs he saw Milton lying on the floor in the bedroom and there was blood on his face and his nose was bent and it was getting fatter. He made a noise when he was breathing, like his father did sometimes when he was asleep in the chair. His zip was shut now.

19

'This is Degree Street, sir,' Harpur said, 'and here's State Square.' He was in front of a blackboard in the Chief's room, pointing with a pencil. 'This is Barclay's. I'm sorry it's only a chalk drawing. We haven't had time to do a proper diagram.'

'Tenderness is going to hit that?' Lane said. 'Tenderness? I thought he only moved on certainties?' Lane was still pretty new to the Force, but he worked hard, absorbed all the dossiers. Iles used to say that the Chief might know fuck all about detection but was a beautiful reader.

'That's how it used to be, sir, yes,' Harpur replied, 'but – '

'Tenderness never moved on banks at all until now,' Iles said. 'There've been some changes. For him, it's an emergency. This is a criminal acting out of pattern, no longer like a pro. We must give thanks to the Lord – and to Hubert Scott for letting us know in advance what Tenderness will attempt.'

'Well, Scott's done well, no question,' Lane replied. 'Can't take it away from him. His outburst at the leave-taking becomes not merely understandable – almost a credit. As he saw it, his work was being depreciated by all the suspicion and the inquiry. It's one of the classic dangers in going undercover, of course. Some people will believe you've really turned villain. If this information is accurate, it must obviously change the whole thrust of Adrian Bundy's investigation. It's active proof Scott went undercover and couldn't avoid taking the money if he was to be credible. I'll breathe a word to Adrian.'

'I do feel that would be much to the point, sir,' Iles said. 'It's what is due to Scott, and yet an act of generosity on your part, too, and totally in character. I don't think I've ever heard the perils of undercover roles more graphically put.'

'No doubt about the accuracy, sir,' Harpur told Lane. 'We've had observations going inside and out since Scott's tip. Tenderness, Ditto Repeato and a new lad, Vernon Pitt, were down earlier today doing a bit of planning, one at a time, all looking as tense as buggery. Reg was driving but didn't go in. So, he'll be the wheels, as we'd expect. We've got pix of them casing the bank.'

Lane was without a jacket and wearing an open-necked, short-sleeved, whitish tennis shirt. Standing, he came around from behind his desk to join Harpur near the blackboard. He had taken his shoes off and shuffled a little awkwardly because the heavy, cream coloured socks he was wearing had worked loose on his feet and the slack flapped about as he walked, like a clown's shoes. Informality in dress was very much one of the Chief's things. He thought it important to emphasize the civilian nature of the police and was uneasy about anything smelling of smartness. Another of Iles's sayings was that the Chief's mother had been frightened by a brigade of guards' band while bearing him, and that this had got through to his psyche.

'Where will you put your marksmen?' Lane asked.

Despite Iles's contempt for Lane, in many ways Harpur found it easy to deal with him. Anyway, Iles despised most officers superior to himself, as well as all below. The Chief knew about the disasters with police guns, the deaths and injuries by mistake – of course he did – but he knew, too, that police guns were here to stay and never quibbled or pontificated in a case where they might be needed. Barton, his predecessor, invariably did. Harpur had always liked working with Lane, in fact, and not just because of armament; the Chief could be sharper and tougher than he looked, and generally aimed to behave decently, towards his own men and women, and even towards the villains. He might not be good on clean shirts, but somehow he had clung to an ethic. Now, Harpur showed him how the men would be placed.

'No back way?' Lane asked.

'There is, yes,' Harpur replied. 'but it's through the bank's private yard and surrounded by other private yards. Impossible to get a vehicle close there. And, in any case, they haven't looked at the back. We'd have seen them do it.'

134

'Good.'

Harpur turned the blackboard over. 'This is inside.' He indicated again where he would have armed men concealed.

Lane studied the drawing for a couple of minutes. 'Reg in the car and they'll need to keep a man on the door.'

'That's what we reckon, yes. Len, I should think.'

'So his actual swag party is just the three who visited?'

'We think so.'

Lane thought about it. 'I'd like you to put more armed boys inside, Colin. Three people isn't enough to pull a thing like this and they'll probably realize it fast and panic. Then, the obvious danger is a hostage situation. We must prevent that.'

Iles nodded, as if in wonderment at this shrewdness, and said: 'A hostage situation. That really is a point, Chief.'

'Very well, sir, I'll get two more guns in,' Harpur told Lane.

'I think you should look after this operation yourself, Colin.'

'Of course, sir.'

'I need Tenderness alive – a full, well-reported trial, so everything comes out. I want people to see what we're up against here. I want something to show the bloody Home Office and the police committee and its bloody chairman, Tobin, that this an ordinary provincial patch but that it's getting as rosy as London and we can't fight our gangs with a handful of men and water pistols.'

'I understand, sir,' Harpur said.

'Leave it to Col, sir,' Iles told him. 'He's got a lovely, temperate way with a Smith and Wesson, yet resolute. And he and I and the whole Force are united in the determination to seek recompense for Ivor Wright's balls, not to mention his life.' He leaned forward over the Chief's projecting socks. 'As you say, sir, Hubert Scott has done us very proud on this. We are hugely in his debt.'

Lane grunted agreement.

Iles had a grand, generous chuckle. 'Oh, I know you think I stick up for him because of the Lodge and so on – '

'Not at all, Desmond. I – '

'But this really is a fairly remarkable piece of work. And he's not even one of us now. I'm sure Colin would agree that if this comes off it will be a fine coup. How long have we been waiting to do Tenderness big? Now, here he is, leading his bonny party up the shittiest creek in the history of botched crimes.'

'That's what I mean,' Lane said.

'Mean?' Iles asked.

'It clashes with everything we know about him.' Lane began to sound nervous. He was intelligent and sensitive enough to realize that reading a profile of someone was not the same as knowing him direct. He was probably also intelligent and sensitive enough to see how much Iles monkeyed with him, but the Chief was not sufficiently strong in the job yet to deal with that; perhaps a couple more years. His predecessor, Barton, had never learned how to.

'He's always been a good father, Chief,' Iles said. 'His kind of offal generally are. It's like rats, gifted parents. A child is missing. People don't behave typically in such circumstances. I'm sure you understand, sir; a family man.'

Lane went back to his desk. 'Something of a moral problem here, isn't there?'

Again Iles nodded, as though once more in awed admiration of intellect. 'One knew you would pick that up very swiftly, sir.'

Lane said: 'You tell me Tenderness is after ransom money to buy his lad back. We're going to stop him. So might we be responsible if the boy's kidnappers execute their threat? On the other hand, can we sit back and allow an armed bank raid?'

'May I say that was put with fine clarity, sir?' Iles said. 'It went effortlessly to the heart of things.'

Lane said: 'Oh, I wouldn't – '

'Effortlessly,' Iles insisted. 'And, of course, you did not stoop to use that shagged out, generally inaccurately employed cliché, catch 22. But there is another factor that has a bearing.'

'I don't quite see – '

'As we understand it, the bank will have nothing like the cash on the premises that Tenderness expects to find tomorrow. True, a big transfer is due at the end of the week, but for the moment they are at rock bottom, exceptionally low on readies.'

Lane gasped. 'His information's wrong?'

'That's what we understand, sir.'

'How the hell could it happen? None of this seems right, Desmond. It sounds as if he's been sold – someone as wise and wily as Tenderness?'

Iles shrugged. 'We don't know where his whisper about the bank and the funds available came from, I'm afraid. Scott has given us a lot of material, but not that. It looks as if Mellick has to grab at anything, whether he's checked it out or not. Or there could be a mistake on dates – it happens.'

Lane said: 'So even if he pulled off the raid – '

'He's on a loser, all ways, sir. He might clear a couple of dozen K, but that leaves him nowhere. Whether he manages to do the raid or not – and it's going to be very much not, of course – he still can't come up with the sort of ransom they want. So, we're not endangering the child. Although you defined a moral problem so brilliantly, sir, it does not actually exist.'

'Poor old Tenderness.'

'Exactly, sir. Some might find it odd for a senior police officer to express concern for such a piece of crawling rubbish, but I regard it as perfectly legitimate to feel sorry for him, especially you, sir, with your ability to empathize, and certainly I don't think you should suffer guilt because of that. After all, he is a man, as well as one of the fiercest slabs of villainy we'll ever battle with. It's to your credit, sir, that you can make that very valid distinction. If I may say.'

'Somehow we must find the boy, independently of him,' Lane said.

'Certainly,' Iles replied, nodding once more.

'What are we doing?' Lane asked.

'Widespread random checks so far, patrols, house calls, but without result,' Harpur said. 'Now we're switching to exhaustive door to door.'

'That's the way,' Lane told him.

'And we'd like authority for a phone tap,' Iles told him. 'Tenderness is obviously talking to them, arranging to make the payment, but he'll tell us nothing.'

'I'll see to it,' Lane said. 'It'll take a couple of hours, not longer. Time is not on our side.'

For a moment, Harpur thought Iles was going to clap this observation. He raised his hands together, then let them fall back and, instead, turned to Harpur: 'Well, I think we can say we know rather more about the way to handle this thing than when we came in, Col. It's amazing what a few words of natural insight can do. Thank you, sir.'

He went back to Harpur's room with him. 'Isn't it a poison

what command does to them, Col? When Lane came here he was only a Mick prick. Now, he's a – well, the last thing I'd wish is to be harsh, as you know but now he's a – '

'A Chief?'

'Yes, something like that.' He sat down. 'I worry, Col.'

'About the bank?'

'No, Christ, you can handle that, soft as you are. You've knocked out rougher raid crews than this. No, the child. This poor, backward kid marooned with a couple of panicky apes. Anything could happen to him – could already have happened to him. Haven't we had Bain for young boys?'

'We tried. It fell down. Their parents wouldn't let them testify.'

'The other point; would we have looked harder, sooner, with more zip, if this kid wasn't Mellick's? The sins of the fathers.'

'I've heard of that.'

'It's the Bible, arsehole.'

In the evening, Harpur had first to brief his team and then see the bank staff at a special meeting off the premises, in a room hired from a social club for the occasion. Normally, he would have been going out with Ruth Cotton tonight and he knew she was waiting for a call from him to say where and when. He went to a payphone to cry off. As always when he had to cancel, Ruth sounded as if she did not quite believe he was genuinely tied up by work. Perhaps it was a condition of adultery; one lot of unfaithfulness bred suspicion of more. It did not help that he could never disclose what was keeping him away, and he certainly could not tell her about the bank. But she was a cop wife – twice a cop wife – and ought to understand these things.'

'I'll try and ring you about this time tomorrow,' he said. 'He won't be there?'

'I don't know. He's got something special on. He wouldn't say what – just like you.'

'Oh?' He had told Francis Garland to line up a team for the bank job. Perhaps Cotton was in one of the cars. Ruth might be releasing more than her share of the manpower for this ambush. Yes, a cop wife and a cop lover. 'So, shall I call?'

'If you like. If you like.' There was a tiny pause. Then she said at a rush: 'Oh, I'm sorry, Col. I sound as if I don't care. I care. I care too much. That's why I go so far down when I can't see you. Yes, do call. Please. You don't belong to me, I know that, but – '

'I'll call, Ruth.' Now and then he felt eager to escape her gloom and edginess. Didn't he have a couple of other things to worry about? 'Perhaps we can make the weekend some time.'

'Yes, I'll try.'

'I must go. I've got a lot on. All dull and routine but it has to be done, and done tonight.'

'Take care.'

He hated those words. They could be either a bit of empty politeness, or they would sometimes point to real dangers, and make them seem worse. 'It's a habit with me, love. Why I'm still whole.'

Garland had already begun talking to the team when Harpur arrived at the briefing. Cotton was in the front row. By now, proper coloured drawings of the streets and the bank interior had been done and were displayed on the walls, plus a collection of big blow-up pictures of Tenderness, Ditto, Reg, Len and Vernon Pitt, mug shots and full length. Garland paused for a moment, but only for a moment, as Harpur came in: Garland would never voluntarily give up a platform. Harpur sat down at the back. There were twenty-six men, about half of them uniformed.

Garland was showing how Degree Street would be closed off as soon as Tenderness and his people entered the Square. It would be done first of all with police vehicles, to be replaced later by two JCBs, parked abreast. 'Bringing the JCBs in will mean noise and could scare them off before they're committed to the raid,' Garland explained. 'We want this crew inside the bank building so no fucking defence wig can say they were out on a sight-seeing drive, with guns for pot-shots at cats. It would be best if we could do them here,' he said, pointing to the bank's street door and entrance hall. 'That would mean minimal danger to the bank staff. Only members of the public who happened to be in the hall or on the stairs would be at risk. There'd also be less likelihood of a member of the bank staff losing control and possibly distracting us or getting in the way. It's a pain, but we've had to put these people at the bank fully in the picture. Normally, that would be right out, of course. But we had to place people among the clerks this morning to observe. Mr Harpur and I will try to reassure them, but it is a complication, no denying that.'

'Security?' someone asked from the floor.

'They've been told and told, by us and their own bosses, that they're not to talk to anybody outside about it, not family, even. They won't have had long, anyway – only today. It is another hazard, though, yes. If Tenderness gets an inkling, he might call off. Only might. He's desperate for the money he believes is there. I think we'll be all right.'

Garland generally did. It was one of his best strengths, though there were others: he had a brain and not too many nerves and he knew how to point a hand-gun. He began to allocate positions. Cotton had charge of the road block. He would be armed but his position was safe enough and Harpur felt relieved on two counts; first, for Ruth, and second because he would not be working close to Cotton himself. He liked to see as little of him as possible. Cotton probably felt the same. How much he suspected, Harpur could never tell.

When Garland began to talk about armament Harpur stood and went to the front himself. This was something he liked to brief people about personally. Garland shrugged and gave way.

'We'll have eleven people with Magnums or Smith and Wessons,' Harpur told them. 'That's plenty of fire power, even if they've got sawn-offs, which is likely.' He went to the blow-up pictures and pointed to Mellick and Ditto. 'We worry about these two particularly. Both are inveterates and capable of anything. On Vernon Pitt I'm not sure. We've heard of small stuff only. But he was probably on the trip to Aylesbury when Ivor passed away, so he might have taken part in some true heaviness. If it comes to shooting, we should be ready to blow away Tenderness and Ditto first, possibly Pitt. Reg will be in the car and out of things. And if I know Len Quant, he'll be scared helpless. We ought to be able to take him undamaged. It's important to come out of this kind of operation with one enemy intact; shows moderation. I've got to tell you, we're a bit in the dark about how they'll behave. These are protection people suddenly blossoming into a new career, like a whore turning housewife, and there's no guides for us. Ditto is extremely useful with a Walther, so don't mess about if he points something at you. It won't be a stick of liquorice.'

Harpur coughed and changed his tone of voice. 'Here beginneth the second lesson, again,' he said. 'All the well known restraints about use of firearms will, of course, be in operation. It's not quite, "Don't fire until you've been hit at least twice," but pretty close. I'll give them the "Armed police" bit three

140

times as soon as I'm out of the car, once for the judge, once for the jury, and once for *The Guardian,* and you'll all hear. The rule says you only fire if you think your own life is in danger or that of a colleague or a member of the public's. So, I'm repeating the rule to you now. All hear me? Good. That's quite enough of that, then.'

20

In Mellick's long lounge they had a couple of shortened Beretta shotguns and three 9mm, 15-shot magazine Colt pistols laid out on sacking on the reproduction Boulle writing table, what Vernon always called a *bureau plat,* or something similar. Near by, stacked on a leather chesterfield, were the grey-green boiler suits and navy balaclavas. Looking at it all, Mellick fought to keep clear in his head the connection between what they hoped to do with this equipment and the return of Graham. It was not easy.

Vernon picked up one of the shotguns and held it at the waist, pointing towards the closed curtain. He looked as if he knew what he was doing, as if he had used one before. He might not be all spiel, dude gear and twenty-four hour cock availability. Vernon put the weapon back.

Ditto said: 'What I wish is that bastard Scott was coming with us tomorrow, right in there, where the safe is. That's what I wish.'

'We don't need him,' Mellick replied. 'What good would he be? He's a bloody tipster. What's he know about hitting a bank?'

'No, but, what I mean – I'd like to see him put his heart and long-life guts where his mouth is, that's all,' Ditto said. 'I don't like it, not no longer. It all come so easy, too easy. We leans on him and next thing we got a bank to do, and, Christ, look where it is. It come too easy, Tenderness.'

'He've always done us right,' Mellick told him. 'Didn't I hear you saying that yourself to Vernon. What's changed? You was firm.'

Ditto said, 'Yes, I know, but – '

'You wouldn't chicken, Ditto, would you?' Jane asked gently. 'I

know you wouldn't. This is not just a raid. This is Graham's life.'
Jane could always get through to him.

'No, not chicken. Ditto don't chicken,' Ditto said in a rush. 'I
knows why we're going and I'll do it. But that Scott, maybe he
don't seem right, not this time. Maybe Vernon could be on the
ball this time. I said different, I know, but maybe this time he
could be on the ball. All right, Hubert have always been right
about what's going to happen, but that wasn't about banks, was
it, that was about all the business side, the clubs and that, and
when I thinks about it now, he don't seem right this time, that's
all. That kind, always thinking, and they're thinking about theirselves, that's all they cares about. Well, who else, he been CID all
his life? He's going to do people favours?'

'It isn't no favour. He's scared,' Mellick said. 'Anyway, we got
to go on.' He waved to indicate the weaponry and clothes. 'And
Len and Reg out picking up a couple of nice cars. Ditto, you know
we can't wait.'

'Well, I know, Tenderness. I'm worried, that's all. I can't lie.'
Ditto walked over to the guns and for a moment Mellick thought
he was going to imitate Vernon and try a Beretta. But he looked at
the pistols. 'I'll be using the Walther, anyway. I don't need one of
them. The Walther – I'm used to that, got the feel, and it don't
ever fuck up.'

Vernon said: 'Best use new stuff, Ditto, then ditch it somewhere. Ballistics can't do much then. They'll have you on the
dossier for a Walther. It's a trade mark, it's a risk. A Walther says
Ditto. Did you ever see *The Friends of Eddie Coyle*?'

'Who? I don't know him. Don't know his friends. They use
Walthers?'

'Vernon's right, Ditto,' Mellick told him. 'We got big perils
here, yes, but we got to try to cut them, best we can.'

'What do I know about Colts?' Ditto said. 'Guns never been
tried – I don't like it. Colts? I never used a Colt.'

'You got a bit of night-before nerves, Ditto,' Jane said. 'It's only
natural. It's a good sign, really. You'll be great on the day. If you
didn't have no nerves now it would only mean you wasn't thinking about things enough, and then it could all come as a hell of a
shock when you're going in there, and you could go to bits. It
happens to people, real hard people.'

142

'I got nerves myself,' Mellick added. 'This a bloody big outing. But this time tomorrow, we'll be laughing about it.'

'And Graham will be back,' Jane said.

'And Graham will be back,' Mellick agreed.

Vernon sat down next to the boiler suits. 'Well, we ought to take into account that Ditto could have a point, about Scott, I mean. All right, and it's been a point made by me, too. We ought to cater for the possibility that Scott's not on the level.'

Mellick saw Jane lift her head sharply and stare at Vernon with a sort of horror on her face, as if she had been betrayed. Occasionally, she looked very bad these days, hardly recognizable. Since Graham went she had been neglecting herself, and Mellick spotted lines of grey in her dark hair. Worry and sleeplessness dragged at her skin, making the bones of her jaw and nose jut sharply.

'I'm not saying back down,' Vernon went on. 'Nothing like that. We've got a job, and it will be done. But we can make provisions. Scott? We all know he's deep in the mire. We could be his way out. He used to talk to us on the sly, so he could talk to anyone.'

'Provisions, what provisions?' she still looked and sounded suspicious.

Mellick saw she had thought she could rely entirely on Vernon and was in deep pain at his words now. They had something going, these two, no question. He felt sick and sad, even if she did have grey lines in her hair. They could come out easy when everything was all right again.

'This would be tactics, that's all,' Vernon replied. His voice became very tender, and for that moment he was obviously speaking only to her.

'Tactics?' Mellick said. 'We can't start changing things now. We got it all worked out.'

'All worked out.' To Mellick, Ditto seemed fine again suddenly, back into the old habit of seeing everything the way he ought to see it.

'Yes, it's great,' Vernon replied. 'But we ought to have a fall-back plan. We should take the worst scenario we can think of, and cater for it. I always believe in doing that.'

The sod sounded like Napoleon. 'What worst what-you-call-it?' Mellick asked.

'Well, if it's known about, that's the worst that could happen, isn't it? If they're waiting for us. Suppose Ditto's got it right and Scott's talking.'

'Oh, that was just a bit of nerves,' Ditto said. 'Don't take no notice. That was what you said, Vernon, you was the one who started that. I just let it get to me for a minute, that's all. Don't put it down to me. It's you. That was just nerves. I mean, Hubert Scott, he always done us right, so why's he going to change now? We give him a good fright when we called on him, so he got to do it right for us. He's not a bad old sod, Hubert. I know he been police, but he's not a bad old sod. And we give him a real good fright, so he'll be all right.'

'Of course he will.' Jane smiled her thanks at Ditto.

'Just in case,' Vernon said. 'What's the use of shutting our eyes?'

'Sometimes if you open your eyes too wide you see things that's not there,' Mellick told him. 'Frighten yourself so much you can't move.'

Vernon said: 'If Hubert's been talking – just say he's been talking, because he wants a bit of top rank help to get out of this inquiry – if he's been talking, what are they going to do when they hear about this raid? It's obvious. They won't try to stop things. They want us on the job, don't they? They want us nailed. So, they'll let us into the Square and then they'll block off Degree Street, I mean, really block it, not just cars, something heavy-weight, maybe a loaded truck, or some big road repair machinery.'

'Christ,' Ditto muttered. 'That's a trap, a real trap, Tenderness.'

'Sure it is,' Vernon said. 'They put a unit there with armament and some at the bank, so even if we get out with the money and away, we're in a sandwich. That's no good to Graham, Tenderness.'

'No good at all to Graham, Tenderness,' Ditto told him.

'We've got the money but we can't use it,' Vernon said.

'Got the money but can't use it for Graham, Tenderness,' Ditto argued.

'It's one of the risks,' Mellick answered. 'We knew that from the start.' But he could see he was losing Ditto. He might even be losing Jane. This was the first time he had ever let her in on a business meeting, and he began to regret it. But how could he have kept her out when it was all about Graham?

'The only thing, the only reason for hitting this place, is to get the money for the ransom,' she said. 'So, what are you trying to tell us, Vernon? What new plan?'

'We must have an alternative ready, Jane.'

'What alternative, Vernon?' Ditto asked. 'What alternative?'

'We'll be able to see early if they're blocking Degree Street,' Vernon replied. 'If they're watching us, they'll move in there immediately, maybe with cars first, because they won't want a din. They've got to close it off at once, not just to block us in but to keep the public out. What they don't want is a lot of people and cars, ordinary people and cars. They've got to be careful when there's shooting likely. So, if we see them close the street, we go to number two plan.'

'What number two plan, Vernon?' Ditto asked.

'Obviously, we leave a different way.'

'Yes?' Ditto said.

'Oh, Jesus, you mean out the back, through the bank?' Mellick asked. 'I looked at that. It's into a yard. We couldn't get the car close. We're going to be carrying bags, heavy bags, a lot of money, we got to have the car close. In any case, we can't go in that way, from the back, because someone is going to see us coming on foot through the yard. We'll be in the boiler suits and wearing balaclavas, don't forget. Every alarm in the place would be banging away before we reached the building.'

'Yes, we must go in through the front, I agree,' Vernon said. 'That's the only possible for surprise. Not exit that way, though, necessarily. If we had an extra car, it could be left as near as we could get it to the back. All right, Tenderness, it's not ideal, but at this stage we'd be looking for a way out of a trap, not perfection.'

'No driver,' Mellick answered.

'I can drive.'

'What I mean, Reg is going to be waiting in front. He got to be in front.'

'Yes, what about Reg in front?' Ditto asked.

'This would be only a last resort plan,' Vernon said.

Mellick's head cleared suddenly 'Christ, you mean leave him, like them two at Aylesbury.'

'I know it's rough and I know he's been with you a long time, Tenderness, but, look, what we'd be trying to do is cut our losses, make the best of a bloody disaster.'

Mellick started to shout. 'No. No. That's not on, no way. Reg – Jesus, we been through all sorts together, and he've looked after me in some real tough spots. What the hell you saying? You joins my outfit no time ago out of nowhere in a green shirt and you're telling me to drop one of my best boys, just hand him over to the law. Reg is not like them Aylesbury muck. You got a kidney, saying I'd do that to Reg.'

'Look, I knew you wouldn't like this, Tenderness. Of course not. Although I haven't been here long I've seen the way you think about your people. It's great. But, if it came to the worst, Tenderness, and we – '

The telephone rang. For a moment, Mellick felt paralysed, then he got up from his armchair and crossed the room to answer it. As soon as he lifted the receiver he could hear the voice at the other end talking to him.

'Sick of waiting, Tenderness. You're messing me about, you're playing some game, I bloody know it. I been too easy with you, that's my trouble.'

'No. We're nearly ready now, I swear.'

'Nearly, always nearly. You can't put your hand on a couple of hundred K, no trouble? I don't believe it. You don't like to part with it, Tenderness, that's your trouble. I heard that about you. You're hanging on, hanging on, hoping for the police, or something. They're swarming, I know it, I seen them through the window, but they missed us, Tenderness, went right past us, the soft buggers. I sees them near the other phone box, too. You been talking to them? You got them listening on this line, Tenderness? I told you no, didn't I?'

'It's not true, still no police.'

'You ask your wife if I'm messing about, ask her, she'll tell you.'

'I know you're not messing about. Of course I do.'

'When, then, the money?'

'Tomorrow.'

'All of it?'

'Yes.'

'You sure? No more tomorrows? The whole lot?'

'Yes.'

'What you don't realize – I want to help you, don't I, Tenderness? I comes out here night after night in these stinking phone boxes just so I can have a quiet word with you, and you just fools about. It don't make sense, Tenderness. It don't show any regard for your own flesh and blood, that's what I can't understand. You ought to be grateful, but you mess me about instead.'

'Yes, yes, I'm grateful. We all are.'

For a while there was silence.

'Are you still there?' Mellick said.

'I'm here. I'm trying to sort out if I can believe you.'

'Please, I swear – '

'Well, all right. I'll wait. Tenderness, I'm going to believe you, just once more. I'm going to call tomorrow again. Tell you how to deliver. That'll be the last – one way or the other, you got it?'

'Yes. And Graham, is he all right?'

'Yes, Podge is all right. That's what I calls him, Podge. He's with me here.'

'With you?' Up until now, his voice had been strong, but it left him suddenly and he could only manage a whisper. 'With you now? Please, can I talk to him?'

Jane stood up and came across the room to Mellick, half holding out her hand for the phone: he saw she could not prevent herself doing that.

'Can I talk to him, just for ten seconds?' Mellick said, a little louder now.

'I mean, with me, in the car.'

'Could you get him? But he was hearing the dialling tone again. He replaced the receiver and put an arm around Jane. 'Sorry, love.' In a few moments they both went back to their chairs.

'You told him it was coming?' Jane asked. She was whispering, as if her voice had gone, too.

'Yes.'

'And he sounded all right, I mean, pleased?'

'Yes.'

'Coming tomorrow? Everything?'

'All of it, yes.'

'Why does he bring him out in the car?' Vernon said. 'That's dicey. Milton must be with him or they'd be afraid he'd bolt. That means three of them driving about looking for a phone that works. They're taking risks.'

Jane stood up again and came and kneeled in front of Mellick. 'Bernie, love, it's got to work at the bank, got to, hasn't it? He's losing patience, that's obvious. We could hear his voice. He's frightened, he won't wait for ever. Like Vernon says, they're doing crazy things. Maybe if we had told the police when it all started, they would be spotted. But you wouldn't have that and it's too late now. So, it's got to be tomorrow.'

She put her head against his leg and he was conscious once more of the greyness in her hair. It did not matter. She was still all he wanted. But what the hell did a kid like Vernon see in her?

'It'll work,' he told Jane. 'Don't worry.'

'I know you can do it.'

'We've got it all worked out.'

'Yes.' She lifted her head and looked at him. 'But, darling, you ought to listen to Vernon – I mean, just about that plan in case things go wrong. That's all. When he first mentioned it, I didn't like it myself, but maybe he's right.'

'Ditch Reg?'

Vernon said: 'They're not going to be hard on him, Tenderness. He's only wheels. He won't do any rough work himself.'

'We kill someone, he's an accessory, you know, that, you smart bastard.'

'We've got to get the money out, Bernie,' Jane pleaded.

'So, say goodbye to Reg. God. And what about Len?' Mellick asked. 'He's going to be on the front door. We leave him, too? Is that another bit of the fucking master plan?'

'Yes, there's Len,' Ditto said.

'Well, I thought about Len. I thought about him a lot', Vernon replied. 'He could be banging off at the police, so we ought to try to get him away, yes. Maybe he could run with us to the back if we gave him a shout and he was fast enough. Depends how quick he reacted, really.'

'You mean, don't tell him about this second plan, though, until things go wrong and then let him take his luck?'

'He's close to Reg,' Vernon said. 'You tell Len and you might not have a team at all tomorrow, Tenderness. Anyway, we'll all be taking our luck at the bank.'

'Len and Reg talk a lot, Tenderness, it's true,' Ditto said.

Mellick moved his legs out from under Jane and stood again. 'Christ, I feel like a bloody fink even listening to this. These boys, they're not just people who work for me, these boys are friends.'

Vernon said: 'I know, I know, Tenderness, and if things go fine tomorrow – '

'If things go fine,' Jane said, 'we'll all be laughing tomorrow night, Reg and Len and you three and our boy, Tenderness, our boy. That's how it got to be. But it's if there's a slip up, or if you haven't got surprise, that's the trouble, isn't it, love?' She went and stood close to him. 'We can't leave Graham's life to luck.'

'It would be hard to leave Graham's life to luck,' Ditto said.

'Bernie, when all this started I thought you had the money, and no trouble. It wasn't going to be sweet giving it to these swine, but no trouble. Well, you haven't got it, we all know now. So, where are we? You got to get it, it's as simple as that. And if you got to climb over a few when you're doing it, that's too bad.'

She gripped his hand. It was as though she was saying that if he brought her son back things could be all right again between them, even if he had bugger all in the bank, and even if she had been taking comfort from an outsider.

'So, please, Bernie, think about what Vernon says.'

'I could go and get a nippy vehicle from somewhere tonight,' Vernon said. 'Put it in place.'

'Yes, that's a good idea, isn't it, Bernie? Can Vernon go and pick up a vehicle? I mean, that don't commit nobody to nothing, do it? But the car's there then if you want it, that's all. Things go all right, you just forget it. The owner will get it back nice and quick, and no vandalization. He'll be real pleased. Yes, Vernon, you go ahead and get it. That's right, isn't it, Bernie?'

'Like it don't commit us at all, Tenderness,' Ditto said. 'That's not hurting Reg and Len, just picking up an extra car and putting it handy. I'll go with him.'

Mellick did not answer.

'So they're going now, Bernie. There's not too much time.'

In a while Vernon and Ditto went out of the room and he heard them drive away.

She put her arms around his waist and pulled him to her. Her body seemed alive and clinging, the first time she had been like that with him for months. In a way, he found it disgusting, as if he had just traded two men to get her love again.

'Let's go to bed, shall we, Bernie?' she said. 'We've got a few hours. Suddenly, I really want you. There's all this trouble – Graham and this thing tomorrow, all that going on and not able to think about anything else, but suddenly all I want is to go to bed with you. Do you understand it?' She giggled. 'I don't myself. All I know, it's real, so real.'

Perhaps he did understand. He allowed her to draw him by the hand upstairs. She felt good for a few moments, so it was only kindness to let her hang on to that. She had made herself believe what she wanted to. That was not like Jane, but despair did rough things to people. Why smash her bit of happiness by pointing out what she would usually have seen at once for herself? She had heard the fears about Scott, she had heard that State Square might be a trap. Those risks she recognized. So, why didn't she spot that the promise of a bank stuffed with money ready to be turned into ransom for Graham was probably wrong, just a bit of come-on?

21

Graham Mellick lay huddled against the spare wheel in the boot of their car. It stopped and he heard the door slam when Dave got out and his footsteps as he walked away. After a while he heard him come back and then the car moved again. The smell in the boot made him cough and he cried and called out now and then because he was so afraid in the darkness.

When Dave had made him go in the boot he said: 'Sorry, Podge. I've got to telephone and I can't leave you with him now.' He meant with Milton, the boy knew that. It was because Milton had been touching him on the trousers. But after the fight Milton did not try to do that again. Graham thought Milton knew that every time he did Dave would hit him.

But sometimes Dave had to go out of the house. That was why

150

he said, 'I can't leave you with him now.' The boy tried to stop Dave putting him in the boot and he tried to shout but Dave had a towel and put it over Graham's mouth. He could not bite.

The car was in a garage when Dave made him get in the boot. Graham had not known of the garage. It was the night. They went out of the house through another door, not the one at the front where there was the high bolt, and into the garden. He saw grass. When they were in the garage Dave pushed the doors almost shut, but there was something wrong and they did not close properly. Graham did not know the colour of the car. He thought it might be yellow, but could not be sure.

Now, the car stopped again. He heard the door slam and then the lid of the boot went up and it was not dark. When he looked up he saw Dave and they were back in the garage with the light on and Dave helped him out. 'That's the last time, Podge,' he said. 'Tomorrow. You'll be all right tomorrow.' Dave took him back into the house and Milton came down the stairs to see them.

'Tomorrow,' Dave said. 'He got it. I just had a very nice talk with him and he says tomorrow for sure.'

Then Milton started laughing and he caught hold of Dave's hand and shook it. Now Milton seemed to like Dave and the fighting did not matter. Milton and Dave began to dance, like people on the television, holding each other, but on the television it was a lady and a man and there was music for them. Milton started to sing sometimes when they were dancing. When he sang, his mouth was open very wide and the boy saw blood in the front and one of his teeth was not there any longer. But he knew Milton did not care.

22

Harpur went to look at the telephone box with Iles in the Assistant Chief's new Orion. Iles had a cassette player in the car and they listened to a tape of Mellick's conversation, recorded off the telephone tap. At the end of it, the Assistant Chief said: 'You shouldn't be out at this time of night, dear Col, when you have the bank appointment so soon. And Garland. He's with you tomorrow and is up here, too, yes? You people can do too much. That's how we get shoot-bang-fire accidents. Was that definitely Ancient Dave talking to Tenderness?'

'I'd say so.'

'He doesn't sound too bad, not unhinged, yet. Starts a bit rough – that "sick of waiting" stuff – but he levels off and gets almost matey. In fact, there's a nice sort of balance in some of those sentences.' Iles imitated the voice, giving it a sing-song tone: '"You ought to be grateful, but you mess me about instead." Like a Bessie Smith blues lyric. If he's talking fast, it's only because he's worried we might be listening and doing a trace, sharp old bugger. He was probably away from the box a good four or five minutes before we had a patrol there.' He assumed Dave's voice and then Mellick's: '"You got them listening on this line, Tenderness?" "It's not true, still no police." Ah well, best you don't know, Tenderness.'

'Yes he was gone, but there'll be good leads,' Harpur said. 'It's not very late. There might have been people around. We should be able to get something on the car, at least.'

Iles drove without speaking for a while. Then he said: 'Of course, it will be on your mind that we don't really want to recover Graham Mellick tonight, Col, or even locate him.'

'We don't?'

'You love to play dumb and untainted, don't you, so it's left to me to spell out the rough and shady aspects of our trade?'

'I'm not with you, sir. This is a kid being held by potential nutters, one of them possibly a child molester. Shouldn't we try to be quick?'

Iles laughed. 'You're bloody priceless, you know that? But fair enough. What you'll say is that I've got the rank, so I take the brutal decisions. You don't have to defile your mind.'

'With what, sir?'

'With strategy. If we pick up Graham Mellick tonight, what's the first thing we have to do?'

Harpur had seen from the start how the Assistant Chief was thinking but, as Iles had said, Harpur meant to make no input himself. 'See he's all right, I suppose. Feed him. Get him to a doctor.'

'How true. What else? What else, you prevaricating bastard, is immediately to notify his parents he's free. All right, Mellick's a

152

piece of refuse, but he still has to be told his kid's safe. We'd be dealing with him as a frantically anxious parent, not a candidate for thirty years in a top security jail. And what happens to the bank job in State Square then? Tenderness wouldn't need the money any longer because there's no ransom to pay. Banks are not his kind of work, and he and his people know or half know that this could be a disaster outing for them. Is he going to continue, for the hell of it?' Iles waited for an answer.

'Tenderness tries nothing for the hell of it.'

'Thank you. So we lose our chance of taking him, Ditto and the rest in one of the most foolproof ambushes ever donated to a police Force by Fate and prime information. We likewise lose the chance of neutralizing the Bundy inquiry and putting our colleague Hubert Scott into the clear; if there's no bank raid we can't say we were tipped off about it by him, from his undercover knowledge. Is the reasoning going too fast for you? It's in all our interests to undermine Bundy as much as possible, and if it helps Hubert as well, that's excellent.'

'Yes, I see that but – '

'You're going to say we're talking about the safety, possibly the life, of a child.' His voice had grown warm and understanding. 'You have a very fine, humane streak to you, Harpur, and I think you should cherish it. My own thinking is that this would not really be a sizeable risk. They've held this boy for a long time now without hurting him, as far as we know. One more day would not be so critical, would it? You'll say, Who knows whether it would? I certainly take that point. You'll argue that these are thugs who might be at the very end of their self-control.' He nodded. 'That's very reasonable, very reasonable. But my own thinking is that this is a warrantable gamble, in view of the likely all round gains. Are we ever going to nail Tenderness any other way?'

Harpur said: 'If we did find the boy tonight, couldn't we hold him somewhere safe, look after him, without telling Mellick?'

'You know we couldn't, don't you? That would be almost certain to come out, and Bundy and the media would put two and two together and start asking very direct questions about the timing of events. If it was shown that we had deliberately not disclosed his rescue so the raid would go ahead, how would it look? We'd come out of it appearing not just monstrously callous but as *agents provocateurs*. We don't want that, at any price, Col.'

153

'No, sir, but I still think – '

'That's how I see it,' Iles replied. He reimposed silence. 'I worry about the boy, but some gambles have to be accepted in our work. I can accept them.'

They were approaching the district where the phone booth had been pinpointed by the trace. Iles replayed the last section of the tape. 'He says, "He's with me now," and then backtracks when Tenderness asks to talk to the boy – "with me, in the car." Could he really leave him in the car while he makes a three-, four-minute call, and that's supposing he didn't have to wait for the booth? What guarantee he won't bolt, even a slow-minded child like this one? Some of them are sharp enough about practicalities, anyway. He couldn't risk tying him and having him seen. There's no way of locking someone into a car, is there? He might have had him in the boot. That's been done in a kidnap. Or did he drug him? Would Dave be up to that?'

'Probably not.'

'He must have known Tenderness would ask to speak to the kid. Why say he was there if he didn't intend bringing him to the phone? Was it just a tease, to get Mellick worked up?' He set the tape going from the top again and crouched forward over the steering wheel to listen very carefully. When it ended once more he said: 'Yes, possibly a tease. Do people realize, Col, that in most serious crime we're dealing with savages capable of absolutely anything? Do they, do you think?'

'They're beginning to.'

'If we told Tobin about that conversation the only question he'd ask is what right we had to tap and trace. That's what we're up against, and they're supposed to be on our side.' For a while he was silent again. Then he said: 'I suppose Milton could have been looking after him in the car. Should we be asking around the phone box about a vehicle seen there with three people in it, two men and a boy?'

'Perhaps they don't trust each other. Graham Mellick is money in the bank, so they both want to stick to him.'

'Except the money isn't in the bank.'

'Why else bring the kid out?' Harpur said. 'Ancient Dave's not a fine mind, but even he would see he was putting the risks up.'

'He might be afraid to leave the boy with Milton Bain for other reasons.'

154

'I'd thought of that.'

'You had? You can speak about such things to me, you know. I'm over twenty-one.'

'Here's the box, sir. The boys are around the corner.'

Iles drove past the telephone booth and turned off. An unmarked Fiesta was parked a little way up the street. When Iles stopped, Francis Garland came quickly from the car and spoke to Harpur through the window. 'We've got people watching the booth, sir, in case he comes back, and we're trying to find two cars seen near it at about the right time, one we think a red Volvo saloon, the other a yellow Cavalier, old style. We might have a bit of the registration for the Cavalier.'

'How many people in these cars?' Iles asked.

'Only one in both cases. I know he said he had the boy with him, but is it true? And he could have been carrying him in the boot. Of course, we've no idea how far he had driven. He probably uses a different box each time, distance no object.'

'Impeccable analysis, Francis,' Iles said.

Someone in the Fiesta flashed its lights very briefly and Garland looked about urgently. Harpur saw nothing moving. Garland walked swiftly back to the car. Iles and Harpur left the Orion and followed him. When they reached the Fiesta its driver was finishing a radio conversation, with Garland listening through the window.

'There's been a call from a member of the public,' he told them, straightening. 'He was crossing the road between cars stopped at traffic lights in Aubade Street and thinks he heard someone coughing from the boot of a yellow Cavalier. Male, he believes – can't say more than that. The car pulled away before he could do anything but he got the number. It squares with the fragment we already had. The car turned off into the Redbrick housing estate, at Painter Avenue. He took the trouble to walk up to the corner of the Avenue and look, but couldn't see the Cavalier.'

'This is good,' Harpur said. 'Redbrick's not a big estate. Private?'

'Yes,' Garland replied. 'Quite select, right alongside the foreshore.'

'So there'd be garages.'

'Yes.'

'Bugger,' Harpur said. 'The Cavalier might not be on view.'

155

'Look, Colin, Francis, I worry about you two,' Iles told them. 'I want you to get some rest now. I can't have you going more or less straight from one quite taxing operation to another. I'll take charge here.'

Harpur did not want to leave it to him. He had an idea the Assistant Chief would make sure the search went slowly enough to guarantee no find of the boy until after the bank ambush. That could be dangerous for Graham Mellick. 'We'll be all right, sir.'

Garland said: 'Yes, don't worry about Colin and me. It's fine, sir, I wouldn't want to miss – '

'I insist. You and Colin go and get your heads down now,' Iles replied. 'I can handle this. It won't be the first house to house search I've handled. Really, lads. You leave it to me.'

23

In the morning, Graham felt excited. Milton said he would make a big breakfast because it was a great day. First, he and Dave played darts, both of them laughing a lot and talking to the boy. It was a great day and a big breakfast because Dave had a nice talk when he went to the telephone, Graham knew that.

He liked the smell and noises that came from the frying pan. He liked fried bread and bacon, not eggs, but if Milton gave him eggs he would eat them because he was always very hungry in this house and because he did not want to make Milton angry.

When Milton put the big breakfast on the plate there was a lot for Graham, fried bread and some bacon and two eggs. They all had red sauce. Dave touched him, but it was not on the trousers. Dave put his arm on his shoulders and said, 'Podge is a grand lad.' And then he said, 'Home today, Podge.'

That meant he would not be staying in this house but going to his mother and father. He wanted to go, but Sam the dog was not there now and his mother never gave him red sauce with breakfast. He thought she thought red sauce was not needed, like 'fucking'.

They had lots of cups of tea, more than four. While they were drinking them, Dave suddenly held up his hand and Graham knew it meant to keep quiet. Dave wanted to listen. Milton stood and went to the side of the curtains again, looking out. 'Nothing,' he said.

But Dave said: 'At the back. The garage.' Then he got up and went downstairs very quietly and Graham heard him open that door at the back of the house. They waited and soon Dave returned. He still had a cup of tea in his hand. Graham did not hear him shut that door at the back of the house. When Dave came in he said: 'Nobody.'

Milton was still by the window and he said: 'Nothing here.'

And Dave said: 'I was sure.'

The boy knew Dave meant he was sure he heard somebody by the garage in the garden, or a pig. Then Dave whispered: 'They might want a peep at the car. They know the fucking car.' He was afraid somebody would hear him, or a pig.

Milton said: 'How could they know it?'

Dave was listening again: 'Yes, how? You could be right,' he said.

Graham knew what that meant, when Dave said 'Yes, you could be right,' to Milton, he meant nobody could know what their car was like, because they kept it in the garage. But the garage doors would not shut. Dave and Milton stayed by the curtains again, looking at the street.

Graham could not eat as fast as Dave and Milton and he was still finishing his breakfast. He ate everything. He did not like the colour of the eggs in the middle, it was like the colour of the car, but he ate them. He put the red sauce on the eggs and then they were a different colour.

When he had finished, he saw some fried bread on Milton's plate. Graham's mother used to say to leave something on the plate if you did not want it. She said it was like a pig if you ate everything just because it was on the plate. If there were pigs in the street and they came in here they might eat everything they could see. It was not a big piece of fried bread on Milton's plate, because Milton had been biting it. If pigs came they might eat that.

He wanted that small piece of fried bread because there was still some red sauce on his plate and some on Dave's plate and he could dip the fried bread in it. Then he picked up the piece of fried bread from Milton's plate. When he did that he was looking at the men but they did not see him. He dipped the piece of fried bread in the red sauce and ate it. It was very nice.

He looked again at Dave and Milton, but they were still at the window. He wanted to go before Milton saw the fried bread was not there. He might be angry. The boy stood up quietly. Then he walked very slowly to the door of the room. If Dave or Milton saw him he would say toilet. His mother told him always try to go to toilet in the morning.

When he came to the door of the room it was part open and he went out. He took the stairs slowly. He wanted to go fast because Milton and Dave might come after him, but he feared making a noise. Downstairs he did not go to the door with the high bolt on it, but the other one. It was open. Dave forgot to shut that door when he came back, because he was so worried.

He went and stood on the grass. He was afraid. He knew that if he left he must go in the street. He did not know how to find the house where his mother was and he did not know if there were pigs in the street. He was not sure if pigs were bad or good, and if they would hurt. Dave and Milton thought pigs would hurt and they were afraid, he could tell, so he was a bit afraid of pigs as well.

But he was afraid to stay in this house. When they were at the farm, Milton used to talk to him and he was a friend. Graham did not mind if he had a cigarette in his mouth or about the hairs in his nose. He was not a friend now.

He knew that sometimes in the streets there were buses. He went on a bus with his mother one day because the car was broken and it took them to their house. But his mother gave the driver some money. It was needed. Sometimes the boy had money in his pockets and now he urgently pulled out all the things he had on him, searching for coins.

When he was searching like that he dropped the little soldier, the one on the horse with colours on his hat, which he had kept in his pocket. It was still like a friend and guardian to him and he looked for it desperately in the long grass but could not find it at once. And he did not want to stay long in this garden because Dave and Milton might come looking for him. He gave up searching for it now.

He did not find any money in his pockets. He did not want to go in the street because there might be pigs, and he did not have any money to go on the bus. He felt confused again but hurried across the grass and climbed over a big wall. He dropped down into another garden, then climbed another wall there and found himself in a third. This one had bushes and trees and he crossed it quickly and rested for a while behind some greenery at another wall.

Suddenly, while he was waiting, he heard a man talking very close by. He could not see who it was because the voice came from the other side of the wall, but he knew it was not Dave or Milton. The man said: 'Moving up to their garden now. Over.' Then there was a noise like when the radio went wrong and whistling and he heard a lady talking, but could not understand what she said.

He was afraid that when the man said 'Over' he meant he was going to climb over the wall. If he did he would see him and he might take him back to Dave and Milton. People did not like it if children were in their garden. Sometimes, children went into the gardens near the school and a lady came and told the teacher, she was so cross about weeing in her pond on the goldfish.

So, he ran away from that wall very quickly and went to another part of the garden, where he hid again in the bushes. He watched that wall where he heard the voice. A man climbed over quickly, and then more men, he could not tell how many. Some of them were policemen, he saw their silver buttons. The others did not have silver buttons but they were with the policemen. They did not see him.

They went across the garden and then they climbed a wall, going the way he had come. He did not know which garden they were going to. Perhaps they were looking for pigs. If pigs were in somebody's garden the people might not like it and they might send for the police. Graham did not call them because his father did not like police and told him never to tell them anything and never to talk to them.

He climbed another wall, and this time when he reached the top he did not see a garden but a street. For a while, he stayed on top and looked for pigs, but could not see any. Then he jumped down.

When he was in the street he could hear something, and after a few minutes recognized it as the sound of the sea. Sometimes his mother and father took him to play on a beach and he liked it, so

159

now he decided to try to find the sea. He could not see it but when he walked he could hear it better.

He came to the end of the streets and houses and found he was walking on pebbles. He could still hear the sea, stronger now. He had to climb up the bank of pebbles and began to feel hot after going over walls and walking. He knew about climbing because of the frame in his garden at home, but walls were harder. Then, when he reached the top of the little hill of stones, he saw the sea. There were very big waves, he liked that.

He started to laugh because he loved the sea and because he could not see Dave or Milton or any pigs. He felt safe and free here and ran down the other side of the bank of pebbles to be near the water. He wanted to go in the waves.

24

Harpur got up early and went to make the breakfast for Megan and the girls. He had not slept well, unusual for him, regardless of stress and anxieties. But this job, this ambush, looked too easy. In the middle of the night, Megan had groaned a couple of times and then muttered: 'What's wrong with you?'

He had been trying to keep still and not show his restlessness. 'What? What do you mean?'

'You're lying like a corpse.'

It did not seem possible or deserved or likely to have someone like Tenderness Mellick on toast, and in bed Harpur found himself rehearsing and re-rehearsing to himself the details of how things were supposed to go in State Square today, and looking for the gaps. Yet, it ought to work. After all, this was not Mellick behaving like Mellick, and anyone could see why; he was a man in despair, acting as if he had no options, no time, no exit from fierce, unfavourable odds, a man running his head against Fate's brick wall. It could happen to anyone, even to people as clever as Tenderness. All the same, Harpur fretted.

He had run other bank parties, acting on information received, received usually from Jack Lamb. Sometimes things had gone nicely, sometimes half nicely and sometimes they had been appalling, very dangerous cock-ups. Cock-ups could come in any number of varieties; you could miss all the raiders or some of them, or you could shoot an old lady or her whippet, or you could end up dealing for hostages. Because he had heart and knew about caring, the Chief would regard the last two as far and away the worst outcomes, and perhaps he was right. Iles would not agree. He thought caring was for Mother Theresa and Meals on Wheels. In any case, he made a point of bonfiring most of Lane's ideas, especially the liberal ones. Iles would be exceptionally enraged if Mellick or any of his people slipped out of this corral.

Harpur was doing a big fry-up this morning, eggs, bacon, black pudding, the lot. It was something of a ritual when he had a promising day ahead. His daughters loved these meals. Today would be a super delight for them because, not only was there the breakfast, but he would not have time to drive them to school; they hated arriving at John Locke Comprehensive with what they called 'the pig prince', and even though he always dropped them around the corner from the gates they would leave the car quickly and never glance back. Hazel had given him some crap jargon once to excuse their behaviour: 'At our age, it's well known that acceptability to the peer group is paramount,' she said.

'The peer group – that the name of one of the mugging gangs?' he had replied.

Now, he heard all of them stirring upstairs as he began to dish up.

There was a special element in this bank project that had helped keep him awake most of the night: Robert Cotton. He would not have picked him for this operation and saw now that it had been a mistake to leave to Garland the selection and allocation of men. Francis was clever and sensitive and pretty well in the know about Harpur and Ruth Cotton, but not even he could understand all the intricacies.

Originally, Harpur had thought of Cotton as being reasonably well away from the worst of it, running the road block in Degree Street. Now, he was not so sure. The plan for the ambush concentrated on taking the gang either in the hallway of the bank or, if that did not work properly, at the only exit from the Square. Not all of them might break away, but if some did and Reg brought their car up to the block there could be a lot of shooting, as they abandoned the vehicle and tried to get through on foot. Anyone in front of the bank might be a target, and anyone at the road block. By that stage they would be pretty frantic, blasting off everywhere.

All the assumptions were that they would come in and leave that way. True, there was a back exit and Garland had put a token couple of men to watch there. But if the reconnaissance trip was anything to go by, Reg and the car would wait at the front and he would carry them clear. Garland had given one mobile unit the job of trying to box Reg in while he waited outside the building, but Reg knew a bit about driving and it might not work. There could easily be a blast-out in Degree Street.

Harpur knew Cotton's dossier; he was not short of guts and he believed a leader should lead. These were grand qualities for a sergeant, but it had become one of Harpur's main fears that because of them Cotton would be hurt, or worse. Harpur wanted none of his people hurt but his worries over Cotton had become obsessive. He did not understand them altogether. Partly it was the dread of seeing Ruth a police widow again and her sons without a father once more. That was reasonable enough. He suspected there might be something else, though he did not care to examine it too exactly; if she was made free again it would raise all the old questions of what he should do about her, and of how much they were tied together, and he still would not know the answers. He was not ready to move on that. Perhaps he never would be.

When he told the girls he could not take them to school, Megan said: 'Meeting?' She would already have seen in the big meal a sign of something special ahead.

'Yes.'

She looked up from her breakfast for a moment at him, reading his face, but said no more.

'What will you be discussing, new methods of harassment?' Hazel asked.

'Isn't this your, well, sort of friend?' Jill said. 'The informant?'

Harpur looked around quickly and saw Jack Lamb standing smiling at the glass door of the kitchen. He had his new companion with him, Helen the infant punk. Harpur opened the door and they came in, Lamb waving largely to Megan and the girls. He had been to the house twice before, and knew he could always rely on a glacial reception from Harpur's daughters, and not much better from Megan. What he had come to say must be very important.

'Excuse us, won't you?' Lamb said. 'It's rough turning up so early, I know, but Helen and I are motoring to the races at Cheltenham and I wanted to look in and give Colin a few tips.' He stood, huge and benign, in front of the dresser, his frame almost covering it. 'Megan, grand to see you. I've some fine pictures in the house at the moment that I'd love to show you, Tissot, Kees van Dongen, yes, and Calvaert.'

'Edward Calvert?' Megan asked, 'of Appledore? Isn't Anita Brookner an expert on him – the *Hotel du Lac* dame?'

'No, not him. Much earlier. Denis Calvaert, Flemish.'

'Ah, also known as Dionisio Fiammingo,' Megan said.

'Oh, God. Listen to her,' Jill said, 'Is this set up? Who you trying to kid, you two? God, a mother who drools education and a father who's a heavy. Isn't there a decent middle way?'

'You have a remarkable mother here,' Lamb told them. 'A remarkable wife, Col.'

'How do you come to have the pictures?' Hazel asked.

Lamb beamed at her. 'I remember when you were no bigger than this,' he replied, holding his hand just above his knee. 'Now, womanhood beckons.'

Helen said: 'Jack has wonderful contacts.'

'Yes?' Hazel replied. 'Would we know any of them, I wonder.'

'A private word, Col?' Lamb asked. 'Helen can talk to your family about culture generally. She's really into *l'art fang*.'

'Prime,' Jill said.

In the living room, Lamb asked: 'Will your kids join the police?'

'You're joking.'

'They ask all the right questions.'

'Police are about getting the answers.'

Lamb sat down. 'A breakfast call! But I had to catch you before you left – '

'That's OK.'

'For State Square.'

Harpur was silent. Lamb's displays of knowledge often flattened him.

'It's all right, Col. This isn't widespread.'

'How?'

'Someone I know saw Tenderness having a look at the bank

and you having a look at Tenderness. And you've got people watching his house, haven't you? You'll follow them in?'

'But the timing? How did you get that?'

'I didn't. I just have. I assumed it must be very soon, because the boy's been gone so long.'

'Jack, you ought to join us.'

'I would, I would, if I wasn't a martyr to art and other lovely things. I've always had these two elements tugging and tugging inside me – did I want to protect the peace, did I want to be an aesthete, and for the moment I'm afraid the things of beauty won. Are you paying enough attention to the back of the bank, that's really my point, Col? I know the front looks right, Reg waiting there and so on, I heard about the run-through, but I wonder, and so does my tipster. I mean, I'm aware Tenderness is under cruel pressure, but he's never been a suicide pilot. And the new boy, Vernon – he's bright, his eyes are wide open. I hear very good things about him from afar. When the shit hits the fan he's the one who's brought his badminton racket to crack it back.'

'The rear's no good to them, Jack. We've had a good look at it. Well, of course we have, we've had muck-ups at other banks that way before, but – '

'My information is – and this is really why I'm bursting in on your family scene, Col – my latest is that Vernon and Ditto left a perky looking Granada 2.8 in Bear Lane late last night. In case you don't know, that's behind the bank. Just those two. Maybe Reg knows, maybe Len. I wouldn't bet on it. Silver. It's a B reg. I've got the full number here. If you ask the computer it will tell you it was nicked yesterday evening, I should think. They've parked it very carefully with its nose towards Date Street and away.' He handed Harpur a slip of paper.

'They'd dump Reg, and maybe Len?' Harpur asked. 'I don't believe it. Tenderness was always an *esprit de corps* lad – a bastard, but good at looking after his own.'

'Tenderness is in the mincer, isn't he, Col? Mincers change the nature of things. Anyway, all you have to do is see if the Granada's there. Bear Lane. If it is, return it to the owner right away. That's what police are for. If it's not there, I've obviously got things wrong.'

When they went back to the kitchen, Helen seemed to be doing well at winning over Megan and the children. She was illustrating steps in some ballet routine, holding a bacon sandwich, while the others applauded.

25

Mellick said: 'Jane's cooking us a big breakfast. It's a help, a day like this.'

'Smells great,' Reg said. 'We ought to do this more often, then.'

Ditto laughed. 'Yes, do this more often. I like it. Do this more often and a big breakfast every time.'

Mellick would have liked him to keep quiet. Ditto's laugh sounded cracked and nervy, and even more cracked and nervy than it ought to be before a bank raid. Would Reg and Len pick up something? Mellick said: 'Bacon and eggs this morning, champagne tonight.'

The weapons were still laid out on the writing table in the lounge, but under a blanket now, you couldn't tell who might be around the garden and squinting into the windows. Nobody had ever done much writing on that writing table and it was nice to see it getting some use at last. The boiler suits and balaclavas had been moved a while ago to the boot of the Mercedes.

'Breakfast?' Len said. 'Jane won't mind if I don't eat, will she, Tenderness? It's not because of anything, not nerves, nothing like that. This morning – it's just like any other day to me, no sweat. I never haves no breakfast, can't take it, that's all. Just tea. But a lot of tea. Well, that gets everything moving, don't it, it's well known. It's like a medicine to me, tea.'

'We know you're delicate,' Mellick said. 'Always have been.'

Ditto laughed. 'We all knows how delicate you are, Len. Very delicate.'

Vernon seemed to notice the special jumpiness in Ditto and cut in to stop him talking any more: 'Don't do anything that might upset you, Len. What we don't want is you throwing up in the bank door so we're all skidding about like Torville and Dean when we come out the front with the money.'

Ditto laughed. 'Too true – skidding about out the front with the money like . . . who's them two you mentioned, Vern? Is that

Harry Chate, the one they calls The Dean because he had some bird against a font?'

'I'll go and give Jane a hand,' Vernon said. 'Big catering job.'

Watching him walk from the room towards the kitchen, Mellick realized suddenly that he was afraid of Vernon. For a moment, he felt stunned. It was years since he had feared anyone, yet this cock-happy, tinselled kid, full of words and cheek could scare Tenderness Mellick. Who would believe it? Well, *he* would, for one, but he did not know how the hell it had happened. He was going to have to do something about it, though, before long. Vernon had some bright sides but there was more than a handful of reasons why Mellick could not wear him. He might be useful today, that was all.

Ditto must have read something in Mellick's face. 'He've just gone to help Jane, because of all the plates and that, Tenderness. He's not a bad kid.'

Mellick turned to Reg and Len: 'We all go in the Merc from here. And then you two got a Montego somewhere, right? We switch to that.'

'They're not so bad, Montegos,' Reg said. 'They picks up very quick and they can hold it.'

'We goes in to the job in the Montego and then transfers after we done it all to a Sirocco, yes?'

'Don't feel too bad about Jerry cars, Tenderness. It can do the business very nice,' Len told him. 'We'll be away, good.'

'Who's making a fuss about Jerry cars?' Mellick asked. 'Don't I run the Merc?'

'A Merc's different. That's, well, a Merc haven't got no nationality, a Merc's a Merc,' Reg said.

'We gets from the Montego to the Sirocco somewhere not too far away and then back to the Merc when it's all clear. Then we comes home, right?'

'That's it, Tenderness,' Reg said. 'It's simple and it's neat.'

'Yes, it's real neat,' Ditto added.

Thank God, he had given up the laughing now.

Reg said he wanted some air and went out for a walk in the garden.

'Reg, he got a lot on his mind,' Len muttered. 'He's out there waiting for us, up front, maybe stuff flying all over the place. Sometimes I think – well that fucking Degree Street, sometimes I think we ought to do the runner from the back. I mean, I knows it's neat and we done the run-through in front, but that fucking Degree Street, it could be a slammer door, Tenderness.'

'Not if we got speed. We got to be in and out like Speedy Gonzales, that's right, dead right,' Mellick replied. 'That way, we're all right. That's going to be down to you, Len. That's why we got to have that front door safe, so we're clear. That's why we're putting you there, Len, because you knows what's what and you can keep it clear for us. I got to have somebody I can really trust there, this is the heart of the outing. You might of thought that going in for the cash was the most important, but no. It's you on that door making sure we gets away fast. Don't let us down. We seen a lot together, Len.'

Ditto laughed. 'Yes, Speedy Gonzales. In and out, no messing. Why Tenderness picked a good one to go on the door, Len, somebody we can trust.'

'If they're watching us,' Len said.

'Why should they be?' Mellick replied. 'I've had my eyes open, and so have all of us. I been keeping an eye around the house, well, of course, but nothing. Look, Len, they don't know a bloody thing. Why they going to be watching?'

'We all been keeping an eye, haven't we, Len? What we seen? We seen nothing.'

'Look, this is your guts playing up, Len,' Mellick said. 'I seen you in enough tricky spots, so I knows you'll be great when it comes to it, but you should eat breakfast, fill a hole, so you don't feel sour and weak. That's what a breakfast is for, a doctor will tell you that.'

'That's what all the doctors say,' Ditto told him. 'Mops up all them rotten juices you gets in the night. It's well known about breakfast.'

'Just tea. I'm all right, it's just a day's work, that's all. I'm thinking about these things, I'm seeing some of the angles, that's all.'

'Bit late now, Len,' Mellick said.

'Yea, it's real late now,' Ditto told him.

Reg came in from the garden and then Jane called them to the kitchen for breakfast. They sat around the big reproduction refectory table, and Len took only tea.

'I understand,' Jane said. 'People are funny about breakfast.

Graham – ' She hesitated as if forgetting for a moment that he was gone, and then the reality hit her. 'Graham can't take eggs,' she went on, very quietly. 'It's the colour, I think, the yellow. He was learning his colours real nice. The teacher said Graham was one of the best in the class with colours, that kind, old teacher, not the one who was touching up boys or the one Graham had to bite, he was such a living bastard.'

'Colour – you never knows with colours, how people will be about some colours,' Ditto told them. 'I got an aunty, nice old lady, nothing provocative, goes like a wild thing, I mean savage, if there's too much turquoise.'

Vernon said: 'As soon as he's back, he'll pick up all that again, colours and so on. It's still there in his mind, it will just need bringing out again. Bit of prompting, that's all. You'll see, Jane.'

'Yes, of course it will come back, Jane,' Mellick told her. 'You're so patient with him. He learns very fast from you, much better than school.'

'I seen it,' Ditto told her, 'much better than school. He laps it up from you, Jane. You got a way. Patience.'

Mellick said: 'Look, Jane, they might come through on the phone again while we're out getting the money. He said he'd call today, it could be any time. You can deal with him, can't you?'

'Of course.' She had not eaten any of the breakfast, or even taken a cup of tea.

'Just say we're getting it, it's a matter of a couple of hours, that's all.'

'Yes.'

'Not *how* we're getting it.'

'Am I an idiot?'

'Just say we've popped out down the bank to get some money,' Reg told her, and laughed.

Ditto laughed, also. 'Yes, at the bank geting some money. That won't be no lie.'

'Try and be calm with him, love,' Mellick told her. 'Think of it like a business deal. You've helped me good on a lot of those. You got a way.'

Ditto said: 'Yes, you got a way, Jane. You got a way teaching the boy and you got a way helping do deals, anybody can see that.'

'If he gets rough, shouting, swearing, all that, still keep calm,'

Mellick said, wiping his plate clean with fried bread. 'No good at all shouting back, not yet. One day, maybe I'll be able to settle with him, I likes to settle, eventual, but not now, he's strong. I mean, he's just like he always was, he's half crazy and weak as gnat's piss, but that's why he's so strong now, if you can understand me. We got to play it like that.'

'Don't worry, Bernie. I know.'

'He can really smell the money now, Jane,' Vernon said. 'That makes people wild. It can do it to all sorts, but especially to someone like this guy who I gather is half way there already. Don't let him upset you, that's all. He's never seen real money, and now it's nearly here under his nose, so he's going wild.'

'It's like my aunty with turquoise,' Ditto said. 'Real wild, a sweet old lady.'

They went back into the other room and Reg and Len took one of the sawn-off Berettas each. They wrapped them carefully in brown paper, thoroughly enough for concealment when they were changing to the Montego but not so tightly that it would take any time to bring them into play. Mellick had a sports bag for his and he left the zip open. He had carried a sawn-off before, but never used one, and he had not even carried one for ten years, maybe more. But he could do whatever was needed. He took one of the Colts as well. He liked to feel something in his pocket.

Vernon chose another of the Colts. 'Come on, Ditto,' he said. 'Don't get superstitious about the bloody Walther. If they trace you, they trace all of us.'

'It's a fact, Ditto,' Mellick told him. 'The Colt's a nice weapon. It won't let you down.'

'I don't call it fucking superstitious. What you mean, superstitious?'

'Just you haven't thought it through,' Vernon said.

'Thought it through where? I got a Walther. I seen it do right by me, so where's the thinking? I don't need no thinking.'

'Leave the Walther, just today,' Mellick told him. 'I'm asking you, for me.'

Ditto picked up a Colt and held it as if it were coated with slime. 'It don't seem right, that's all. It don't seem as if things will go right if I got this.'

'That's what I mean, superstitious,' Vernon said. 'The Walther's become a lucky charm.'

'This lucky charm can blow a man's head off good. You ever heard of a lucky charm can blow a man's head off? You talk shit. I heard of a lucky charm, a rabbit's paw. I never pulled out no rabbit's paw to put the frighteners on somebody.'

'Leave it,' Mellick said.

Ditto put the Colt in his pocket, took the Walther from its shoulder holster and placed it on the table. He touched it once, then walked to the other side of the room and sat down. 'This Colt will be good,' he said. 'The thing about the Colt is no bugger can trace it, it's new. The Walther – everybody knew if it was a Walther it was Ditto.' He spoke like somebody who had just worked out a clever set of new ideas for himself. Mellick had often seen him turn himself inside out in that way. It did not matter. In the job he did, Ditto's mind was less important than some other things. He wasn't asking to be made Pope or put in charge of N.A.T.O.

'That's good thinking, Ditto, bloody good thinking, I reckon,' Vernon told him. 'You know a thing or two, anyone can see.' His voice was all over Ditto and making him sound like a Nobel prize winner for bank jobs.

Vernon knew a bit about leadership and making the boys feel bright, that one. 'We're away, then,' Mellick said.

'Have a nice day,' Jane called.

They drove to pick up the Montego. Mellick kept an eye behind and told Reg to watch the mirror, but they saw nothing to worry them. It was not easy to be sure because of so much mid-morning traffic. After a few miles, Reg said: 'The only thing staying with us, an old Ital with a woman in it by herself.'

'Yes, I saw that,' Mellick replied. 'They're not going to use a woman in a banger on a job like this.'

'She's gone into Tesco's, anyway,' Reg said, not long afterwards.

They had left the Montego in a multi-storey car park. Quickly they made the transfer and moved off towards Degree Street and State Square, Len in front with Reg. In a quiet road very near to Degree Street they stopped and pulled on the boiler suits, without getting out of the car, and put the balaclavas around their necks, ready to be drawn up when they arrived.

'Looks OK,' Mellick said as they drove into Degree Street.

Ditto brought the Colt from his pocket and put it ready on his lap. 'Looks great.'

'Nothing in front of the bank. We got luck,' Mellick said.

'A minute then I thought I saw the sodding Ital in the mirror,' Reg told them.

Mellick looked back. 'No.'

Ditto looked back, too. 'No. Clear.'

They were into the Square. 'All right, Reg, let's have the speed now, get that spot right in front. Balaclavas up.'

Reg covered his face and then hit the accelerator. His Beretta was on the floor of the car alongside Len's feet. They were up to nearly sixty for the last couple of hundred yards. Mellick was staring all ways, trying to spot anything that looked wrong, some police face and police haircut and police clothes among the people on the pavement around the front of the bank, or some car full of heavy chins, or some van with too many aerials. That fucker Hubert Scott; who'd trust a cop, even a bought cop? As they hurtled towards the bank, Mellick knew he was searching above all for one face, waiting for him, that ape who was up the house, nosing and throwing his weight about, Colin Harpur. Information went to that bugger, somehow. Nobody knew where it came from, but it was good. He did not see him now, though, thank Christ.

They were out of the car, Len first, then Mellick with Vernon and Ditto behind him. Reg was screaming something as they stopped. He did not hear it all, but he got one word, the one that counted. 'Ital.' He took a glance back and saw it coming into the Square from Degree Street, with the woman still at the wheel, but all the other seats occupied now by men. Behind it was a blue-lamp Rover. He felt his guts go like ice.

So, after all, it was a sell, a trap, and Hubert Scott had done them. There would be no big cash here. Then, for a second, as he charged forward, he experienced something that was almost satisfaction. For the sake of Jane and Graham, he had tried, he had put his head into a spot that he knew from the start was a peril. He had done it, not thinking about himself, because that was what you did if you had a woman you wanted to keep and a kid you wanted to save.

They had to go on. He kept right behind Len, waving the

Beretta about in case anyone in the way turned out brave or turned out police. He saw faces that were terrified and cowed and dazed, men and women, but none that looked as if it would give bother. Somewhere, though, there were going to be a lot of faces that would give bother.

'Len, we're fucked,' he yelled. 'Forget the money. Fight through to the back. There's another car.'

'What?'

'Another car.'

Len was in the doorway and hesitated, waiting for Mellick to come up with him. 'What other car?' he bellowed. 'What about Reg?'

The hallway to the bank was empty. That was wrong, too. They must have cleared people. This was where it was going to happen. From behind them he heard a man shouting: 'Stop. Armed police. Drop the weapons. Armed police. Armed police.' He knew the voice.

Ditto and Vernon arrived. 'Through,' Vernon screamed. 'We can't go back.' He ran into the hall and suddenly there were men at top of the stairs, coming down, men in combat gear and carrying handguns. Len went with Vernon and, still running, pointed the Beretta up the stairs and fired. A man in the gear sank to his knees on the stairs and his handgun skidded down and landed on the marble floor in front of Mellick. The man would have rolled after it, but two behind grabbed him when he had slipped only a couple of stairs and pulled him back up. The other police in the group paused at the top and then there were four shots from up there, two men firing, and Len fell at once, with the Beretta under his body. Vernon ran on, still holding the Colt.

It looked clear. Ditto started to move after him, also holding a Colt, and then Mellick saw him glance back to see if he was coming. But Mellick suddenly found he could not follow, could not ditch Reg. Although he wanted to, his legs refused. You couldn't leave a man like that. He turned and saw that Reg had the shotgun pointed out of the window and was holding back a party with Harpur in the lead. They had taken cover behind police vehicles that had swarmed into the Square now. He could see Harpur, a pistol in his hand and lying on the pavement alongside one of their Fords.

Mellick did not know whether Reg had fired, or if he had managed to scare them by the sight of the gun and shouting. The engine of the Montego was running and the doors to the pavement stood open, ready for them to come back with the money, just as it had been planned. Reg had everything right. There would be no money, but you did not leave a man who always did everything right, regardless.

He ran out of the bank and back toward Reg and the car. He heard firing coming from the left in the Square but could not see exactly where. They were all round. They would never get a job as easy as this again: target practice.

He fell into the car alongside Reg and slammed the door. As he leaned back to pull the rear one shut he saw that Ditto had changed his mind and was following him. He had been hit high on the left arm and there was a wide blood stain on his boiler suit. Staggering a bit, he kept coming, and he still held the Colt in his right hand. The mouthpiece of his balaclava was soaking, as if he had dribbled or retched because of the pain. Mellick got out and helped him into the back, then climbed in alongside Reg again. 'Go,' he shouted.

'Len? Vernon?' Reg said.

'Go. Len's hit. Forget Vernon.'

Reg pulled the shotgun in and put it on the floor. The Montego surged away. Ditto groaned in the back.

'Christ, look,' Reg said.

Mellick saw there had been time for them to replace the car blocks across Degree Street with two JCBs, their grabs facing into the Square. 'Get right up to them. Then on foot.' He turned and saw two cars and a van behind them, Harpur in the front of the leading Sierra. 'Ditto, we got to run in a minute. You all right?'

'I can run.'

Reg brought the car up to the JCBs and braked. He grabbed his Beretta and the three men jumped out. Someone was yelling 'Armed police' from behind the barricade and he could see a sergeant in combat gear sighting a revolver on him, two-handed. Behind, the three police vehicles pulled up and he heard men running and yelling.

Reg galloped towards the side of the street, to get around the JCBs and Mellick and Ditto went after him. There was a burst of firing from behind and Reg fell, slowly, sliding down against the side of one of the JCBs. Mellick and Ditto skirted him and came out behind the barrier, and there he saw the sergeant again, still with the pistol up in a two-handed hold and about to fire. Ditto saw him too and stopped and raised the Colt to knock him out first.

Mellick watched him squeeze the trigger, but the Colt did not fire. There was not even a click. The hammer failed to move. He saw the sergeant shift his aim and then there were two shots and Ditto fell heavily against Mellick, knocking him to the side as he fired himself at the sergeant. Something struck him hard on the head from behind and for a moment he was conscious he would fall across Ditto. Then he felt his mind and eyes and legs all going.

26

Graham remembered that his mother used to say it was all right if he went near little waves, but big waves could knock boys over and take them away. This sea was big waves, and that was why they made a noise when they came on the stones. He liked them, and his mother was not here now. If he took his shoes off and his clothes the waves would not wet them. He would leave them on the stones. He would not take all his clothes off to go in the sea because his mother said that was not nice. People might come and see him, so he would leave his underpants on.

When he went in the sea with his mother and father his mother brought a towel in a bag to get dry afterwards. He did not have a towel but he had a vest. If he made himself dry with the vest it would be all right because he would put his sweater on and nobody would know he was not wearing his vest. He decided he would not throw the vest or underpants away afterwards just because they would be wet. He would keep them and they would be all right when they dried. When he had been in the waves he would take the underpants off and put his trousers on quickly because there might be people, and they did not like it if a boy had no clothes on. That was called rude.

27

'Haven't I told you, Col, command knackers them,' Iles said. From all I hear – well, from you, from others – from all I hear, there was a time when Lane had real balls.'

'Yes, he was great, and witty with it.'

'So, what the hell happened? Look at him now.'

Harpur was sitting with the Assistant Chief on the soil in someone's garden, their backs against a low brick wall.

'He insisted on taking this over personally,' Iles said. 'Bumper panic. You know what he's like about hostages – and kids. He could have had a great career as a nanny.'

'Well, you took it over from me, sir.'

'The difference is that I'm not a wanker.' He brushed earth from the leg of his suit. 'Christ, am I paid to spend my time in mud? It's like being at Ypres.' Half a dozen men waited in the garden, keeping below the level of the wall. 'We've had this place circled for, what, nearly two and a quarter hours now. He won't move. Good God, you've knocked a bank raid on the head in the time and still managed to get here for the action.'

'I felt I was entitled.'

'Don't trot out your bloody bargain basement irony on me, Harpur.'

'Garland's tidying at the bank, quizzing Tenderness and counting the dead.'

'And we got the young genius and cock-about-town, Vernon, as well?'

'We moved the Granada he had waiting and just hung about for him to turn up.'

'Did we get a tip about that car?'

'Yes.'

'Hubert Scott again?'

'No.'

'Who?'

'A contact.'

'Someone you don't talk about.'

'That's it, sir.'

'So nobody's going to know where it came from?'

'No, nobody.'

'So, you could say it came from Hubert – when you see Bundy in the investigation. That would be the bank raid itself and the getaway scheme. It would make him look a damned good undercover boy, and be excellent for all of us.'

'I suppose so, sir.'

'All right, I've got special loyalties to him, I wouldn't hide that, how could I from you? But it's not just the Lodge, is it? I mean, it will make the Force look sharp and formidable.'

'I suppose so, sir.'

'Well thanks for the promise, and for being so sodding enthusiastic, as usual, Harpur.'

Iles stood up and very cautiously peered over the wall. 'It's this open back door that's upset Lane. He said it meant Ancient Dave was about to take the kid out again in the car and it would be easier and safer to let him do that and then collar him on the road.'

'Sounds shrewd.'

'Except it hasn't fucking well happened, has it? I've heard of softly, softly, but Lane's so soft he melts. You've heard of the Hemingway thing, grace under pressure? Lane comes close, but it's grease under pressure. And who knows what's going on inside the house while we hang about being subtle? They're there, all right. We've seen curtain movement.'

He sat down again on the ground.

'Have they got a radio?' Harpur asked.

'We don't know what they've got, except the Cavalier.'

'If they're tuned local and hear about the bank fiasco – '

'We haven't released names to the media, for Christ's sake, have we? Not said we've got Tenderness?'

'No. But Dave or Milton could put two and two together, couldn't they? Or some bloody reporter might dig out names for himself. If those two hear that and realize the kid's suddenly worthless—'

'They could do anything. Bright, Col. I hadn't thought of it, Lane hasn't. I always said you had a first-rate second division brain.' He brought out his walkie-talkie.

176

'Where is the Chief?' Harpur asked.

'In a house opposite, at the front door. I'll give him a call, make your point.' He seemed about to speak to Lane but then put the walkie-talkie away suddenly. 'Oh, bugger him. He'll froth and find reasons for hanging about. We want this kid now.' For another second Harpur watched him contemplate again a call to Lane. Then he said suddenly: 'You and me, Col, through the back door. It's still open. They're a couple of thick jerks. We can handle them.'

'If this – '

'Of course it will work. You're not scared of the Mick?'

Iles stood up again and was over the wall in a second. Harpur followed and they ran hard for the open door. Today he should have been on bonus. He still had the .38 with him from the bank outing, but left it in his pocket.

Iles led quickly through the kitchen into the hall and pointed up the stairs. He bounded to the top, making no sound, with Harpur right behind. On the landing they paused for a moment while Iles took his bearings, and they both listened. There were no voices but they heard a faint, series of sounds from behind a closed door. They seemed to be in groups of three and were like gentle blows from a small hammer on a yielding surface. Iles carefully took hold of the knob on this door and glanced around to see that Harpur was ready.

He brought out the .38. It was the sort of situation he dreaded, the sort that every policeman with a gun dreaded: a room where you did not know what you would find, except that it would be a mixture of the dangerous and the innocent, and you might have only a speck of a moment to sort out which was which. Read all about it in the papers. He took a two handed stance with the gun. Iles threw the door open and stood clear to give Harpur full sight.

He saw Ancient Dave and Milton at once. They were in the middle of a shabby room. Blankets lay in one corner. Milton was about to throw a dart at a board hanging next to the fireplace, and Harpur understood what the sounds had been, metal on cork. They both turned and stared at him.

'What the hell?' Dave said.

'Keep still,' Harpur yelled.

Iles rushed into the room and stared about. 'Where's the boy?'

177

'Boy? What boy? What's going on?' Milton asked.

Iles pulled the dart from his hand and jabbed it hard into where his balls would be and then did it again. Milton bent over and screamed, before collapsing into a chair. 'Where's the fucking boy?' Iles howled.

Dave said. 'We don't know about no boy.'

Iles turned to him with the dart out in front. Blood shone on it. 'You want some?'

'Mr Harpur, I knows you, this one I don't know, you lets him do this?'

'Graham Mellick, Dave, just say where he is,' Harpur replied.

'Tenderness's boy? I don't know nothing about that. Is he gone?'

'Christ, I'll kill you,' Iles said, and moved towards him a few steps. Dave cowered back but Iles stopped suddenly and turned away. Harpur heard him hurry through all the rooms in the house, pulling cupboard doors open, shifting furniture. Harpur put the gun into his pocket again, went to the window and drew back the curtains. He stood there for a few seconds so Lane and his team could identify him and know the waiting was over. He wanted other people here before Iles returned and did more damage.

'Where's the keys of the car, Dave?' Harpur said.

'What for?'

'I want to look in the boot.'

'What for?'

'Just give me the keys, will you?'

He handed them over. 'You think the boy's in there?'

'Is he?'

'Of course he's not.'

'He's been in there.'

'Who says?'

'That's why we're here.'

Milton said: 'Dave, I told you it was bloody crazy taking – '

'Keep your mouth shut,' Dave snarled.

'Go on, Milton,' Harpur said.

'Nothing,' he replied.

'The Assistant Chief will be back in a minute.'

'Nothing.'

'You got nothing,' Dave told Harpur. 'No kid, nothing. Even if you had him, how's he going to sound in a court, a dumbo kid and we deny?'

'Is he alive?'

'Who?'

'The boy.'

'What boy?'

There were footsteps on the stairs and in a moment Lane and a couple of sharp shooters came in. Lane had on one of his army surplus combat jackets and a navy bobble hat. He was sweating heavily and there were large wet patches under his arms. He looked very angry. 'Harpur, how in God's name do you come to be here?'

Before he needed to reply, Iles returned. 'We can't find the boy, sir,' he told the Chief.

Harpur went downstairs and out to the garage. He opened the boot of the car and searched thoroughly, but discovered nothing. On his return to the house he looked closely at the garden for any sign of recently disturbed soil or turfs: a grave. He did not find that, but something red and blue gleamed in the long grass of the lawn and he bent down and picked up a mounted Lego warrior wearing a plumed helmet. He had seen others like it at the farm house.

When he reached the bedroom Lane and Iles were alone with Dave and Milton. Those two were seated on the uncarpeted floor. The Chief and Iles had taken the only straight-backed wooden chairs.

The room smelled stale and small clouds of dust moved whenever anyone took a few steps. Lane had removed the bobble hat and was questioning Dave. 'Tell us what you've done with the boy and we might be able to help you in court, Dave.'

'What boy? What court?'

Iles said: 'Listen, you piece of – '

'I'll handle this, Desmond,' Lane told him. 'There are ways to deal with these things. My God, this other man says you stabbed him in the genitals with a dart.'

'What dart?' Iles replied.

'Dave, Milton,' Lane said, 'there's nothing in this for you now, holding stuff back from us. All I'm concerned about is the life of a child.'

'We don't know nothing about no child,' Dave replied.

'We know you've held him,' Lane said.

'You don't know nothing. You'll never stand it up,' Dave answered.

Harpur opened his hand and showed him the Lego trooper. Dave stared at it and kept quiet, but Milton grunted and said, 'Christ.'

'What is it?' Lane asked.

'I've been thinking of who you remind me of in that gear, sir, and the heat, and so on,' Iles said. 'It's Alec Guinness in *The Bridge on the River Kwai*. They gave him a very saucy time, the Japs, remember?'

'What is that, Colin?' Lane said.

'A toy. There were a lot of them where we found Rick the Intelligent dead. Graham Mellick brought one of them with him here.'

Dave laughed. 'Oh, come on, Mr Harpur, that's the oldest bloody trick in the book. You brought a pocketful with you, did you? That don't wash, not one scrap.'

'What happened to your nose, Dave?' Iles asked. 'You've been bitten? Love games, you and Milt?'

Lane shouted: 'Are you accusing Mr Harpur of planting evidence, Dave?'

'Of course I am. He's great at it. You all are. What's it mean, anyway, a toy soldier? So, there was some at this farm wherever it is. You say Rick was there, dead. So what? I mean, it's regrettable, but what do it mean about us? All right, we know Rick, we knew Rick, but if he's at a farm, what do we know about that? You going to prove all that because there's a toy soldier here? Don't make me laugh.'

Iles said: 'You know the law, you know juries, you know about the failure-to-convict rate, I'll give you that, Dave.'

'You'll have scrupulous treatment from all my men,' Lane told them. 'What we have to prove we'll prove, and we'll prove it properly, fairly.'

'Like just happening to find the bit of Lego,' Dave said.

Lane turned to Harpur: 'Colin, I want you to assure me, and assure Dave here and Milton, that there is no question of a plant, absolutely no question. I think that's something they can reasonably ask for.'

'I admire it, sir, your fine regard for integrity, and that other quality you mentioned: scrupulousness,' Iles said. 'Would there were more Chiefs like you. Don't you think so, lads?' he asked Dave and Milton.

'Colin?' Lane insisted.

'It was in the grass.' For a foolish second he thought of mentioning, too, the charred fragments of pictures and notes he had taken from the farm grate, but quickly decided against: nobody must know he had been there alone, nobody except Lamb, who had pointed the way. 'I was looking for something else and found it by accident.'

'Thank you, Colin,' Lane said, 'for answering and for not taking offence.' He turned to Dave and Milton again. 'You heard Mr Harpur. I believe him. Now, please, for your own sakes, tell us where the boy is.'

'What boy?' Dave replied.

'Yes, what boy?' Milton asked.

Lane grew almost enraged. 'I'm trying to be fair with you. You're – '

'As to tying them to the farm and to the murder of Rick the Intelligent, there's something else,' Harpur said. This was why his early visit to the farm had to stay secret.

Iles had been looking despondent, but revived now. 'What's that, Col?'

Harpur said: 'Rick was a great one for rings.'

'Yes, I know,' Iles replied.

'Some had obviously been removed from the body. The marks were clear on the fingers.'

'Yes,' Iles said.

Harpur put his hand into his pocket and brought out two diamond cluster rings and an amethyst. 'These were hidden in the boot of their car,' he told Lane.

'Great, oh, great, Col,' Iles said.

Dave jumped up from his chair and seemed about to throw himself at Harpur, but Iles stood quickly and punched him twice, one heavy blow low in the stomach with his left and then a jab on the side of the jaw. Dave fell on the floor, still conscious and Iles bent down and picked him up by gripping a handful of his shirt.

He pushed him back into his chair. 'Our grey hairs don't go well with violence, Dave, but sometimes it just seems inescapable.'

'I never took them rings, I would never take no rings from a dead, anyone knows that,' Dave mumbled. 'Oh, Christ, this is a stitch-up, a stitch-up.'

'You're going to tell the Chief this is another plant, are you?' Iles said. He put his face down close to Dave's. 'Is that what you're going to tell my Chief, my kindly, decent Chief, who's doing everything possible to make things reasonable for you, you fucking murdering, abducting grave robber?'

Milton said: 'Them rings was still there when – '. He stopped.

'When what, Milt?' Iles asked, sweetly.

Harpur, leaning against one of the grubby walls, said: 'You've lost the boy, haven't you? This dumbo, as you call him is too smart for you.'

The Chief, Iles and Harpur watched Dave and Milton taken away later and Lane gave orders for a proper search of the house and garden and everywhere nearby.

Then he said to Harpur, 'Colin, show me exactly how you found the piece of Lego. I'm sorry, but a great deal is going to turn on it.'

They went into the garden. 'Here,' Harpur said.

Lane stared at the grass.

'Do you want me to show you where the rings were, too, sir.'

'No, no,' Lane said. 'No jury's going to believe *they* could be a plant – simply not believable. What police officer is going to remove rings from a corpse and keep them for evidence?'

Iles nodded. 'Quite, sir.'

'We've got them, no doubt of it,' the Chief said. 'Those finds will be conclusive.' He left a little later.

Iles said: 'I ought to apologise, Col. That business about your not being first division. The rings – magnificent. That's long-term planning, the mark of the highest management potential. Pre-science is it called? Admirable. When I do my textbook on policing methods, the key chapter will be:, Think jury, think jury, think blind and bent British juries and make sure you bring them something no fat QC can jinx. If I may, I'll cite the rings, Col.'

'It was just routine, sir – to search the boot.'

'You don't say.'

They drove out together to Mellick's house on Elms Enclave.

Jane Mellick answered the door and Harpur was shocked to see how much worse she looked than when he last called; thinner, paler, her eyes more sunken.

Iles said: 'Can we come in, love? There's a few shocks for you, I'm afraid.'

She did not move aside at once. 'I'm waiting for – '

'Look, we know what you're waiting for, Jane,' Iles said gently. 'There's going to be no phone call. They don't get phones in the cells.'

'You've found him?' she whispered, almost smiling.

'We've found *them*,' Iles said.

'I don't understand.'

'We don't understand, either,' he replied.

Now, she did let them in and led to the long, elegant lounge where Harpur had seen the party guests. As soon as they were there she spun around to face them, her face haggard with anxiety, waiting to hear what they had to say.

'Both your men are all right, Tenderness and Vernon,' Harpur told her. 'Tenderness, a bang on the head, nothing grave. Ditto, Len, Reg, not so lucky. Reg might live. The others have gone under, I'm afraid.'

'But Graham?' she asked. It was as if she had not heard Harpur speak about the bank party.

Iles crossed to a writing table and looked at a blanket lying there. He bent down and smelled it. 'Had weaponry on this? I hope we're not going to have to do you as an accessory. Not a bad piece of repro. Good enough to fool some. The blanket's genuine.'

Harpur said: 'We believe Graham escaped somehow, probably from a house on the Redbrick estate.'

'You think he's alive?'

Iles said: 'Sit down, love, will you?'

She did, but crouched forward on the edge of the chair staring at him from those large, dark, sleepless eyes.

'Yes, we believe he is,' Iles told her. 'He was last night. We're pretty sure he went with Ancient Dave in the car. And we've been watching the house since early today, so we don't see how they could have – well, where he could be if he's not alive. We've got a huge search out, door knocking, doing streets and gardens, the foreshore.'

'Foreshore?' she said.

'Redbrick is right on to the coast,' Harpur said.

'He's fascinated by the sea,' she murmured. 'And he has no fear, none.'

'Can he swim?' Iles asked.

'A couple of strokes.'

'I think we might drive up there, Col. Mrs Mellick could come with us.'

'Oh, please,' she said. 'Please. God, I wish we had spoken to you earlier.'

'Tenderness has his own way of looking at things. I understand that,' Iles replied.

In the car she said: 'That sod Scott set up the bank trap, did he?'

'We get a lot of information, Mrs Mellick,' Harpur said. 'From all directions.'

'Scott has retired, you know,' Iles told her. 'We wouldn't have contact now.'

When they reached the foreshore the three of them left the car and climbed over the heaped pebbles towards the sound of the sea. Jane Mellick was in heels and stumbled hopelessly until Iles picked her up and carried her to the top. It was almost high tide and they watched as heavy waves crashed down on the stones, dragged some back with a long, echoing rattle, then threw more up the beach with the next incoming breaker. Harpur saw her begin to weep.

Iles had brought field glasses from the car and spent two or three minutes scanning the beach in both directions. 'Four of our search parties,' he said. 'If he's playing down here, they'll find him, Mrs Mellick, rely on it.' But she was looking at the sea and still weeping.

In the evening there was a big, impromptu party at the club for all the people who were on the ambush and Harpur dropped in for a while. The Chief appeared briefly, but he had been to see the widow of the inspector killed on the bank stairs and looked very worn. He did his bit for a while with people of all ranks, buying drinks, listening to their tales, then disappeared. Iles arrived late and set himself up at the bar with his usual port and lemon. He did not seem to want company.

Ruth's husband, Robert Cotton, was very drunk, just about conscious but bent over in an armchair with the boys he had led at

184

the barrier. Cotton had killed a man today and had been almost killed himself. He deserved a drink. Maybe not everyone in the world would worry too much about the death of Ditto Repeato, but if it was the first time Cotton had shot someone, or even the second or tenth time, the shock might still undo his seams. The shock always turned Harpur sick and he was glad not to have opened fire today.

He went out and called Ruth from a pay phone.

'I heard you saved Robert's life,' she said.

'I hit someone over the head from behind. Nothing valiant. Can you get out?'

'Should you leave the party?'

'Not really. But I don't want a confrontation with Robert when he's drunk. Might lead anywhere.'

'Can't you come over? The kids are asleep. He said he'd be very late.'

'Yes, he'll be very late.'

In a way he liked going to their house, hers and Cotton's in Canberra Avenue. Of course it was risky and of course it was especially treacherous, yet it seemed to give their relationship a kind of extra solidity and warmth, something that could be missing in an hotel or the back of a car. He liked to feel there was a family nearby, Ruth's two boys and Cotton's daughter. To his surprise, really, he had found that for him, love-making had to do with families, with children, although he did not want anything like that to happen with Ruth, and although making love to her was a betrayal of his own family. He could not sort it out, but he knew he was always content in her bed.

She was thinking of families, too. 'This woman, not knowing where her child is – still not knowing, it's appalling.'

'I think he'll be all right,' he said. 'He must be tough, he's wily enough to escape. He's lying low.' He didn't tell her about the way Jane Mellick had looked at the sea.

On his way home, he drove to Redbrick estate and toured the streets slowly. If the boy was really as wily as he had said, and hoped, he might decide to move at night. He saw some police patrols, but not Graham. Outside the house itself there was a constable on watch in a car and Harpur talked to him for a little while. Then he left his own car and went to check for himself that the house was properly secured; the finger print and forensic people would resume work there tomorrow. It worried him particularly that the garage could not be properly shut and he went to look again at the car and make sure that the doors and boot were locked.

While he was standing near the car, he heard a small sound from somewhere at the rear of the garden and he moved quietly to where the garage doors hung partly open, so he could look out. For a moment he saw nothing, but then he spotted the crouched shape of a boy edging skilfully along by the wall, picking his way slowly over flower beds to the neglected lawn. He was carrying something in one hand, something white that looked like a bunched up cloth or undergarments. When he was up near the house on the lawn he stopped and seemed to begin searching the grass, getting very low in the darkness, and using his free hand to part the blades so he could see down to the soil.

Watching him, Harpur felt a huge rush of joy and relief. It was a joy that sprang from something larger and deeper than simply seeing a child safe after great dangers. This child, with all his supposed limitations, had thought his way and worked his way to survival. On his own he had beaten his enemies, escaped from evil. Maybe the dark wouldn't win, after all.

Harpur moved out very quickly from the garage and, before Graham could straighten properly, had hold of his arm. The boy struggled fiercely. Of course, he would think everybody connected with this house was one of those enemies and part of that evil, and would fight to stay free.

'I've got something for you, Graham. What you're looking for,' he said.

The boy took no notice, but, bending suddenly, fixed his teeth with savage force into Harpur's wrist. The pain almost made him let go. Instead, Harpur quickly opened his other hand and pushed it close to Graham's face, so the boy had to look at what was there. 'You missed him?' he managed to say, showing the Lego trooper.

At once, he felt the bite relax and in a moment the child gently took the soldier. Graham smiled and closed his hand over the model, seeming to squeeze it tightly. Then he bent his head again and for a moment Harpur feared he would be bitten once more, but this time the child kissed him on the wound.

28

Bundy said: 'Tell me about Hubert Scott then, Mr Harpur.'

'First-rate man, sir. A great loss when he went out.'

'What sort of first-rate?'

'Undercover, especially.'

'Undercover where?'

'In an outfit run by Bernard Mellick.'

'Tenderness?'

'That's right, sir.'

'Scott's told me about this. Incidentally, he's full of your praises.'

'I'm grateful.'

'Says you're a fine leader, fine family man, fine copper.'

'Nice of him.'

'You look after each other?'

'We all try to look after each other in this Force, sir. The Chief's a great believer in team effort.'

'Mason?'

'Scott?'

'Yes.'

'Yes, I think he is,' Harpur said.

'You?'

'No. Never fancied it.'

Bundy looked at some notes. 'You may know that Scott had heavy infusions of funds from Mellick over a long period.'

'That would follow, sir. He had to appear a genuine bent officer.'

'That's what he says.'

'And it worked, sir.'

'Yes?'

'He tipped us off about the bank raid. We've been trying to nail Tenderness for years. He puts himself into a dead-end for us. We wouldn't have liked to miss that.'

'No.'

'And Scott came up with a tip about a secondary getaway vehicle. We could have lost some of them.'

'Yes, Mr Iles told me about that.'

'It was incomparable information, sir.'

'Mr Iles a Mason?'

'I believe he might be, sir.'

'Yes, I believe he might be, too.'

'Is it important, sir?'

'I don't know. Is it important?'

'We've landed a lot of heavy people, with the loss of only one man. That seemed important, sir. Without Scott it would have been impossible.'

'What about the money?'

'Which money, sir?'

'The take money – the take money he had to accept to keep his cover intact.'

'What about it, sir?'

'He can't give it back. He's spent it,' Bundy said.

'That would follow, sir. These people, Tenderness and the rest, they have a fast life style. Scott would need to match it, wouldn't he?'

Bundy smoothed his face with his hand. 'Sometimes I wonder why the hell I'm doing this inquiry, Harpur.'